The WRITINGS ═══ *of* ═══ SILVANUS

Dana George Cottrell

ISBN 978-1-68197-848-2 (Paperback)
ISBN 978-1-68197-849-9 (Digital)

Christian Faith Publishing, Inc.
296 Chestnut Street
Meadville, PA 16335
www.christianfaithpublishing.com

Printed in the United States of America

Many thanks to Penny Cottrell, Carol Martin, and Jeannie Martin for their editing support.

CONTENTS

Introduction..7

Chapter 1   The Copper Mine.................................15

Chapter 2   Beth-Gebar...20

Chapter 3   Like Father, Like Son........................26

Chapter 4   Hermes 36

Chapter 5   The Evangelists.................................47

Chapter 6   Stephanie 57

Chapter 7   Our Weddings.....................................71

Chapter 8   Greece..85

Chapter 9   Jerusalem...109

Chapter 10 The Shipping Trade 119

Chapter 11 Hermes Moves to Neapolis..............127

Chapter 12 Amphoras 141

Chapter 13 My Second Trip to Jerusalem............156

Chapter 14 Amphora Production 163

Chapter 15 The Market Place 170

Chapter 16 Rachael Marries Stephanos............181

Chapter 17 The Enterprise 190

Chapter 18 The Artist Community 195

Chapter 19 The Trip North 202

Chapter 20 The Inheritance 212

Epilogue 223

INTRODUCTION

I first met Nicholas at the university. We were both studying to be electrical engineers. During the last two years of schooling, we and a couple other students rented a house from one of the mechanical engineering professors. As we closed in on graduation, Nicholas invited me to his home in Piraeus, Greece. He comes from a wealthy family of shipping magnates, and not having visited Greece before, I took him up on his offer.

Nicholas met me at the airport. His family had a fairly large, beautiful home that overlooked the Aegean Sea. Because of my five years of friendship with Nicholas, the family was looking forward to meeting me. His sisters and relatives from all over the area were there to greet me. We spent the first evening having a fabulous meal in a rather large dining room and discussed touring Athens while drinking wine on the veranda. Nicholas had everything planned out.

I couldn't help notice that their home looked like a museum. There were decorated vases, urns, and pottery of all kinds and shapes stuck in every nook and cranny. However, they were arrayed in such a manner so as to not make the house appear cluttered.

The first day of touring was spent at the acropolis and a fairly large museum. Nicholas said that if I really wanted to see ancient Greek architecture and ruins, we should take a three-day land tour.

While waiting for the evening meal, I noticed a decorated urn sitting in a glass case and asked Nicholas about it. He said that it had been passed down from generation to generation, and according to a museum curator, the urn was a Phoenician amphora, based on the artwork and color of the fired clay. He took it out of the glass case and showed it to me. I didn't want to touch it for fear of dropping it and splattering someone's ashes all over the carpet.

Nicholas said that he didn't think that it contained ashes but was tempted many times to unseal the top and see if there was anything inside. I suggested that we carefully open the top and check it out. I mentioned that there could be an ancient treasure map inside. Normally, he would never do such a thing. At the university, I was the guilty one who seemed to lead everyone else astray, from making elder berry wine and beer to making a tesla coil that disrupted TVs throughout the dorm and disrupting unruly neighbors with low frequency sound.

I believe it was the iodine paste on a piece of paper that got him into trouble. I talked Nicholas into throwing the paper into the wastebasket next to the professor's desk. When the paste dried, all it took was a slight breeze, and the paper exploded, making the professor jump and drop his notes. Nicholas got into trouble over that, and I thought he would never forgive me for it. We still laugh about it when sitting around drinking wine.

I told him that removing the wax top should be fairly simple. All one had to do was heat up a cork screw and twist it into the center of the wax and then heat up a small knife and cut around the edges while lightly pulling on the corkscrew. You could tell that he didn't want to do it, but curiosity got the best of him. When no one was around, we carefully carried it out to the workshop and began the process of removing the wax plug. The corkscrew went in quite easily, but cutting the outside edge was a bit difficult. As we cut into the wax with the knife, the melted wax would solidify as the knife made its way around the edge. Eventually, after cutting around the edge several times, the wax plug pulled out. It was heavier than expected, as there seemed to be something attached to it. As we slowly pulled out the wax, there appeared to be a scroll attached to it. It was a long piece of wood with some sort of paper wrapped around it.

When Nicholas realized that it was a scroll, he very carefully laid it across two blocks of wood so as not to damage it. We were both excited about what we found. Nicholas said that the smart thing to do was to take it to a museum curator whom he knew and let him unroll the paper. He said that museum curators know how to handle these kinds of things. We very carefully removed the wax from the wooden handle of the scroll and reinserted it into the urn, making sure that no one would notice that it was tampered with.

Nicholas drove us to the museum the next day. I held the scroll by the wooden ends as he maneuvered his way through traffic. One drop of the scroll could mean disaster. In my mind, I pictured the scroll hitting the dashboard during a sudden stop, and the paper shattering into a thousand pieces.

On the safe arrival at the museum, the curator said that it was a papyrus scroll, and that there was someone in the lab that had experience in working with such items. He said that it would take a week of working with it before identifying what and if anything was written on it. We left it with him and spent the rest of the day touring different sites and having lunch at his favorite café. I kept telling him that it was a treasure map, and that the curator was going to be the first one to get the treasure. Nicholas said that it was most likely an ancient writing of no significant value.

Nicholas encouraged me to extend my stay another week to see what was on the scroll, if anything. The scroll was spread out under a glass enclosure in a dark room illuminated with some sort of violet light. The curator said that the words on it were in ancient Greek with uppercase characters and were probably written sometime in the first three centuries. He said that detailed lab tests on the paper and ink would need to be performed to narrow down the time frame. Unless the writing appeared to be of significant interest, he wasn't sure that anyone would take the time and effort to perform the tests.

Nicholas asked the curator if he could interpret what was written, and he said that he and the lab technician were able to figure out most of the writing. He said that he had to go to the library to figure out some of the words but basically said that it appeared to be written by a man named Silvanus and seemed to reference several urns hidden in a cave next to a spring in a village called Beth-Gebar. The curator said that he could find no reference of a village named Beth-Gebar in Greece or anywhere else. The only other clue was that the writer cautioned anyone from retrieving the scrolls until after hostilities between the Jews and Romans have ceased. That indicated that Beth-Gebar was probably located somewhere near Israel.

Given that the amphora was Phoenician, based on the artwork, the scroll most likely came from the Lebanon area, perhaps Tyre or Sidon. The base of the amphora had the letter P stamped in it. It was most likely the Phoenician letter P, which probably identified the maker. It could have been the Greek letter rho, but a Greek letter on a Phoenician amphora didn't make sense.

Nicholas asked me if I wanted to visit Lebanon and research the museums there in hopes of locating Beth-Gebar, and perhaps the cave where the urns may be hidden. I told him that my new job limited my vacation time, and that my funds were low. He offered to cover the flight costs to Beirut and pushed me to extend my vacation. Reluctantly, I agreed, although I had no interest in going to Lebanon because of the turmoil in that region.

We rented a small car in Beirut and began checking museums from there and to the south. The museum curators were very accommodating. The museum in Beirut had a jar that was stamped with the letter P on the bottom, and compared to our picture, the letter seemed to be the same size and shape of the one on the amphora. We found several pieces of art in the Sidon museum that were stamped with the maker's logo on the bottom, even a glass figurine. There were a half a dozen amphoras with the logo. The curator said that there may be others in storage, and we were welcome to look at them.

As we moved further south, there was a small museum in Sarafand that had several amphoras similar to the one in Nicholas's home. They all had the logo stamped on the bottom. The Tyre museum had a couple amphoras with the letter P, and that was it.

There was nothing further south. We decided not to enter Israel but instead focused on the coastal area between Tyre and Sidon.

We crossed the Litani River and wondered if that was the spring that was mentioned in the scroll. We'd have to study the Greek word used for *spring* to see if it could be translated as *river*. Just north of Sarafand, which is the modern name for Zarephath, I noticed a pipe leading down the embankment that appeared to feed under the road. The only place to stop was about a quarter mile down the road. We walked back to the pipe and up the embankment. There was a very small stream of water feeding into the pipe. We wondered if that could be the spring mentioned in the scroll and decided to walk the area and check it out. There were houses nearby to the north, but the land around the stream seemed vacant. There appeared to be some ruins to the right, a couple of old foundations.

Nicholas suggested walking to the top of the hill to see if we could spot a cave in the area. There was a foundation of a large building at the top. I brushed away some of the dirt and noticed the letters alpha and omega on a couple of the tiles and suspected that it was the ruins of a Christian church. The view from the top was fabulous. There was a small village and harbor to the northwest.

We noticed that the path disappeared about three quarters of the way down the hill. The hill was sandstone, and erosion over the years had covered the south side. Nicholas noticed a small hole further around the hill. We checked it out, and it looked like a small animal hole. It went in fairly deep, and we didn't have a flashlight to see how far it went.

There was a bed and breakfast place in the village. We spent the night there. Nicholas asked the owner, Artemis, if he could borrow a shovel. Artemis gave him one but told him that digging for artifacts is a no-no. If the authorities caught us digging without a permit, Artemis said that we would not see daylight for several years, and that was before we went to trial.

The name of the village is Az Zahrani. I asked the owner if he ever heard of a place called Beth-Gebar. He said the name sounded familiar, and that it could be the name of the old village that existed south

of town. He suggested that we talk with the rabbi at the local synagogue, as he knew the area history better than anyone. Artemis said
that the rabbi didn't speak English, just Arabic, French, and Hebrew.
Fortunately, Nicholas spoke French, so off we went to the synagogue.

The rabbi was aware of the area history and confirmed that the
original name of the village was Beth-Gebar, but the location was
more to the south of the village. The village was relocated due to
occasional flooding from the nearby wadi. We spoke with him about
our quest, and he said there were a few artifacts in the storage room
that we could look at. We found a couple amphoras and checked the
bases for the logo. Unfortunately, there was no logo, but the artwork
was very similar to that in our picture.

We asked him about springs in the area, and he said that the
only spring was the one that we spotted by the road. He said that a
pipe runs from the upper part of the spring to a holding tank near
the village. With that, Nicholas and I decided to search for the cave
at night when no one could see us. We purchased a flashlight and
headed to the sandstone hill. The ground was hard but loosened up
as we dug further into the hole that we discovered earlier. It turned
out to be the top of a cave that seemed to have collapsed over time.
We weren't sure what kind of critters lived in the cave and slowly
crawled across the rocky debris. We could see the cave floor but nothing of consequence could be seen. I noticed two rooms off to each
side. The floor to the left appeared dark and dirty.

The one to the right was covered with a layer of dust and sand.
We had to move several large rocks to get into the one on the right. It
was empty except for a pile of dirt at one end. I brushed away some
of the dirt and encountered a pile of rocks. With curiosity, I removed
some of the rocks, and lo and behold, a dirty clay jug of some sort
was buried in it. We unearthed the whole area and found nineteen
sealed urns. One urn had the logo on the bottom.

Needless to say, we were both quite excited. Our next task was
to figure out how to get them to Athens. Nicholas called his dad
and explained the dilemma that we were in. At first, his dad was
upset that we tampered with the urn in the glass case. However, after
hearing what we found, his dad was filled with the same curiosity

that we had. The plan was to transport the urns to Beirut and smuggle them aboard one of the company ships. That was the easy part. Unfortunately, the ship was not heading to Greece. The ship was used to transport water, and its regular route was between Turkey and Lebanon. Once the urns were aboard ship, we flew back to Athens. I left a day later and made it back to Boston. Nicholas's father flew to Turkey in his private jet and picked up the urns. Being in a small airport where everyone knew him made it easy to transport the urns from the ship to the plane.

The nineteen urns contained twenty papyrus scrolls. The curator forced Nicholas to learn how to translate ancient Greek into modern Greek and how to properly handle ancient artifacts, especially papyrus scrolls. It took Nicholas about a year to translate them. He said that the scrolls were about a family who moved from Judea and settled in an area near Beth-Gebar. The author was Silvanus, and he wrote about his family history while living there. The time frame seemed to cover most of the first century. Nicholas wondered if there was a connection between that family and his, based on the urn being passed down through generations of his family.

I couldn't read Greek, so I asked Nicholas if he or someone he knows would be willing to translate the scrolls into English. Nicholas said that a summer hire at the museum would probably do it for some extra cash on the side. He agreed to pay for it, as I had no money to speak of. I told him that I would pay him back in a year or so. My engineer salary was not all that great compared to my cost of living.

Once I received the translations, I smoothed out the English and put it in book form. The scrolls written by Silvanus gave an account of his family's move from Judea to a small village along the Mediterranean coast in what is now Lebanon. As the story line progresses, the focus becomes more and more on Silvanus's younger sister Rachael, who grew from being an unkempt, fearless little girl to becoming the most wealthy and powerful woman in Greece, impacting both Greek and Roman economies. I took poetic license and translated Rachael's nick name as Ragamuffin. It was the best way to describe the little girl who had unkempt hair and wore dirty clothes. She became my favorite character in the book.

Chapter 1

THE COPPER MINE

Silvanus, son of Matthias, son of Gaius, son of Jonathan to my descendants. Having lived along a thoroughfare traveled by Roman soldiers, rebel forces as part of the Jewish resistance, Syrian raiders, traders of all sorts, dignitaries, and folks traveling to or from something for one reason or another. I felt it was time to document the stories passed down by my forefathers as well as those of my own experiences. Rabbi Zachias gave me a scroll to work with. Rain squalls were moving in from the sea and to escape the rain, I retreated to the desk in my bedroom. I used a couple of decorative onyx stones to hold the scroll in place. My younger sister, Rachael, whom we call Ragamuffin, stepped in out of the rain, wondering what I was doing. During the explanation, she was admiring one of the onyx stones holding down the scroll. In the process of picking up the stone, the scroll rolled and landed on the oil lamp and caught fire. With a deep breath, she sighed her usual apology. After sending her off to her mother, I began the following account of my great grandfather, Jonathan, albeit, on a partially burnt scroll.

Grandfather Gaius often spoke about his father, Jonathan. The most notable tales revolved around his participation in the conflict with the Arabians. Cleopatra, in her support of Mark Antony in Egypt, convinced the Arabians to attack Israel. The intention was to weaken the Roman army in that region in hope of defeating Octavian forces who were trying to solidify control of the empire in Rome. Unfortunately, Mark Antony was later defeated in the Battle of Actium.

Following battles with the Arabians, Jonathan would scavenge the battlefields for spoils of war. He preferred swords and any item made of metal that could be used in his family's metal working business. On occasion, he would deliver wounded soldiers to their respective villages and would hide as much plunder as he could with the men in the carts. On his last journey, he was confronted by a centurion named Cassius who discovered the hidden weapons and accused Jonathan of supplying weapons to the Jewish resistance.

Needless to say, Jonathan was arrested and enslaved at a nearby copper mine overseen by Cassius. Jonathan described the forced labor conditions as horrible, to say the least. He was lowered into a deep hole by a rope and wasn't allowed to come to the surface unless he and his team met their quota of copper ore. The mine tunnels were small, cold, and damp. The tunnels went every which way as they followed copper veins. The lack of airflow made it difficult to breath.

While on the surface, Jonathan noticed hundreds of men spread out over the ground smelting copper ore. The ore was in small pieces, and the bellows were small and crude, being operated in a foot peddle fashion. The small amount of copper released from the ore was combined and refined in a large smelter.

Jonathan befriended one of the Roman soldiers and would often talk with him during meal times. On one occasion, Jonathan mentioned how inefficient their smelting process was and offered to improve the process if Cassius was interested. The soldier mentioned it to the centurion, and it wasn't long before Jonathan was summoned by one of the guards and taken to Cassius.

Cassius asked Jonathan how he would improve the smelting process, as his superiors weren't happy with his production rate. Jonathan suggested adding leather valves to the bellows to improve airflow over the coals and to create a higher melting temperature. Jonathan knew that gold and silver were by-products of copper smelting and suggested that the centurion acquire the by-products before shipping the copper ingots to Rome to be further refined.

Jonathan also knew that centurions looked for ways to increase their personal wealth before retiring or returning to Rome and suggested that he could design a method to strip most of the gold and silver from the copper before being shipped. Cassius's eyes lit up and became quite interested in Jonathan's method of extracting the gold and silver.

Jonathan told him that he would have to make an iron cone into which the molten copper is to be poured. Gold and silver being heavier than copper would settle at the tip of the cone, whereby a metal worker could cut or knock off the gold and silver for later refinement. Cassius liked the idea and asked where he could get the iron cones. Jonathan said that he could make several of them at his family's forge, and all he needed was some iron to work with.

Cassius said that he had no iron to spare, and Jonathan suggested that the iron swords that were taken from him could be used to make the cones. Cassius smiled as he summarized what Jonathan was suggesting. He was to trust Jonathan with the swords that he was arrested for, allow him to return to his village, and trust that he would return with the iron cones. After a lengthy pause, the spirit of greed took over, and he decided to take the risk.

Following many days at the forge and a lot of hammering, Jonathan was able to make several iron cones. He faithfully returned to the copper mine. Cassius wasn't too surprised to see him. Cassius could read people quite well, and Jonathan was one person whom he believed in. With some help from the smelters, Jonathan demonstrated how to use the iron cones. Cassius was breathless when he saw the first tip of gold and silver. He told Jonathan not to mention this to anyone and gave him a denarius along with his freedom.

Shortly after returning home, Jonathan married Lois and had three sons, Gaius, Joseph, and Demitrius. Gaius was a homebody and served as an apprentice under Jonathan. He married Priscilla and had five children: Matthias, John, Benjamin, Naomi, and Elizabeth. Joseph and Demitrius were more adventurous and worked the caravans that traveled to Damascus in Syria and to Tyre and Sidon along the coastal route. They served mostly to guard the caravans from looters. Jonathan had trained them to be excellent sword fighters, training that he had received from the Romans. Joseph and Demitrius fell in love with Sidon and had made friends with several of the merchants who offered to help them set up their own businesses.

Grandfather Gaius was born during the reign of Herod the Great. The Roman Republic had just transformed into the Roman Empire with Augustus Caesar (Octavian) being the first emperor. Augustus confirmed Herod as king of Judea, although, for all practical purposes, he was king of all Palestine and had been appointed as king of the Jews by the Roman senate. Herod was not well liked. Herod expanded the temple in Jerusalem, broke many Jewish laws, and promoted Hellenism by introducing Greek style games, Greek temples, forts, and palaces. He also built an amphitheater for gladiatorial fights, which offended the Jews. He even selected who was going to be the high priest. After his death, the Romans appointed politically reliable priests. Herod devastated the rural society by confiscating subsistence farms (family farms) and turned them into large estates for high yield, single purpose crops for export. Wholesale land confiscation, heavy taxation on farmers, and other taxes such as salt tax, fishing polls, custom duties for transfer of produce from one region to another, taxes on manufacturing, and the uprooting of agricultural families who were deprived of their land forced people to relocate. Unhappy with the turmoil under his reign as king and the loss of the family farmland, Gaius and his two brothers, Joseph and Demitrius, decided to leave Judea. With several donkey carts, a couple of pack animals, and backpacks, they headed north along the coastal route.

Jonathan remained behind. As a coppersmith, he did not want to part with smelting and refining copper and making copper utensils and vessels to be sold to the local villagers. Jonathan was excellent at refining the metal to the point that he could separate out the silver and gold. Unfortunately, most of the crude copper was sent to Rome along with other resources such as tin and marble. He didn't want to give up his trade as of yet despite the fact that he had little material to work with. He promised to join the family when they were settled. Jonathan and his wife, Lois, eventually moved to Sidon to live with Joseph.

Chapter 2

BETH-GEBAR

S ilvanus, the son of Matthias, the son of Gaius, to my descendants. After Abigail, Mary-Beth, and I finished watering the garden, I thought it would be a good time to take a break and write concerning grandfather's journey from Judea to Beth-Gebar. Rachael joined me as she was escaping some teasing from her sisters. She never stopped talking and wanted to know everything that I was writing. I got rid of her by sending her off on assignments such as getting me a bowl of stew or some grapes from the vineyard. Rachael was a servant of servants. She loved to retrieve food from the garden or fruit from the trees. She eventually made up with her sisters and left me alone.

As for the journey from Judea, my father Matthias, along with his two brothers Benjamin and John, and his two sisters Naomi and Elizabeth, remember the trip as being very hot, dusty, and tiring. While Gaius and his brothers traveled north toward Sidon, taxmen tried to extract a toll from his brothers as they passed through Tyre even though it was obvious that they were transporting their personal household goods. His brothers, being experienced traders, had recommended a certain route around the main road to avoid the tax collectors, but unfortunately, the tax collectors were wise to this strategy. Gaius walked to the front of their little caravan and inquired of his brothers as to the problem. While listening to their response, Gaius noticed suture marks on the arm of one of the taxmen.

The suture marks reminded Gaius of his experience as a surgeon's assistant during his participation in a conflict with the Arabians. Herod the Great engaged in several conflicts as he solidified his kingdom. Rather than be conscripted into Herod's army, Gaius, at the suggestion of his father, volunteered to support the surgeons at the rear of the battlefields. It was a position that rarely resulted in death or injury. While there, Gaius gained a reputation as a fast and efficient surgeon. He found that the surgical equipment was quite cumbersome to use. During a short visit to his village while transporting injured soldiers to their villages, he got together with his father, Jonathan, and they decided to improve on the needles used for suturing wounds. The current needles were large and tended to make large holes for the thread to go through. It took a long time to make the stitch. To cut back on time and the size of the hole, and not to mention less pain, they made a fishhook shaped needle (without the barbs and with a small eye in one end). Each side of the needle was of equal length. The new design was small and easy to use. It took a while to get the manufacturing process down, but with patience and a lot of delicate hammering, Gaius and his father made a dozen or so needles.

Gaius employed the new needles during his surgeries and was able to complete the sutures in half the time with less scarring. He applied honey to the stitches. This seemed to prevent infections as the wounds healed. A lot of soldiers died from infected wounds. The chief surgeon was impressed and took him under his wing. Hundreds of soldiers were treated at the hands of Gaius.

Gaius asked the tax collector who did his stitches, and before responding, the taxman recognized Gaius as his surgeon. Following humble greetings and a couple of war stories, Gaius and his brothers were able to pass toll free.

As they neared Beth-Gebar, a small Phoenician fishing village, they stopped at a spring to water the donkeys and to give everyone a refreshing break. Grandfather Gaius noticed that there were no residents in the area of the spring. He climbed up the sandstone hill and followed the spring for quite some distance. He saw potential there as a place to settle. It seemed quite isolated from Beth-Gebar, and he inquired in the village as to who owned the property. With no ownership claims, Father decided to make it his home. Gaius couldn't understand why the village was located on a wadi in which water flowed during the seasonal rains rather than around a spring that appeared to flow year round. Perhaps the suitability as a small port was the reason.

The port was nothing to speak of other than being capable of supporting a fishing village. He spotted wells in the village. Perhaps they supplied enough water to satisfy the needs of the villagers. There were few Jews in the village. The village was still overpowered with pagan influences with Athena as their main focus of worship. They seemed to have adopted the Greek gods. Other gods were not accepted because the villagers hated the Romans and disliked the Egyptians and peoples of the east. The village mayor made it a point to put a bust of the reigning emperor in the town square to appease the Roman troops who visited the village during their southern and northern marches. When the troops left, the bust was removed, and Athena was put back in its place. The soldiers never noticed that the bust was of Julius Caesar and not the current reigning emperor.

The location was great. Neither the Roman procurator of Sidon nor Tyre claimed the small village. There was no military praefect in the village to act as the chief of police to enforce civil order or to collect taxes. Because it was not a port suitable for importing goods, no import tax was collected. All imports were taxed by Roman law and came into such ports as Sidon to the north or Tyre, Caesarea and Joppa to the south. Smuggled goods usually ended up being taxed as they made their way up and down the coast. Imported goods lacking documentation were confiscated at the entrance of any legal port city or cities along the eastern trade route. Smuggled goods were usually taken across the coastal range to avoid detection and ended up on the black market in some way, shape, or form. The village mayor profited quite well from this illicit traffic.

Given that the property was outside of the Palestinian borders and not under the responsibility of any procurator, also not to mention being outside the village, there were no land and head taxes to pay. From that point of view, it was a nice location. Wealth accumulated from taxation was funneled to Rome and was used to turn Rome from a city of bricks to a city of marble.

Octavian ruled the empire after the death of Julius Caesar. He was later dubbed Caesar Augustus. Under Caesar Augustus's Pax Romana, there was general peace, prosperity, and good government. Palestine seemed to lack all of these. He implemented many construction projects throughout the empire.

There appeared to be small caves carved into the sandstone cliffs. Gaius suspected that the area was inhabited at one time. They camped a short distance away, between the road and the cliffs that bordered the sea. The camp and especially the site where they eventually settled had a beautiful view of the Mediterranean.

Joseph and Demitrius were traders at heart. Their plan was to continue on to Sidon. They remained at the camp for six months. During which time, they helped Gaius build a home, a stable, and fencing for the donkeys and goats. They left their goats with Gaius prior to leaving for Sidon.

Over decades, the property progressed from being a rundown hobble next to a spring to a flourishing estate consisting of a garden, vineyard, fruit and nut trees, and trees grown for firewood. Gaius wanted a house with a view of the sea, so he carved out a nice place on the south side of the sandstone hill. The side of the hill was one wall and sandstone blocks made up the other three walls. A veranda faced the sea. The veranda was just outside of Gaius's bedroom, and the bedroom was curtained off from the kitchen. A large dining area separated the kitchen from the main entrance.

A fire ring was constructed near the main entrance. The spring flowed next to the building area. Near the fire ring, steps led up to one of the caves in which a bedroom was carved out. The bedroom could sleep four, and this was where the girls, Elizabeth and Naomi, slept. My sisters—Abigail, Mary-Beth, and Rachael—would eventually inherit this room. A guest house was built a short distance from the fire ring. The guest house was where my father, Matthias, and his brothers, Benjamin and John, slept. It eventually became my bedroom unless visitors were offered a place to stay. It had four beds arranged in each corner. Gaius carved a small room into the sandstone on the sea side of the hill. It could be accessed from the veranda. He and Priscilla eventually made that their bedroom when father married Mariam.

The outhouses were a problem at first. Gaius located them on the other side of the spring so that the outflow didn't contaminate the water. People had to walk a fair length across a small wooden bridge to get to them. During harsh weather conditions and during darkness, the trip was no fun to say the least. To appease the women, Gaius installed a large pipe that redirected the spring water closer to the main house. The newly formed stream emptied onto the road below. There was a culvert below the road where the original stream flowed. A new one had to be constructed to manage the new water flow. Two outhouses were then built closer to the buildings. With pipes, rocks, cement, and fill dirt, they were quite sanitary. It was not a good idea for anyone to drink what little water that flowed in the old stream path.

Father directed the good water that flowed to the road into two areas. He designed and constructed a water trough for horses and donkeys that traveled the road. In the other area, water poured into a bowl for travelers to drink from. Father found an area further inland that had a decent clay deposit. He figured out a way to make clay pipes, and over the years, he connected the whole area with an elaborate network of water pipes. One system ran to the southern field to water the livestock. Another flowed to the area where Gaius first camped on the other side of the road. Water was directed through that system when visitors camped out in that area.

There was a waterfall upstream from our home. Grandfather Gaius and Father built a pool below the waterfall. It eventually became big enough to bathe and swim in. The hillsides next to the spring were terraced off and planted with fruit and nut trees. A vineyard was planted near the field to the south. The garden area was on the other side of the spring near the vineyard.

All the grain was used up by the time Joseph and Demitrius departed for Sidon. They had contacts with merchants in Sidon who were going to help them set up a business. Gaius found a way down the cliff to the sea shore. A few deep areas near the cliffs yielded plenty of fish. Goat's milk, a few fowl, and fish were the main staples until a garden was planted. An occasional deer supplied venison. Wild honey and berries were plentiful.

The garden consisted mainly of onions, beans, squash, beets, cucumbers, melons, and cabbage. Our trees produced apricots, lemons, oranges, figs, olives, almonds, and pistachios. Joseph sent grain shortly after getting established in Sidon. The village rabbi would occasionally stop by and bring fruit, nuts, and wine. The rabbi grew fruit and managed a vineyard on the synagogue property. The synagogue was small but adequate for the contingent of Jews living in or near the village.

There was no demand for Gaius's trade skills. As a metal smith, there was no metal to work with. Also, it took time to construct a smelting furnace. Coal for the furnace could be purchased if there was a decent source of money. The village had no need of a carpenter or a mason.

Chapter 3

LIKE FATHER, LIKE SON

Silvanus, son of Matthias, son of Gaius, to my descendants. The ill winds were blowing hard today. Everyone remained undercover to shelter themselves from the dust and the wind. Hermes, our volunteer servant, continued to teach us Greek. Rachael mastered the language better than the rest of us. She was most excellent when it came to learning languages. The rabbi taught her how to write in the Hebrew-Aramaic language used in Judea. Grandfather Gaius gave the following account while sitting around the campfire the night before.

Grandfather Gaius needed a financial breakthrough. The big break came at a time when he was standing on top of the hill next to his home. He could see a fair distance up and down the highway, along with the village and its moored fishing boats. It was here where he and Priscilla would watch the sunsets over the Mediterranean. One day, while alone and praying toward Jerusalem, he noticed a contingent of Roman soldiers to the south. It was a combination of foot soldiers, horsemen, pack horses, horse-drawn carts, and a chariot.

Gaius watched as they approached the spring. The riders drank from the spring first and then watered the horses. As they moved on, the foot soldiers took their turns at the spring and waited for every-one to finish before forming ranks and continuing on their march. Next, the cart handlers stopped at the spring followed by another group of foot soldiers. There was a fair distance between the horse-men and the first group of foot soldiers.

As the horseman paralleled the village, Gaius noticed movement in the valley just east of the village. As he watched, the whole field seemed to move as if a huge gust of wind had hit it. To his surprise, spears and arrows were directed toward the horsemen as a huge num-ber of people covered with hay to disguise themselves rushed toward the road. As a fierce battle ensued, the foot soldiers, being alerted by the commotion, ran toward the battle. Unfortunately, most of the horsemen, including their commanding officer, were slain before the foot soldiers could reach them.

The soldiers broke into two ranks, and with close quarter posi-tions and with spears and swords in hand, they attacked the raiders on two fronts. Gaius hiked over to the saddle that connected the hill that he was on to the hillside that was closer to the valley. The sad-dle was a better vantage point to view the battlefield. As the Roman archers arrived, there was an array of arrows going both ways. The Romans archers were more organized in that they concentrated on targets in small groups, whereas their foe was shooting at individual targets or at the rank and file groups that seemed well protected using their shields.

Both sides seemed to run out of arrows and were seen picking up expended arrows and shooting them back at the enemy. Eventually, a group of Romans, made up of remaining horsemen and cart handlers (mostly servants), formed a front that flanked the enemy from the south. Generally, servants stayed out of harm's way, but given the cir-cumstances, they were inducted as warriors. The Romans eventually kept up a relentless pursuit and drove the enemy east up the valley and disappeared around the ridge.

It was late afternoon when the soldiers returned. They showed no mercy to the wounded enemy. They did keep a couple prison-ers, probably for interrogation purposes. The rest of the evening was spent setting up camp and dealing with their wounded. It was at this point that Gaius saw an opportunity. He remembered how Jonathan would scavenge for weapons and anything made of metal from the battlefields. As darkness settled in, Gaius sneaked down the hillside and began to collect valuables from both the Roman bodies and the enemy. He took money bags, gold and silver ear and finger rings, swords, knives, spears, bows, and arrows. His take was somewhat limited as he had to stay invisible to the Romans encamped by the road. He stashed his plunder in a crevice along the hillside and covered it with brush and whatever debris he could find. He waited for the moon to rise so that he could move about at night and collect as much plunder as he could.

Before twilight and not wanting to be seen, Gaius headed up over the saddle toward home. He suspected his family was quite worried, being aware of the previous day's conflict. When Priscilla saw Gaius, she was in tears as she ran and hugged him. When she became aware of the commotion, Priscilla and the children went to the top of the hill to see what was going on. When she did not see Gaius, she became quite worried and stayed up all night waiting for him. Gaius had slept part of the night at the edge of the field.

Priscilla noticed that Gaius was carrying something in his uplifted garment and inquired as to what was in it. Gaius showed her some of the gold jewelry that he had collected, explained what he had done on the previous evening, and told her to keep quiet concerning his foray. With a short laugh, she said, "Like father, like son." After feeding the children, Priscilla—through exhaustion—retired to the bedroom. Gaius hid his spoils of war and decided to walk up the road toward the Romans and offer his assistance as a surgeon based on medical experience gained when he assisted the Jews and Romans in their fight against the Arabians.

The Romans were quite eager to accept his assistance as a surgeon. His surgical bag had little in it. He used their wine to cleanse the wounds and used their honey to seal the wounds after he stitched them with his special fishhook needles. His surgical skill captured the attention of the head Roman commander. Villagers stayed away during the conflict for safety reasons but congregated at the battle site in the morning. Gaius spoke with the officer in command and suggested that the villagers would help with burying the dead for a few sacks of grain. Some of the grain carts would have to be emptied anyway to carry the wounded, so the officer agreed. A messenger was sent to the Sidon garrison to inform them as to what happened and to request assistance.

About fifty-seven Romans were killed in the battle, most of them during the initial attack. The attackers were identified as Syrian raiders. It was suspected that they were a mix of Jewish rebels and Syrians, but everyone essentially agreed that Jewish rebels weren't involved. At least forty or so raiders were killed. Once the Roman dead were buried, the army continued on their northern journey. They left it up to the villagers to track down the Syrian bodies and bury them.

Gaius noticed that they left behind a chariot. It was damaged to the point that it could not be used for travel. There was also a large iron cooking pot on the side of the road. Gaius claimed both of these items as his. The villagers divided up the sacks of grain that were left for them and began to scavenge the valley for valuables and weapons left behind. The Roman soldiers had already stripped the Syrians of their valuables. That is, except for what Gaius had accumulated the night before.

Gaius rolled the big iron pot back to his home and then returned for a sack of grain and an amphora filled with barley flour. With some help from the villagers, he was able to move the chariot to a spot near the stables. It had a broken axle. It would be awhile before he could tool up to repair it. He realized at this point that conflict had its benefits. After getting a good night's sleep, Gaius retrieved his remaining trove of armament that he hid on the other side of the saddle. The next few days were spent scouring the valley for items that the other scavengers may have missed. He found mostly arrows, a couple more bows and a spear. He came across a couple of bodies that others had missed and found a few coins and a couple of gold ear rings. He buried the bodies the best he could and returned home.

The chariot was a bit odd. It was obviously of Egyptian design. However, it had some Syrian markings along with some subtle modifications. The Romans had replaced the leathering and colors to best match their military ornamentation. It was probably taken from a Roman versus Syrian battlefield. Fixing it would take time. However, it still needed a couple of horses to move it. Horses which Gaius didn't have and couldn't afford at the time. Nevertheless, it was a prize to behold.

The villagers began to show a lot of respect for Gaius. At first, they were puzzled by his willingness to help the Romans, but when he negotiated grain for burying the dead, this was a most excellent move, as there was a shortage of grain during that year. The grain fields along the valley were small. Any change in weather conditions would make or break their yearly need. Fortunately, being a fishing village, seafood was a good backup in time of grain shortages.

Money was always in short supply. The local fishermen would sail to Tyre or Sidon to sell their catches. For all practical purposes, there were no taxes. When the village was in need of maintenance, the mayor's wife and daughter would visit the homes of the villagers and solicit money for the project. Most people gave something, usually a denarii or two.

The village rabbi showed his appreciation by delivering a basket of fruit. He planted many fruit trees around the synagogue and was proud of his produce. When in season, it was not unusual for the rabbi to bring some of his first fruits to Gaius and his family. The fruit consisted of apples, figs, apricots, grapes, and pomegranates. Many times when visiting the synagogue, Gaius would return with almonds and pistachios. Although not grown by the priest, many village Jews tithed these nuts from their produce. Gaius gave him a tenth of the grain that he acquired as a tithe. It was the first time that Gaius could realistically begin paying tithes again.

Gaius casually mentioned to the rabbi that he had acquired a small arsenal of weapons from the battlefield, and that if anyone had need, they could purchase them for a reasonable price. The Romans controlled most mining and manufacturing. Slave labor was used both in mining and manufacturing. Thus, acquiring weapons was quite difficult. Weapons could be acquired from the east, and many weapons such as swords could be purchased on the black market, for a hefty price of course.

It didn't take long for the word to get out, and Gaius gained the reputation as an arms dealer. It was the first source of income for the family. Although welcomed at first, the reputation presented a bit of uneasiness because of the risk of being discovered by the Romans. Gaius's name began to filter through such groups as the Jewish and Syrian resistance, not to mention the underworld of thieves and robbers. Rumors spread that he led a ruthless band of outlaws operating mostly in the Palestinian area and was using his newly acquired home as a hideout. How these rumors spread, only God knows. When walking in the village, the people always treated him with respect. Gaius became a good source of money for the marketeers.

With his newly acquired wealth, Gaius began developing a metalworking business. Smelting gold and silver was his first task. Although the gold and silver that he acquired from the battlefield were fairly pure, he wanted to melt it down into talents with proper standard weights. His father, Jonathan, gave him molds that allowed him to make some silver drachma and denarii coins. Being a counterfeiter was not necessary but added excitement to his business. It was a way of thumbing your nose at the Greeks and Romans. Silver and gold held its value by weight regardless of the shape it was in. Coins seemed to guarantee purity. As one can see, a skill in metal working had its side benefits. The rabbi's eyes would always light up when Gaius dropped silver and gold into the box, whether it was in the form of shekels, drachmas, denarii, or just plain ingots.

Gaius needed a place to store food and contraband. He expanded on the cave that existed next to the girls' room. It was a place to go when one wanted to cool down from the summer heat. He carved two side rooms. One was for storing weapons and his gold and silver. He blocked it with a wooden storage shelf that moved when certain pins were removed. The other was the cold room. The rest of the cave was for storing stuff that may or may not be of any future use.

The cold room was used for storing ice. When the small lakes would occasionally freeze over in the mountains, Gaius would travel with donkey and cart as far as he could go and cut big pieces of ice—some thin, some thick—and cart them back to the cave. He used sawdust and cedar boards to insulate the ice. The ice would usually last until late summer. Some years, there would be very little or no ice at all. Thin ice usually melted before he returned home. The ice served to make cool drinks in the hot summer and was a novelty for guests who dropped in after a long hot journey. It went a long way in winning and influencing friends. The spring itself was quite cold. I'm not sure that the trips to the mountain lakes were worth the trouble. There was not a whole lot to do in the winter, so the trips were mostly made to fill in the time. If there was no ice, Gaius would always cut down a tree and bring back firewood. This preserved his trees for use as lumber and such around the home site.

After several years, Gaius wanted to replace the sandstone blocks used for constructing the house with hewn stone. Limestone was plentiful. Most houses in Judea were built with limestone. The poor in the outlying places lived in huts made from dried mud. Marble was a popular stone to use. However, Rome placed a great demand on marble for its construction projects, which left very little to be had. The family argued over replacing the sandstone blocks because most of the quarries seemed to be mined using slave labor. The slaves were a mix of Jews, Syrians, Arabians, and Egyptians. They were not treated well. The slave code of ethics popular in Rome did not apply throughout the empire. The constant wearing away of the current sandstone blocks and the need to continually sweep sand collecting on the floor persuaded Priscilla to side with her husband on replacing the blocks.

Gaius had to go to Tyre to acquire the blocks. Finances dictated a few blocks at a time. Several years later, there were enough blocks stacked in the backyard to rebuild the main house. The guest house was replaced about three years later.

Gaius kept some of the armament for himself. Once sold off, it wasn't long before money was in short supply again. There was plenty of food from the fruit trees and garden. However, material was needed to continue building up the property and improving his metal work.

One day, while observing a small contingent of Romans stopping to partake of the spring water, the commanding officer spied the open area ahead and told his men to camp there for the night.

Gaius walked down to where the commanding officer was standing and invited him and three of his top officers to join him for dinner.

The officer accepted. Before the four officers showed up, Gaius arranged to have Elizabeth and Naomi wash their feet and for Priscilla to prepare a meal fit for a king, which consisted of a meaty stew with freshly baked bread. The boys gathered some fruit, some of which was made into lemonade. Just as the officers arrived, the lemonade was served with ice. They looked at each other in shock, as no one served drinks with ice in that part of the world.

After showing them the home site, he offered them a stay in the guest house. They accepted the offer. The boys would have to sleep in the kitchen. They weren't too happy about that. The girls did an excellent job in massaging and washing their feet and gave them clean sandals to wear. After a nice meal, they spent the rest of the evening around the fire ring, drinking wine and sharing news of the empire.

In the morning, the girls showed them the pool where they could bathe. The pool wasn't big enough to swim in at that time but was adequate for bathing. After a nice breakfast, the officers asked Gaius how much he charged for the accommodations. Gaius told them that there was no charge for guests invited into his home. He stated that he was glad to have visitors, and that they were welcome to stop by any time they were in the area.

The officers marveled at this and thanked Gaius for his hospitality. One of the officers slipped the girls a couple of denarii as they left. Gaius later found two amphoras of wheat flour at his doorstep. Having found Gaius's generosity a bit overwhelming, they felt that a gift was necessary prior to leaving the campground.

This activity soon became a family tradition. They found that providing free hospitality actually was rewarding. There were times when travelers were invited in, and they obviously had no means to leave a departing gift. This didn't matter because travelers brought news, and news was always welcome. Besides, serving the poor meant gaining favor with God.

The villagers were not too happy with Gaius's relationship with the Romans. He would tell them from time to time that it was good to keep your friends close but wise to keep your enemies closer. It was amazing how many gifts were received for providing free hospitality to travelers. Gaius more than tithed from the gifts, as there was always excess food, dishes, pots, pans, and even clothes given to them. Most of these items were imported from Egypt. The rabbi took good care of the Jews in the village, and even distributed food and items to the nonbelievers in hopes of gaining some friends and perhaps a few proselytes.

This novel approach to improving our welfare has lasted through three generations. With a lot of digging and the cementing in of some rocks, Father improved on the bathing pool. It was actually big enough for children to swim in. He also built a bathhouse that was great for the winter time. No one wanted to jump into the ice cold pool water, except for father who was a bit on the crazy side.

Father rigged up the big pot that Gaius acquired from the battlefield so that it could pour hot water into the spa that he had built. Those who wanted to take a bath would build a fire under the pot and then pour the boiling water into the cold water in the spa. The spa had a pipe from the spring to feed it. About two pourings were enough to make the spring water warm enough to bathe in. My father and mother would always have us pour extra hot water for them. The water was never hot enough for mother. The spa had a drain at the bottom.

The main issue was having enough wood to heat the water. The small forest to the east of the property would be depleted in a few years if we continued to use wood to cook food, feed the fire ring, and heat the spa. To compensate for this, the children would hike down to the waterfront and scavenge driftwood along the shoreline. The salty wood made for sparkling flames in the fire ring. Occasionally, Father would take the donkey and hike up the valley for quite some distance and cut down a tree. Between the donkey and him, they would drag a log all the way back home. Father always wished he had a horse, as the donkey just didn't cooperate on these kinds of tasks. The donkey seemed fit to pull a cart, but when it came to dragging things, his character and mannerisms changed. Both Father and donkey always appeared stressed after hauling a log home. No one would talk to him until he had a meal and some time to destress.

My job was to cut up the log. Hermes would help me. It took forever. The iron saw seemed to get dull after a few cuts. The saw teeth constantly needed sharpening. Between sawing wood and hammering iron, I was in good physical shape.

The spa was a hit with guests. The Roman officers really like their hot baths. Father and I often wondered if the Roman officers didn't plan their stops at the campground just to take advantage of the spa in the winter or the cool pool water in the summer. Obviously, our family enjoyed the prosperity. The Romans referred to our house as the House of Gaius, and one of the Roman officers actually gave Gaius a sign that read "The House of Gaius, a friend of the Romans." The sign was attached to the lower gate and could be read from the road.

We always removed the sign after the Romans left. Other travelers, as well as the villagers, would not be amused with our apparent friendship with the Romans, especially members of the Jewish resistance. The sign immediately went up when a contingent of Romans were seen approaching. The increase in wealth allowed for tiled floors, marble furniture, and some good grade of limestone for building a house on the other side of the spring.

Chapter 4

HERMES

Silvanus, son of Matthias, son of Gaius to my descendants. Today was not one of my best days. I tore my robe on a tree branch and later on stubbed my toe on a rock. While complaining to mother about my unfortunate mishaps, my twin sister Abigail and my younger sister Mary-Beth both annoyed me by simultaneously, emoting deep sighs and telling me that they felt real bad for me. With that, I decided to retreat to my room and continue writing concerning our family adventures. Rachael retrieved a scroll from Rabbi Zachias earlier in the day while discussing religion with the rabbi. She was upset with the rabbi because he would not let her sit with the boys during their tutoring sessions. Rachael, in her Ragamuffin role, stopped by and did her best to console me. As always, she would grab my arm and lay her head on my shoulder, and with a deep sigh, she would say, "I love you, Silvanus." I could never figure out how she could start the day with clean clothes and a fresh look and end up with dirty clothes and unkempt hair. Her sweet, compassionate character was in contrast to her daily activities. After bidding her good-bye, I decided to write an account of how our humble servant, Hermes, joined our family.

My two uncles, Benjamin and John, left home early and went to work for their uncle Joseph in Sidon. Beth-Gebar didn't have a whole lot to offer them in terms of work. Uncle John was a hard worker and a smart businessman. Joseph and Demitrius really liked him. Benjamin, on the other hand, couldn't stay put in any one place. He was too adventurous. He had joined the Jewish resistance and survived on a little bit of work here and there. Benjamin was the black sheep of the family. He showed up on occasion, usually needing food and money. After a few days of socializing with the family, Grandfather Gaius would slip him a few shekels, and soon afterward, Benjamin would be off to places unknown.

Naomi and Elizabeth married Jews in the village. They visited quite often and helped mother raise us children. The variety of food was limited in the village, and their father, Gaius, always handed them food from the garden when they left. The close contact with family members seemed to create a peaceful atmosphere. Sidon wasn't too far to the north. John and his wife would often walk the distance and spend the night. However, when they had children, the visits became few and far between.

The villagers were hardworking, nice people. Mother went to the village often to visit friends and relatives. One of the children usually went with her. Abigail loved the walk. Aside from looking at and smelling flowers along the way, she would stop and have tea and muffins with either Naomi or Elizabeth while mother made the rounds with her friends.

As time went on, Abigail would take Ragamuffin for a walk in the village. Mary-Beth was quite shy and preferred to stay at home. When mother was with them, she would always avoid walking next to Penelope's home. Penelope always screamed and yelled at anyone coming near her flowers. She had flowers growing everywhere.

Apparently, Penelope's husband never returned from a fishing trip, and she blamed the villagers for not making an extra effort to try and find him. She made a living selling flowers in the summertime and making shawls during winter.

When Abigail was without Mother, she would always walk next to the wall outside Penelope's home and smell the flowers. Penelope's screaming and yelling fell on deaf ears. Abigail would always look up and compliment Penelope on her flowers. When Ragamuffin was with her, she would squeeze Abigail's hand in such a way as to tell her that they should leave and not to continue annoying Penelope.

Abigail always made it a point to ask Penelope questions about her flowers. Eventually, Penelope's loud voice sweetened, and it wasn't long before Abigail was invited in for tea and sweet bread. Her change in attitude could be seen as she walked through the village. Penelope even let Ragamuffin and Kaysi (our dog) watch over her flowers while she and Abigail went shopping in the village. Persistent kindness seems to prevail over disturbed minds.

In general, life was fairly routine and peaceful, at least until one day when I was twelve years old, I took the donkey up the valley looking for firewood. On that day, I heard a barking noise as a fox ran out of the brush and ran toward me. It immediately turned and ran off in another direction. He scared the living daylights out of me. If that wasn't enough, I could hear horses off at a distance. It wasn't normal to hear horses in that area. I decided it was time to head home. As I made my way toward the main road, a group of about forty riders passed by. They looked at me as they passed and stopped at the ridge on the left side as if to stay hidden from the road.

One of the men pointed at me and motioned for me to stop. I led the donkey to a nearby rock and sat down waiting to see what would happen next. Inside, I was shaking from fright, but I didn't want them to know that I was scared. To alleviate the tension, I began to talk to the donkey and pet the back of his neck.

Then, suddenly, they drew their swords and charged over the ridge toward the main road. I ran to the top of the ridge and watched as the riders attacked a small caravan of traders. There were only a dozen or so traders, and Father always said that they generally run when overwhelmed by raiding parties. Raiders were more interested in the goods than in pursuing and killing people.

In this instance, things were different. The traders stood their ground. They positioned themselves on the other side of the carts and pack animals, and as the raiders approached, swinging swords and screaming at the top of their lungs, the traders let loose a series of arrows. I was amazed at how fast they could reach back and grab an arrow, reload the bow, and aim and shoot at the enemy. They were extremely accurate.

As the horsemen ran between the carts, the defenders did forward rolls over the hitches connecting the donkeys and the carts and were quickly on the other side. They immediately stood up and fired at the rear of the horsemen, striking them in the back of the body. There were arrows sticking out of the back of their thighs, their rear end, and all over their backs. The raiders weren't very organized. Because of their inability to reach the defenders while on their horses, the raiders dismounted and attacked the traders. They swung their swords in a crazy, fanatical fashion. The defenders would roll away from them, and as they rolled, they would stab or slice with a knife, land on their feet, and use their swords to parry, block, and slice away at their foe.

The traders were obviously well-trained fighters. It wasn't long before the raiders were routed with their tails between their legs. About twenty-five or so made it up to the valley opposite to where I was watching the conflict. They were not a happy lot. They were yelling and screaming from the pain of their wounds. Some still had arrows sticking out of them. As they turned and glanced back at the caravan, they were helping each other pull out the arrows. Reluctantly, they headed back up the valley and were soon gone out of sight.

The traders didn't show any mercy to the wounded raiders. They had killed about fifteen of them. As I continued down toward the road, I could see that several of the traders were either killed or wounded. I approached one of the men and told him that my grandfather Gaius was a trained surgeon and could help them. They accepted, and I ran home to get Gaius and my father, Matthias.

Upon returning to the scene, some of the villagers began to show up. Father recommended that the villagers take the stray horses to the field south of our home. It was the only place where they could get water and hay. The villagers didn't have horses in that there was little hay in the area, and besides, horses were not needed in the village.

While the villagers were busy tending to the horses, Gaius pulled Father aside and told him to scavenge for valuables and weapons from the dead. Father turned to me and told me to hook up the donkey to our cart and bring it to the battle area. Gaius recommended that the traders move to the campsite south of our home. His intent was to clear the area so that Father and I could maximize our gain as scavengers.

At the camp, Gaius would apply his surgical skills on their wounds. Three of the traders were killed. One was seriously wounded. All the others were either cut or scraped in some fashion or other. It seemed that they were all covered in blood.

Father kept the personal items of the dead traders separate from those of the dead raiders. He had acquired quite a bit of gold jewelry along with a few coins. The cart was loaded with many swords and knives. The weapons thought to belong to the traders were given to them.

The rest of the day was spent burying the dead. The villagers were paid a few denarii for their efforts in burying the dead traders. The traders could care less about the other dead. It turns out that the traders were from northern Greece, and that their ship had to pull into Sidon for repairs. They hired carts and pack animals to complete their journey to Tyre. They were sailors and were in the business for themselves.

Priscilla and Mother baked extra bread and made some extra stew to feed the remaining nine Greeks. They spent the night at the campsite. They obviously weren't used to traveling. They had no tents, cooking utensils, or food to speak of. In the morning, after feeding them breakfast, they gave Gaius a few drachmas for his work as a surgeon and gave a mix of drachmas and denarii to Father for his hospitality. They took all the horses except for two to compensate for their losses. They were to be sold in Tyre.

A seriously wounded Greek appeared near to death. Father offered to care for him until he died. His name was Hermes. He was in bad shape. Lots of deep cuts on his body. He was moved to the guest house. Gaius, Priscilla, and Mother spent lots of time cleaning and tending to the wounds. Hermes was quite feverish and had a hard time keeping down food. Father fell out of favor with the rest of the family for offering to take care of Hermes. In one sense, they felt a call of duty. In another sense, everyone felt they were wasting a lot of time caring for a dying man.

About a week later, Hermes appeared to be getting well. Mariam's diluted juices and vinegar seemed to be working. Lots of wine was used to keep the wounds from festering. Applying honey to the wounds seemed to prevent infection. In any case, Hermes eventually recovered.

About two weeks passed before the Greeks returned from Tyre. They were surprised that Hermes was on the mend. Gaius recommended that Hermes remain with us until his wounds completely healed, and that he could walk without the need of crutches. The leg wounds were the worst. The traders left Hermes his share of the money obtained from the goods and horses sold in Tyre. Hermes said that he would rejoin them as soon as his physical condition permitted.

Meanwhile, Gaius and Father were back into dealing arms. Syrian raiders and members of the Jewish resistance continued to pay a decent sum of money for weapons. One of the Syrian guests noticed Hermes sleeping in the guest house. Father explained that he was our household servant and had fallen ill. No one in the family wanted anyone to know that Hermes was part of the battle. I suspect the Syrians knew where Father was getting the weapons, but all seemed fair when dealing in such business. On one hand, they feared each other, and on the other hand, they respected each other. Father's hospitality, especially the wine, always won out. They saw father more as a friend than an enemy.

Hermes wanted to stay awhile to compensate for the family's hospitality. Gaius told him that it wasn't necessary. Nevertheless, he insisted on remaining for a while. For all practical purposes, since we didn't purchase or hire him as a servant, he couldn't be called a slave or a hired servant. However, when the situation arose, Hermes would act as a slave or servant for one reason or another.

Hermes was a Spartan and a hard worker. He would cut wood, lug water, and having experience as an artisan, he helped remodel the main house. I had set a goal to build steps to the top of the hill. Hermes helped me cut into the sandstone. I would do a few steps every week or so. Hermes tripled what I did. For the steps that were too soft and crumbled, he would take tile and rock and cement in a nice looking step.

We built a cupola at the top of the hill. The dome was made out of palm leaves that were set on straight columns. A minor earthquake knocked it over. The next design included brick arches with a dome made with wood and a thin layer of concrete. It looked real nice from a distance. It was an excellent place to hang out during the summer evenings as the sun went down. The ocean breeze always kicked up during late afternoon.

I asked Hermes where he learned to fight. He mentioned that he was raised in an orphanage near Sparta. One of the older men taught all the boys the art of self- defense. The boys needed a father figure and something to keep them occupied aside from their regular schooling. He was taught to read and write and served as an apprentice in his late teens working in building construction.

He eventually teamed up with Macedonian traders who delivered goods to the Greek port of Thessalonica. The traders were descendants of warriors who fought with Alexander the Great. Training in the art of fighting passed down from generation to generation. There was no love between Macedonians and Romans.

The traders wanted to cut out the middle man in their trades and decided to purchase their own ship and sail to Tyre and sell their goods on the open market. They soon discovered that their choice of boat was bad, not to mention that neither of them were sailors except for one recruit whom really didn't know one star from another. His navigation was the North Star, and that was it. The sailing vessel that they purchased leaked like a sieve. The seller probably thought that he would never see those guys again. The Macedonians will probably kick his butt on their return to Thessalonica, assuming they make it back in their shoddy boat.

Hermes became like one of the family. Gaius asked him to teach us the art of fighting. One never knew when raiders might attack his household. Hermes complied and began by putting us through an exercise routine. Abigail and Mary-Beth joined us. Mother was quite upset over this. She said that a woman's place is in the home, and that it was the man's responsibility to protect them. Nevertheless, the girls became excellent archers. Because of their lack of strength, Hermes taught them how to use small crossbows with short darts. He said that they could lock themselves in their bedroom and shoot darts from the windows and door at anyone who approached. He designed the door to be locked and put slits in the wood that allowed arrows to make their way through them. It definitely would not be healthy for anyone to walk up the steps and try to break into the bedroom. He designed and built a training area and taught everyone wrestling moves and how to use their hands and feet as weapons. When Rachael was old enough, he took her aside and gave her special training. That was a big mistake as Rachael, in her Ragamuffin role, flipped a visiting Roman officer. More on that later.

Hermes was quite the actor. He was an excellent slave when visitors arrived. He exhibited a jovial uplifting character when things were down. He was the resident sage when the family incurred insurmountable problems. He never stopped moving from cutting hay, to feeding the livestock, to fixing this and that, and to helping everyone with their chores. He and the donkey got along very well. There was no issue when hauling logs. He would tell us that when the donkey got tired, he would put the donkey on his shoulders and drag the log by himself. In reality, he used a horse to drag the logs but would tell everyone that he used the donkey. He didn't fool Priscilla or Mariam as they could always see him with the horse from the kitchen or veranda area.

Hermes knew neither Latin nor Hebrew. Hebrew was the spoken language of our household. He eventually learned to speak Hebrew. Everyone wondered why he didn't return home to Sparta. He said that he had no family there, and that we were the closest to a family that he never had. He loved what he did and especially loved us children. He fell in love with one of the Phoenician woman in the village. Her name was Emma. Mother arranged for the two of them to meet. It was a match made in heaven. They were two peas in a pod. Emma became a close family member. Gaius and Father helped

Hermes build a home on the small hill south of the spring. It had a front view of our home site and a back view of the field.

Hermes wasn't the only person to stay at the guest house while recovering from wounds or illnesses. The future procurator of Tyre, Decarus, was passing by. One of his officers, who also was his son, was deathly ill and needed a place to recover. Gaius offered to take care of him. Father treated Decarus with the usual excellent meal and wine. Meanwhile, Hermes and Abigail tended to Flavius, the ill officer. Mary-Beth had a difficult time dealing with sick or wounded people and applied her time elsewhere.

Flavius stayed with us several weeks. Mother treated him with the usual medicine, vinegar three times a day and diluted juices in between times. Flavius recovered in about a week but took advantage of the hospitality and extended his rest and recuperation another two weeks. During this time, Abigail and Flavius hit it off. She was sixteen at the time. Abigail was always washing and massaging his feet. When she detected that he was thirsty or hungry, food was immediately brought to him. When he went to the pool to bathe, she had a towel ready and waiting for him. She was getting to be a pest. Mary-Beth couldn't wash and dry his clothes quick enough. Mother couldn't prepare the stew fast enough, and Hermes could never pour the right wine for whatever occasion.

Father was repairing the chariot that had been sitting around for quite some time. He was pestered constantly by family members in the offering of help or asking when the chariot was ready for use. The family wanted Flavius out of there. Abigail was driving them crazy. Also, mother was not too keen on her Jewish daughter's infatuation with a Roman officer, not to mention the fact that he was not a Jew. Tyre wasn't that far away. It was a full day's walk at a good pace, but I suppose that it would have been unbecoming of a military officer to be seen walking unaccompanied for that great of a distance.

Repairing the axle and some of the wooden pieces was no easy task. There was a lot of working and reworking of replacement parts. Father adorned the chariot with his own leather work. Even though Flavius was a Roman officer, it would not be a good idea to show up at the garrison in Tyre with a Roman chariot. He did keep the spear and bow holder in place and added a place to store arrows. He added a basket to store goods.

Finally, the day of celebration came, and it was time to bid farewell to Flavius. Gaius wasn't quite sure if Flavius was able to leave the next morning. During the evening of celebrating, he had a bit too much wine. Mother was praying that he had the strength to leave. Nevertheless, Father hitched up the horses, and with a shopping list in hand, he and Flavius headed to Tyre. Abigail was saddened to see him go.

The road was a bit rough, but the distance to Tyre was short. The chariot held together quite well. Father did a couple of test runs before embarking on the journey. Abigail was hoping the chariot would break down. She wanted Flavius to spend a couple more weeks. Mother breathed a sigh of relief when the chariot was out of sight. Other than the test runs, Father never drove a chariot before. It was a bit awkward at first, but with some instruction from Flavius, it didn't take too much time to learn how to control the horses. They passed through Zarephath without stopping. It took about four hours with a couple of rest stops before arriving in Tyre. The Romans at the garrison were excited to see Flavius. He had the respect of both officers and soldiers alike. They treated Father as his slave at first, supposing that a civilian driving a chariot with a Roman officer had to be his slave.

Flavius introduced Father as his friend and close companion who was to be treated as his equal. He ordered the soldiers to take care of the horses and chariot. The soldiers looked at the chariot and were scratching their heads wondering who made this make and model.

Father did his best to fulfill mother's shopping list. He had confided with Mariam the night before to purchase a colorful dress for Abigail with two thoughts in mind. One was to help her get over the departure of Flavius, and secondly, a colorful dress told possible suitors that she was available. Jewish suitors I might add. Although, Father and Mother would have her wait a couple more years before getting married.

After finishing shopping, Father was invited to the praetorian for an evening meal. Following a change of clothes which Flavius had provided, Father had a fabulous meal and visit with Decarus the procurator and his officers, which included Flavius who sat at his side. Decarus asked Father if he was a Roman citizen, knowing full well that he was a Jew. Father answered with a no. Decarus was aware of his family's support and hospitality toward the Romans. He told father that as a member of the House of Gaius, he well deserved the honor of Roman citizenship and offered it as a gift to my father. Father accepted the gift with pleasure, as most people paid quite a sum of money to acquire Roman citizenship. The soldiers prepared his chariot for him and with citizenship papers in hand, he departed for home.

Father's return without Flavius was met with celebration. The dress that he purchased for Abigail didn't cheer her up any. However, Hermes leaned over and told Father to tell her that Flavius helped pick out the dress and paid for part of it. It was a small lie, but the sparkle returned to Abigail's eyes, and no one could touch the dress while it was hanging in her room. Much to mother's chagrin, she would not wear the dress, as she was saving it for her next encounter with Flavius. Such is life.

Chapter 5

THE EVANGELISTS

Silvanus, son of Matthias, son of Gaius, to my descendants. I caught lots of fish this morning. Ragamuffin and Kaysi (our pet dog) sat nearby while doing so. She helped me carry the fish up the cliff. After cleaning the fish, I decided that it was time to relax and do some more writing. It's been a couple days since finishing the last scroll. With the help of Hermes, I have become quite fluent in the Greek language. I wasn't sure what to write about. My mind wandered from Abigail's infatuation with Flavius to finding Kaysi to our encounter with Christian evangelists.

With regards to Abigail, it was easy to understand why Abigail fell for Flavius. A good many of the Roman soldiers were tall and handsome. Abigail was tall and quite attractive. They were a good match in several ways. The main issues were that Jews weren't allowed to marry outside of their faith, and it was taboo for Jews to associate with Romans. The Jewish resistance came down hard on any Jew seen associating with a Roman. However, in the larger cities, Roman soldiers were better tolerated. The troops were quite disciplined and time seemed to overshadow Roman dominance.

Ragamuffin was eight years old when she found Kaysi the wonder dog. She was helping Mary-Beth water the garden when she heard a noise in the bushes. She alerted Mary and the two of them investigated the source of the noise. It turned out to be a puppy. The mother was nowhere to be seen. They left the puppy where they found it and went to the house to find some scrap food to feed it. They mentioned the find to Mother, and she told them to stay away from wild animals, and that the dog's mother was probably in the neighborhood.

Nevertheless, the two girls smuggled the puppy into their bedroom. They would feed the puppy a couple times per day and carry him to the garden with them. Ragamuffin always had an excuse to go to the garden, and Mary-Beth had to go with her as her personal security guard. Mother knew what they were up to, but just shook her head and kept silent. She was going to let Father deal with it.

Grandfather Gaius, in a bit of humor, suggested naming the dog Cassius, after the name of the centurion who imprisoned his father, Jonathan. The girls didn't like that name and decided to shorten it to Kaysi. They called him the wonder dog because everyone wondered where he came from and what breed of dog it was. Mother said that he looked like a wolf. One of the visiting centurions thought that he looked like a breed of dog that he saw in Thrace, north of Macedonia. Kaysi followed the girls wherever they went. When they slept, he slept. When they were eating, he was at their feet. He was their constant companion. Kaysi favored Ragamuffin the most. Probably because she was always slipping him food under the table. He was a good snake dog. If there was a snake nearby, he let everyone know. If a critter was under a rock, Kaysi knew it. He was very protective of the girls. Hermes taught him many tricks.

When I fished by the cliffs, Kaysi and Ragamuffin were usually at my side, patiently waiting until I was ready to return home. Occasionally, I would fish near the village, and if I caught several more fish than needed, I would walk near some of the homes along the street that led to the main highway and offer fish for a lower price than what the local fishermen were asking. The fishermen were not happy with me. They had a fearful respect for our family in general.

Rumors had spread about how we were all trained fighters, connected with the Jewish resistance and Syrian raiders, and had close ties with Tiberius Caesar. Most of the rumors weren't true, but Father never refuted them. He liked his status in the village. When one of the visiting children from the village asked father if he really knew Tiberius Caesar, father showed him his certificate of Roman citizenship and told him that Tiberius himself directed Decarus to give it to him as a gift. It was a stretch of the truth, but it had its benefits.

When Ragamuffin was about twelve years old, she, Mary-Beth, and Kaysi would often walk to the village and sit on the pier and watch the fishermen unload their daily catch. Captain Madera had the largest boat. He had converted an old cargo vessel into a fishing vessel.

He would always tell the girls to stay off the pier as it wasn't safe. It was a wooden pier that was slowly falling apart with each storm that rolled in. One day, the captain was carrying a basket of fish, and one of the planks gave way, and he fell flat on his back. The basket of fish fell on top of him. He was covered with fish, and one leg was caught in the hole where the plank was.

Ragamuffin walked over, looked down at him and told him that he shouldn't be walking on the pier as it wasn't safe. He gave the usual grumbling "arrgh" as he tried to pull his leg out of the hole. His sandal strap was caught on a broken piece of plank. Mary-Beth reached down and loosened the strap as Ragamuffin lifted the leg out. He had a deep gash on the side of his ankle.

Ragamuffin told him that her grandfather Gaius could suture the wound. She and Mary-Beth refilled the basket with the fish that had spilled. A couple of fish fell through the hole in the pier. Ragamuffin offered to retrieve them, but Captain Madera told her not to bother.

She and Mary-Beth carried the basket of fish while the captain limped to his home. His cousin delivered the fish to the market as the girls and Kaysi ran to get Gaius. When Gaius arrived, he cleansed and sutured the wound. Ragamuffin held the captain's hand as Gaius did his work. She kept talking to him with comforting words the whole time.

After that, Ragamuffin and Mary-Beth would occasionally meet the captain as he brought his basket of fish to the market. She pestered him the whole way, always cautioning him about not falling into holes on the pier and asking him if he saw any sea creatures while fishing. The captain and his fishing partner would always come up with some tale about a creature with long tentacles trying to grab people off the deck or about large fish trying to upset his boat. Mary-Beth wanted to know what color the monsters were and how big their eyes were. She would ask these questions while holding tight to Ragamuffin's arm. Madera's partner would embellish the stories as they headed toward the market. Ragamuffin would always emote some feelings of awe as they told the stories and then laugh at Captain Madera as she egged him on about more details of his encounters at sea.

Mary-Beth would half believe them, although she knew that they were making up the stories. Nevertheless, when Mother and the girls went to the secluded spot by the cliffs for a late afternoon swim, Mary-Beth would not go into the water for fear of the sea creatures. She told Abigail that she didn't want the sea creatures to see her with no clothes on. The girls would swim in the nude while Mother walked the beach and occasionally waded out to her knees.

Ragamuffin told Captain Madera and his partner that they belonged in a funny farm with their tales of sea creatures. Captain Madera couldn't figure out what she meant by funny farm. He and his partners had short discussions about it. Ragamuffin told Mary-Beth that Father said that a funny farm was a place where the priests took care of the insane, but never told Madera.

One day, she told the captain that his boat looked ugly and was in serious need of paint. She pointed out how all the other boats were painted and had a name written on the side. Captain Madera said that he liked the boat the way it was, and if she didn't like the looks, then she was welcome to paint it. She offered to do so, but the captain said that he didn't allow women on his boat, especially pesky little girls like herself.

Ragamuffin took the hint and bid him a good-bye. A couple of days later, Ragamuffin noticed that the railing on his boat was painted a dark green. She asked the captain why he painted the railing if he liked it the way it was. His excuse was that he didn't want to fray his fishing line as he hauled in fish.

As time went on, she noticed other parts of the boat became painted. The captain always had an excuse for painting one section or another but would never admit to painting his boat because she said that it looked ugly.

Interesting visitors stopped by and spent the night on more than one occasion. News of a man named John who was preaching repentance and that the kingdom of heaven was within reach was spreading northward. The new village rabbi, Zachias, caught wind of it, and when he found out that visitors from Galilea were staying with us and carrying the same news, he hurried over, joined us for supper, and stayed late as they sat around the fire ring, drank wine, and shared stories.

Apparently, a man called John, the son of a priest named Zacharias, was bearing witness of the Messiah who was to appear very shortly. He was baptizing people who made decisions to reject their worldly way of life and follow the ways of the Messiah who was to come. The news was several months old. One of the visitors told us of a man named Jesus who was preaching the same gospel as John, that is, that the kingdom of heaven was within reach, and that the Jews should repent. Many thought that he was a great prophet like John. Apparently, Jesus was performing miracles around the sea of Galilee and was creating a lot of tension among the Jewish leaders. The Sanhedrin seemed to be quite disturbed by his actions.

We knew of the Messiah who was to come, but the details were a bit of a fog. Zachias did his best to tell us of the coming Messiah and was quite interested in the news concerning John the Baptist and the prophet, teacher, and miracle man they called Jesus. You could see the excitement in Zachias's eyes. It wasn't long before Zachias set out on a journey to find John and hear the news directly from the source. Several weeks later, he returned with the latest news concerning John and Jesus. Apparently, John had been arrested by Herod Antipas, the son of Herod the Great. This was at the time when Pontius Pilate was governor of Judea and Tiberius Caesar was the Emperor of Rome.

Zachias was in the crowd when Jesus spoke by the lake. Priests from Jerusalem were there. Zachias knew some of them and inquired as to what John had preached and wanted details on the prophet Jesus who was preaching on the shore.

Some spoke well of him, some were disturbed by his miracles, and others didn't speak well of him at all, accusing him of having a demon. To be honest, Zachias didn't quite understand what Jesus was saying in that he seemed to be speaking in a figurative language that his followers called parables. People were wondering if he was the Messiah and whether he would raise up an army to drive the Romans out of Palestine. Although there was some contention between the Pharisees and Sadducees, this contention was abated, as both sects were disturbed by the presence of Jesus.

Zachias decided to make a couple more trips in order keep up on current events concerning the prophet John and Jesus. Father would take him in the chariot, although the ride appeared to be a bit hard on his back. No one bothered them as they traveled the highways to Galilee. The Jewish resistance would not attack a priest, and would-be robbers were probably a bit hesitant to mess with a man who was armed with a sword, a spear, a visible knife, and a quiver of arrows and a bow. Basically, Matthias was well armed. Albeit, unknown to them, Father was not a trained fighter.

When questioned by Roman soldiers, Father would mention that he was a Roman citizen and would drop a few names when necessary to keep them at bay. Whatever he said seemed to work. When soldiers passed by the chariot, there would be an immediate double take. He amused himself by concocting some story when asked about the chariot. His favorite response was, "It's an Egyptian designed Syrian chariot modified for road use in Herod's kingdom." It either generated a laugh or a shake of the head.

On the second trip with the chariot, news came that Herod Antipas had ordered the beheading of John the Baptist. This did not go over well with the populace, as John had a huge following and was more popular than the Jerusalem priesthood. Following this, the popularity shifted to Jesus, as news of his miracles were reaching into the northern kingdoms. They tried to get as close to Jesus as they could, but the crowds were thick, and those who were sick and needed healing took precedence. Zachias and Father conferred a lot with Jesus's followers, some of whom were called apostles.

The news of Jesus's arrest spread quickly. Shortly thereafter, reports came in concerning his crucifixion. It was a sad day for both Rabbi Zachias and Father. For a while, few visitors stopped in, and news concerning events in Jerusalem were sparse.

One day, a couple of travelers stopped by the spring. Ragamuffin saw them from the wall that leads to the lower gate. She struck up a conversation with them and found out they were heading to Sidon. They asked if there was an inn in the local village. There was none. Ragamuffin told them to wait by the spring and ran off to find someone who might invite them to stay at their place. She found Gaius, and the two of them met with the men by the spring.

The two men gladly accepted the invitation. They were given the normal treatment offered to all guests. They were humble in character and showed much appreciation for our generosity. It turns out that they were Jews from Galilee and were followers of Jesus who was crucified by the Romans. Everyone was excited to hear what they had to say concerning Jesus and John the Baptist. Father told me to run and fetch Rabbi Zachias.

That evening, we got the details of the arrest and crucifixion of Jesus. The two men were traveling north to share the good news concerning the remission of sins and salvation to those who repented. Around the fire ring, they spoke of how this Jesus was considered by them and many others as the Messiah prophesied of old. This message really captured Rabbi Zachias's attention. They told us how we could enter the kingdom of heaven because of the remission of sins set forth by the cross, and that all we had to do was to repent, that is, set aside the ways of the world and focus on a new way of life by developing within us the mind of Christ.

They spoke of the Holy Spirit and ended the evening by laying hands on those who made a decision to follow Jesus. We all wanted to be part of the new kingdom. Some in the group began to speak in strange tongues as we worshipped God. I was a bit skeptical at first, but as they were laying hands on Ragamuffin, I felt a strange feeling in my feet. That feeling rose up and filled my whole body. I wanted to shout for joy, but for some reason, perhaps my shyness, I kept it to myself. That feeling seemed to tell me that these men were men of God, and that the message they brought with them was true.

Rabbi Zachias begged them to stay a couple of days and preach this new message at his synagogue. They preached the gospel of Christ to the village Jews. Some accepted the message, but others for one reason or another didn't. As one of the men said, "It is difficult to pour new wine into old wineskins." When they departed, things returned to normal, with the exception that we decided to gather and pray together on a regular basis before retiring each evening. I'm convinced that a family that prays together stays together. I would pray from the top of the hill on many mornings. Even Hermes, a gentile, was seen praying from the top of the hill.

An odd thing happened one day when a family stopped by the campground. Ragamuffin and Kaysi paid them a visit. She offered our normal hospitality, which they declined. She noticed that the mother was trying to get the attention of one the children who appeared deaf. Ragamuffin offered to pray for the child. To amuse Ragamuffin, the mother agreed to let her pray for the young boy. She placed hands on his ears and prayed in the name of Jesus and asked the Holy Spirit to reach down and restore the child's hearing. It was like lightning struck the child as he motioned to those around him that he could hear. No one could understand him because the boy never spoke, not being able to hear.

The news of the miracle raised everyone's faith, and the boy's father, Peter, decided that the family should accept our hospitality and stop by for an evening meal. Peter was on his way to Caesarea to join a family member who had a restaurant on the waterfront. Father shared the good news of salvation through Jesus Christ to our guests as they sat around the fire ring. The whole family made a decision to follow Jesus. This occurred on the Sabbath. The next morning, the first day of the week, we all gathered and prayed at the campground before our guests continued on their journey. Father gave them some money and food to help them on their way.

More Christian visitors would stop by and speak to us concerning the ways of our Lord and Savior, Jesus. They had nothing in writing to share with us. Mary-Beth wrote some songs and would play them on her small harp. Priscilla played the harp and passed that skill on to Mariam and Mary. We heard that Christian churches were being established in the north. Following some talk around the campfire, it was decided that someone needed to travel north to the churches in search of written material concerning our beliefs and what it meant to be in the kingdom of heaven.

Hermes and I decided to take the chariot and head north. Antioch and Ephesus were on our list. It was quite a distance to Ephesus. Our food supplies didn't last long. Fortunately, we had enough money to buy food along the way. Hermes was only familiar with the road to Sidon. We did that easily in one day. After that, it was a couple of days to Antioch. There, we rested as the chariot vibrated our bones out of their sockets. There was a meeting place where a group of Christians met. They were of a group called the Way. Unfortunately, they had no written material to share, other than the sayings of Jesus passed on by His apostles and followers. They suggested going on to Ephesus and perhaps some of the Greek cities visited by the Apostles.

It took forever to get to Ephesus. We were well accepted by the brethren there, and they took good care of us. Fortunately, they did have written material, albeit mostly the sayings of Jesus. They did, however, have copies of letters from the apostles to other churches concerning the conduct of the church and brethren alike. The believers in Ephesus set about copying what they had so that other groups could hear what the apostles were saying. As such, our goal was to develop within ourselves the mind of Christ, but without guidance, this was difficult. We did, however, still have the law of our Jewish faith and were told that it still stands firm.

We thanked the brethren for what they gave us and made a pact to visit the churches in Greece someday to acquire more written material. The material they gave us included a couple of Christian songs written by one of the ladies who worshipped with us.

The journey home seemed to take forever. We were beset by robbers twice. The first group fled when we surprised them with darts from our small crossbows. They weren't lethal blows. The shock of being hit with them along with Hermes crazy screams and madly waving his sword as he chased after them was enough to scare anyone away. When he stopped, his screams ended, and he laughed as he hopped back into the chariot.

The second band of robbers seemed to be as crazy and fierce as Hermes. The difference was that Hermes was a skilled fighter. I covered his back with what skills he taught me at home. The trouble is, Hermes would roll this way and that way, and shift this way and that way as he used both sword and knife. The knife blade was curved and very sharp. They met my match when it came to sword play. I did all I could just to keep from getting injured. A lot of clanging of swords, but no scores on any of my opponents.

Hermes inflicted many wounds. The robbers decided that they had enough and made a swift departure. I shook like a leaf for quite some time after the incident. Hermes leaned over to me and whispered into my ear, "Your sword play was excellent. You did well on your parries and blocks. In the future, put a knife in your free hand, and use your feet to take out their knees." His voice had a calming effect. In the excitement, I forgot to grab my knife. A valuable lesson learned.

The rest of the journey was uneventful, except that the chariot wheels were beginning to wobble from all the use. We had to take it slow from Antioch on. It took several days to recover from the journey; however, it was well worth it.

We all read the copied letters. Mother and Mary-Beth adapted the new songs to the harp. We got some writing material from Rabbi Zachias, and Hermes copied the letters word for word, as he was quite proficient in reading and writing Greek. We planned on delivering copies to the believers in Judea. Rabbi Zachias copied them into the Hebrew language and shared them with his congregation. He gave us a few copies in the event we encountered Hebrew Christians on our visits to the south.

Chapter 6

STEPHANIE

Silvanus, son of Matthias, son of Gaius, to my descendants. I must write about Stephanie and my trip to Caesarea. While hiking down to my favorite fishing spot, I noticed a small fishing boat rocking in the waves along the shore to the south. It was quite stormy the night before. The boat must have broken loose from its mooring. It looked like one of the small boats normally moored near the village. I waded out and rowed the boat around the small peninsula toward the village. It took awhile as the boat was heavy, and paddling with one oar was a challenge. The wind was still fairly strong and tended to push me toward the shore. As I approached the beach, I saw a girl sitting on the pier. She waved as I approached. As I neared the pier, I couldn't help notice how beautiful she looked. She rivaled my sister Abigail in beauty and form. I asked if she recognized the boat, and she said that it belonged to her father. She had a sweet voice. I asked where her father moored the boat, and she pointed to an anchored wooden float.

I was already wet from wading out and getting into the boat, so jumping into the water and wading ashore didn't bother me. Normally, I would take off my outer garment to keep it from getting wet, but it wasn't appropriate to do so with a girl present. Her name was Stephanie. She looked to be about sixteen years old. I introduced myself as we met on the beach. She walked with me toward the village. She said her father was upset over losing the boat and was preparing to walk the shoreline to look for it. I couldn't help looking at her face. Her eyes sparkled in the sunlight, and she had a beautiful smile when she talked.

We stopped by her house, and she introduced me to her family. Her father was quite excited and very appreciative of me returning the boat. Knowing that I was of the House of Gaius, he felt that he had to offer me a reward of some sort. I told him that a reward was totally out of the question, and that returning the boat was the right thing to do. His wife invited me for breakfast, but given that my clothes were wet, I didn't think it was appropriate to stay. I bid them farewell and told them that I would stop by another time for breakfast, figuring that it would give me a second chance to see Stephanie.

Stephanie was on my mind as I walked home, so much so, that I forgot about the fishing gear that I left by the cliff side. As I approached home, I spotted Ragamuffin and Kaysi entering the road near the cliff. My fishing net was draped over her shoulder. She left the rest of my gear among the rocks where I usually hide it. Apparently, she saw me paddling the small boat toward the village.

When I got home, a few of the Christian brethren were sitting around the fire ring sipping tea and discussing the plight of the believers in Jerusalem. The drought and persecution had taken its toll on them. They were in dire need of food. The brethren were discussing how to get food to them without having it confiscated by robbers, toll collectors, and Jewish leaders who were not too friendly toward Christians. Jewish and Christian hostilities were waning a bit as there was internal conflict within the Jewish sects. The Sadducees were in control of the Sanhedrin as well as serving as the chief priest. The Pharisees were not happy with this situation.

After eating a small lunch, I decided to finish my fishing adventure. Before crossing the road, I noticed a contingent of Roman soldiers approaching from the north. They made the usual stop at the spring. Father greeted them and discovered that the commanding officer, Marcus, was assigned as the new assistant administrator of Caesarea under Pontius Pilate. His son, Cleo, was with them. His son was quite ill and was in bad need of medical attention.

As tradition went, the top officers wined and dined at the house while the soldiers camped nearby. Marcus served as the procurator of the Sidon garrison. His daughter, Patricia, was already in Caesarea. Father offered to take in his ill son and do what he could to make him well again. Cleo was not fit to continue on the journey. Marcus felt that Cleo was close to death and didn't seem to care one way or another whether he stayed with us or continued on. There seemed to be a lack of love between the two of them.

Priscilla was not aging well. However, between her and mother, they did the usual medical treatment on Cleo, vinegar and diluted juices with a tinge of honey. No one was sure what was wrong with him, but it took weeks for him to recover. Upon regaining his energy, he was in no hurry to go to Caesarea. He hung out with the women in the kitchen and didn't mind washing clothes with Mary-Beth. Mary was attracted to him, but Cleo had no interest in her. Mother was happy for that. All she needed was another daughter infatuated with a Roman officer.

Cleo was a bit of an oddity. Whenever he saw a strange bug, he would either sit or kneel down and stare at it for a long time. I asked him about this, and he said that he loved to study bugs, what they eat, what they looked like, and how they moved. He would commit their looks to memory and then draw a picture of them when he had ink and writing material available.

I mentioned that Antonio, the son of a fisherman, was an artist and would most likely share his skills to help him perfect his bug drawings. Cleo was excited over the possibility, so I contacted Antonio and invited him to stop by when he had a chance. The two of them worked well together, and it wasn't long before pictures of bugs were displayed in all the rooms on our property. Rabbi Zachias was kind enough to provide writing material for their artwork. Antonio was an expert at mixing colored inks. Most of his art consisted of birds, mostly sea birds.

The next time the Christian brethren met and discussed getting food to the believers in Jerusalem and parts of Galilee, I suggested hiring one of the larger fishing vessels in the village and sailing to Caesarea. I also suggested that they take Cleo with them, as being a Roman commander under the new administrator in Caesarea, no one will tax the load, and perhaps Cleo could arrange for safe transportation of the goods to Galilee and Jerusalem. Caesarea was the administrative center for Judea and was under the control of Pontius Pilate. He had close ties with Herod Antipas, tetrarch of the region that included Galilee and Judea, and for all practical purposes, he was considered to be king of the Jews. Assigning Pontius Pilate as governor of Judea was a strategic move by Rome. Herod's father, Herod the Great, had close ties with Cleopatra and Mark Antony, and Rome didn't like this relationship as well as the holding on to and promoting Hellenism. Placing Pontius Pilate in Judea was like putting a wedge between Egypt and the Herod family. Pilate spent most of his time in Caesarea. Pilate was not on the friendliest of terms with Herod Antipas. Marcus was assigned to serve as Pilate's assistant administrator.

They liked my idea and set about to acquire grain and other food stuff from the believers in Sidon and other cities of the north, as far away as Antioch. The brethren hired a local fishing vessel that was converted from a small cargo ship. It turned out to be captain Madera's boat. The brethren, mostly fishermen, also volunteered to serve as the crew. Meanwhile, I approached Cleo about having him sail with us to Caesarea, not really telling him that we were using him to avoid taxes and such. Cleo did not like ships as he was quite prone to seasickness. He said that if he could handle ships, he would have traveled with his sister, Patricia, and the rest of his family to Caesarea. His father, Marcus, decided on making the journey by land to visit the city of Tyre and get a feel for the people who fell under his administration. Caesarea was a complex political city that was built by Herod the Great.

This created a serious problem. How does one get a person who gets seasick and at the same time doesn't want to go to Caesarea to be with his family to sail with us? I presented the problem to Hermes who had been helping the brethren load the boat. Off he went to the village. Several hours later, he came back with a possible solution to the problem. As it turns out, Antonio was one of the villagers who volunteered to help load the boat. Hermes suggested that I talk Antonio into sailing with the cargo and have Antonio invite Cleo along to continue his art lessons and perhaps draw pictures of any birds or bugs encountered along the way.

I mentioned this to Antonio, and he agreed to go along with the scheme. Hermes helped out by inviting Cleo to help load the cargo. That allowed time for Antonio to convince Cleo to sail with the ship. With some convincing, Cleo reluctantly agreed to sail with us. This was good news for the brethren and even excellent news to mother. Actually, the whole family was anxious to get rid of him.

Knowing that the boat was going to Caesarea, Abigail asked me if I would convince father to let her sail with it. She wanted to see Flavius who had been transferred to the garrison in Caesarea. It was a good move for Flavius in that it placed him in a political circle that had promotional opportunities. Although, Tiberius, being a bit of a Tyrant, made life a bit uneasy. The senate in Rome seemed to be weakening, and eventually lost control when Tiberius was replaced by Caligula.

Abigail had made a scarf for Flavius and wanted to personally hand it to him. I told her that it was out of the question, as the boat was not fit for having a female rider. We both knew that Father and Mother didn't approve of their relationship.

She then asked if I was going. I said that at this point, there was no need for me to go. The village brethren and the crew were going to arrange to get the goods from the boat to Jerusalem, and there was no need for my assistance.

She insisted that I convince Father that I should go, as it was my Christian duty to serve the Lord. I responded with, "To serve the Lord, or to get your scarf to Flavius?" She was taken aback by my comment, but that didn't stop the wheels from turning in her head. She was offering everything under the sun to get me to go, from massaging and washing my feet for thirty days, to cleaning the fish that I caught, to cleaning out the stables. Then it struck me. Stephanie!

I mentioned Stephanie to Abigail and wanted her to ask Stephanie over as a guest. I told her that if she complied, I would do my best to sail with the ship and give the scarf to Flavius, and that I would even keep it a secret from our parents. She immediately agreed. Pushing my luck, I added, "And washing and massaging my feet for sixty days. She told me not to push it. However, as she skipped away, she glanced back and said, "Fifteen days!" and smiled as she walked off.

It was months later before I told her that I had already arranged to sail with the crew to Caesarea. Abigail held up her end of the bargain. She and Mother met Stephanie in the village market place. Stephanie told them to thank me again for retrieving her father's boat. It was a short conversation, but Abigail was able to work in an invitation for Stephanie to visit our home. They invited her mom to come along as an escort and explained that they would have lunch prepared for them.

Mother, Mary, and Abigail set out a nice spread of food. Mary's freshly baked bread became the main topic. Ragamuffin picked some grapes for the occasion, and Mother prepared some hot soup. I sat and talked with the girls. It was more me listening and them talking. It turns out that Stephanie's family members are descendants of the tribe of Asher. Most of that tribe was carried away by the Assyrians hundreds of years ago. Asher means "happy." Perhaps that's why Stephanie is always smiling.

I asked Stephanie if she would like me to show her around the property. She was delighted to have me do so. Abigail, Ragamuffin, and Kaysi walked with us. Stephanie was impressed with the pool and spa. She was shocked that the girls slept in a cave carved out of sandstone. Stephanie asked a lot of questions. Ragamuffin tended to give all the answers. One could tell that she liked Ragamuffin. She kept her left hand on Ragamuffin's shoulder during most of our walk but kept glancing in my direction. We all agreed to get together again when I returned from Caesarea.

I boarded the boat at sunrise the next morning. It was a typical sunny, balmy day. A light offshore breeze was blowing. With a decent wind, we could have arrived in Caesarea by the next morning. Antonio helped Cleo store his belongings. Cleo didn't wear his uniform.

The offshore breeze made for an easy departure. As the wind picked up, we started to make good time. As the ship listed to starboard, I noticed water leaking near the waterline. That was not a good sign. I checked the bilge and noticed a great deal of water in it. If the water rose much more, the bottom bags of grain would get wet. Captain Madera ordered one of the crew to pump the bilge. We all had to take turns pumping, all except Cleo. The seas were not too kind to him. He had a pale look about himself and was leaning over the rail. The rate of water coming out of the pump matched the rate of water coming in.

As the wind picked up, the captain had to cut the sail because the more the ship listed, the more water that came in. This slowed our journey to a crawl. Soon, we—except Cleo—were either pumping water or bailing. As bad as Cleo felt, he did pitch in on occasion. The wind died toward the evening, and we all took a break. We drifted most of the night with an occasional light breeze. By the next morning, we were all totally exhausted.

There was an occasional light breeze in the morning. Captain Madera tossed a copper coin off the bow. He was trying to buy the wind. It must have worked because a strong northerly wind picked up, and we made good time through the evening and most of the night. Again, pumping water and bailing was required. The long wooden rod on the pump broke. That meant wearing ourselves out bailing.

The lights of Caesarea were sighted before twilight. The captain was a good ship handler. A light breeze allowed us to slowly edge into the harbor. There were no piers available, except for the sheltered military piers near the Roman garrison. Those piers were restricted from commercial use. The rock jetties made for a nice harbor. The docks were well sheltered from the sea.

We decided to take our chances and tie up at one of the Roman docks. We had to strip off Cleo's clothes and help him put on his uniform. He was pale looking and still felt ill from the voyage. We groomed him the best that we could and leaned him against the mast. That was a bad decision because as we changed direction, the boom knocked him for a loop. We immediately brushed him off and straightened his uniform, hoping that the soldiers guarding the docks didn't see the incident.

The guards waved us off as we approached, until they saw Cleo's uniform. They helped us tie off the ship as we helped Cleo set his feet on solid ground. Antonio helped hold him up as he staggered toward the guards. Surprisingly enough, he began to quickly recover from his seasickness. He ordered the soldiers to assist in unloading the ship and to keep an eye on the cargo until the crew arranged for transportation inland.

The soldiers mentioned that all cargo must be taxed, and that the ship needed to leave immediately. Cleo mentioned that he was the son of Marcus, the chief administrator, and told them that there will be no tax, and that the ship leaves when he orders it to leave. He told them that we were his friends and were to be treated with respect, and that the crew may come and go as they please.

Cleo mumbled to himself all the way to the waterfront. The crew set about locating their Christian brothers while Captain Madera stayed with the ship. The walk to the Roman garrison was short. Cleo's walk improved as he approached the gates. One of the guards escorted us to the praetorian where Cleo met his father. His father seemed to have mixed feelings on his arrival. On one hand, he was glad that he survived the illness and was alive and well. On the other hand, I got the feeling that he didn't want Cleo around.

A very young and beautiful lady showed up. Her hair was done up in braids, and she had a very elegant look about her. It was Cleo's sister. She was very excited to see him. She stopped short of hugging him as she had on a beautiful, light green dress and didn't want to soil it with Cleo's obvious untidy condition. Cleo commented on her dress as the servants were leading us away. She told him in absolute terms that he was not to touch the dress. As Cleo emoted a deep breath and sighed, she turned and looked back at him and said with a smile, "You can have the pastel colored one that father wants me to wear." Cleo knew what that meant. Marcus had purchased a colorful dress for her to wear when potential suitors were about. Patricia, being somewhat rebellious, found ways to irritate her father by not wearing the dress. If Marcus saw Cleo with the dress, he would instantly toss him into a cauldron of boiling oil.

The servants led us to the baths and gave us all a change of clothes. Cleo wore a robe until his uniform was cleaned. The servants couldn't locate a new uniform that fit him. They found one early the next day.

We all were treated with a delicious meal at the praetorian. Patricia sat between Cleo and I. Antonio sat on the other side of Cleo. You could immediately tell that Patricia loved Cleo, regardless of his effeminate nature. She also knew that her love for Cleo further irritated her father. Patricia always protected Cleo. Marcus did have a high regard for Cleo's administrative abilities. Cleo was also an excellent strategist. On that level, they got along quite well.

Flavius joined us at the dinner table. He was excited to see me. He wanted to know how the family was doing and what Abigail was up to. I told him that I had a gift for him from Abigail. Flavius invited us to join him on the porch after the meal.

Marcus pulled me aside and offered money for taking care of Cleo. I declined the offer and told him that our taking care of Cleo was a gift from the House of Gaius. He would not listen to me and told Patricia to make sure that I was well taken care of. The five of us walked to the porch and sipped wine and ate bread and cheese as we talked in view of the city lights. The stars were bright that night. It was a very pleasant evening.

I asked the servant to retrieve the scarf from my shoulder bag. He complied, and I handed it to Flavius. He thanked me. He noticed that Patricia was a bit chilled and wrapped the scarf around her shoulders. I noticed that he kept his hand on her shoulder just long enough that it made me suspect something was going on between the two of them. That didn't bode well for Abigail. I related how we helped Cleo recover and told them about my family.

Flavius and Patricia talked politics. Apparently, Decarus arranged for Flavius to transfer to Caesarea in hopes of an upward mobility move. Pontius Pilate had governed Judea for almost ten years. It was rumored that Tiberius was quite upset with him because of his harsh treatment of the Samaritans. In the event that Tiberius should remove Pilate from his position, Patricia wanted her father, Marcus, to replace him. She was using Flavius to influence the right people to make that happen. There was a lot of scheming in the local political arena.

When Tiberius eventually called Pilate to Rome, Marcellus was appointed by his friend, Lucius Vitellius, as the temporary overseer of Judea. Eventually, Marullus, a former tribune under Julius Caesar, became the procurator of Judea. It was almost like going back to the political turmoil that prevailed during the reign of Herod the Great. Needless to say, the scheming between Patricia, Flavius, and others never worked out. Perhaps the relationship between Flavius and Patricia was purely on a political basis.

I mentioned that I wanted to purchase a nice dress for Stephanie and told Patricia that a light green dress like the one she was wearing would be perfect. We all agreed to go shopping that next morning. Patricia knew the city well and loved to spend her father's money. Flavius had commitments and promised to catch up with us at one of the cafés on the waterfront.

The early morning was a bit nippy as we ate breakfast and prepared to go shopping. Patricia knew where all the dress shops were. It was a pleasant, sunny day, perfect for strolling through the market place. We found her favorite dress shop. It was full of linen dresses imported from Egypt. They were softer and lighter than the cotton dresses. She asked what color Stephanie's and Abigail's hairs were. Stephanie's hair was dark brown, and Abigail's was a light brown. She suggested a blue dress for Stephanie. Blue dye was hard to get, which made the dress a bit more expensive. The dress that we picked out was more of a bluish-green with lace at the shoulders and back area.

Patricia picked out a black leather belt with a silver buckle inlayed with stones that matched the dress color. She picked out a white cotton dress for Abigail. It wasn't a full-length dress, and it had woven patterns in it. She also picked out a black leather belt for Abigail's dress. The stones were amber in color. Both dresses were quite elegant, fit for a queen.

Patricia paid for the dresses and wouldn't accept any form of payment from me. We found a nice shop that sold towels. She picked out five sets of white bath towels and hand towels, all made of Egyptian cotton. They were for the three girls, Priscilla, and mother for taking care of Cleo.

One of her servants had followed close behind us. At first, I thought that maybe he was a bodyguard. She directed him to take the dresses and towels back to the garrison. Then she led us to her favorite jewelry shop and picked out nice-looking necklaces. One held a gold pendant with a blue topaz in the center. It went well with Stephanie's dress. The other was similar, only with a crystal clear yellow stone.

Flavius found us in the jewelry shop. He asked Patricia who the jewelry was for. He insisted on paying for Abigail's. He wanted to reciprocate on the gift she sent to him. I saw no reaction from Patricia, which made me wonder even more what her true relationship was with Flavius.

We all agreed that shopping had worn us out and that lunch at a local café was in order. Patricia had one in mind. As we walked the waterfront, I heard someone yelling my name. He used my nickname, Silas, rather than Silvanus. It turned out to be Peter, the father of the boy whose hearing was restored at the campsite. Peter had joined his brother in partnership. His brother had owned and operated a café on the waterfront for several years.

He invited us all to have lunch at his café. We all obliged and followed after him. Peter introduced his brother and seated us next to the street so as to have a nice view of the docks and sea. Peter explained to his brother who I was. His brother was a pleasant fellow. He was a bit nervous with Flavius and Cleo sitting in his café. Serving Roman military was not good for business. Patrons tend to shy away from entering the café when military personnel were dining there.

Regardless, Peter took good care of us and made sure we had the best of food. He sat with us for a while and told us that he met some Christian believers and joined their local church, which was held in the home of one of the church leaders. When hearing about the healing of his nephew and the message of the cross, Peter's brother accepted the Lord as his savior and became a member of the church.

When asked as to why we were in Caesarea, I told him about the cargo that was sent down to help the believers in Judea and Samaria who were suffering from the drought. Peter spoke with excitement and told us that our grain was stored behind the café. Apparently, the ship's crew found the local church and asked for help in transporting the food.

Flavius suggested that they have an armed guard with them when transporting food to Jerusalem and Galilee. He mentioned that Joppa would have been a better port for Jerusalem. He also mentioned that troops were being sent to Tiberius near Galilea to help quell the Jewish uprisings and suggested that they travel with them. Cleo offered to connect the brethren with the centurion in charge of leading the troops. They were leaving in a couple of days. He suggested using camels as pack animals as water was scarce. Flavius would arrange for the pack animals.

With all that arranged, captain Madera was anxious to get back home. He found some pitch and cloth to seal the leaking seams. He also arranged to ship some goods to Sidon and wanted the crew to return as quickly as they could. The Romans had the captain move his ship to a commercial dock. The port master let him use the dock without charge per order of a Roman commander. It was probably Cleo. Cleo was excellent at making things happen.

Antonio and I conferred with Captain Madera and decided that the three of us could take the ship to Beth-Gebar, and that the captain could pick up a new crew to finish the trip to Sidon, and then return to Caesarea to pick up the crew returning from Jerusalem. The captain agreed and arranged to have the cargo loaded as soon as possible.

I spent a couple more days visiting with Cleo and Patricia. Patricia seemed to be having a great time. Any chance of getting out of the stuffy garrison was fine with her. We even attended the local church. Cleo and Patricia had a chance to observe the believers worshipping God and laying hands on the sick. They spoke of the miracles performed by Jesus and repeated some of His messages.

I told Peter that Hermes and I traveled north to Antioch and Ephesus and obtained copies of letters from the apostles and also obtained Christian music written by local church members. I also told him that I would have them copied and sent to them when I returned home. He and the others were excited over that. I asked them if they preferred that the material be written in Greek or in the local Aramaic language. Actually, they preferred both languages. Even though Hebrew was the spoken language, most could read and write Greek as it was the business language of the time.

The trip north only took a day and a half as we had fair winds and following seas most of the way. The captain dropped me off at Beth-Gebar and picked up a couple more crew members before proceeding to Sidon.

Ragamuffin and Kaysi made several trips a day to the top of the hill to look for the ship. When she saw the ship, she ran down the long set of steps with Kaysi close behind. The family was quickly informed as Ragamuffin ran to the gate with intentions to head into the village. Mother stopped her and told her not to go alone. Ragamuffin turned and said, "I'm not alone. Kaysi is going with me." Mother knew that arguing with Ragamuffin was a waste of time. Stephanie had seen the ship come in and ran to alert the family. Ragamuffin and Kaysi met her half way. The other family members stayed behind to prepare a meal for us and clean house in the event other guests should arrive. Stephanie, Ragamuffin, and Kaysi greeted me on the pier as the ship docked. It was hugs for everyone. The pier was not in the best of condition. One more storm, and that will be the end. I told them to be careful as they walked and stepped over missing planks.

Stephanie helped carry some of the gift bags. Upon arriving, we were greeted with excitement and celebration, mostly centered on eating and sharing news of our adventure in Caesarea and of course, Flavius. The gifts went over quite well. Abigail and Stephanie were both excited over the dresses and jewelry. Priscilla, mother, and the girls were happy to receive the towels. Egyptian cotton towels were always a gift to behold.

Father and Hermes looked at each other and said, "Where's our gifts?" I had to think of something quick, and my response was, "Oh! I'm so sorry. The vendors refused to sell items intended for Greek slaves and old Jewish men." Before they had a chance to grab me, throw me to the ground, and beat the stuffing out of me, I handed each of them an Arabian knife with an ornamental sheath. Hugs from each of them meant that I was accepted back into the family.

I didn't forget Mary-Beth or Ragamuffin. I had purchased ankle bracelets for each of them. They actually could be worn on the wrist or ankle, but were a better fit for the ankle.

Chapter 7

OUR WEDDINGS

Silvanus, son of Matthias, son of Gaius, to my descendants. With so much going on, I find it difficult to concentrate on writing. Obviously, Abigail and Stephanie were quite excited over the dresses. They spent the afternoon modeling them, along with the jewelry. They were very careful not to get them dirty. Both dresses were ankle length, which were fine by them. Mother wished that the dresses had covered their feet, which was more becoming of a lady, but times were changing. Mother pulled Abigail aside and said that Stephanie's mother will not like the lace-covered shoulders of Stephanie's dress. Abigail agreed but stated that Stephanie looked rather nice in it. Stephanie kept her dress in the girls' bedroom as her home was not the cleanest of places to live.

I talked to father about my wishes to marry Stephanie. He said that I should build a home for Stephanie and me to live in before getting married. I didn't want to wait that long. As usual, when faced with a complex problem, I confided in Hermes. I told him my desire to marry Stephanie and asked if it made sense to have to wait so long. On one hand, he felt that one should endeavor to do so, but on the other hand, that it may take a few years to build a decent house.

I mentioned that the guest house could serve as temporary living quarters while working on the new house. Hermes stroked his beard and tilted his head sideways and said, "Now there's a thought." After that comment, I told him that then there was no reason to not get married sooner. His response was his usual, "Oh, indeed Silas."

I told him that there just has to be a way to convince Father. Hermes suggested that I talk with Grandfather as he was a bit long in the tooth and could be convinced to desire a great grandson before leaving this world and express that desire with my Father. On the other hand, I could talk directly with Father and mention that Grandfather would most likely want to enjoy a great grandson before too long.

I decided to take both approaches. First, I talked to Gaius, and then that evening, while sitting around the fire ring, I decided to mention it to Father. Father leaned toward me and said that Gaius had already approached him on the subject, and after a short hesitation, he said that he would talk with Stephanie's father and see what can be arranged. He mentioned that the new house should be elegant in style, with a mixture of Greek and Roman architecture, and that it could take several years to build. I thanked father for his approval.

At our next meeting with the Christian brethren, we discussed copying the apostle letters and Christian music that we received in Ephesus and delivering them to Caesarea for use there and for redistribution to other churches in Judea and Samaria. Rabbi Zachias agreed to copy them in the local Aramaic language for the Jews who didn't read Greek, and Hermes and I decided to copy the ones in Greek. Zachias was of the Pharisee sect and had a great deal of training and practice as a scribe.

Rabbi Zachias was short on papyrus scrolls and suggested that someone travel to Tyre and purchase a goodly amount of them. Father and I took the chariot to Tyre. While there, we stopped in to visit Decarus. He was happy to see us and inquired as to any news concerning Flavius. I related to him all that transpired in Caesarea except for the scheming between Flavius and Patricia. Decarus was well informed of the political situation and was wondering if it wouldn't be better for Flavius to become governor of one of the larger Asian cities to the north, perhaps Ephesus or Troas.

Decarus pulled father aside and mentioned some issues with the procurator in Sidon. Apparently, the Sidon procurator was expanding his territory and wanted to include Beth-Gebar and Zarephath in his realm. In order to justify retaining the city of Zarephath and the village of Beth-Gebar under his control, Decarus needed to assign prefects to those locations. Basically, the prefect would serve as the local chief of police under the authority of Decarus. Administratively, they would also be responsible for collecting taxes. Normally, a procurator would assign a centurion to fulfill that position, but it wasn't practical for a small village like Beth-Gebar. Decarus was offering Father, now a Roman citizen, the position of praefect over Beth-Gebar. Father didn't like the idea of being the local tax collector, but Decarus told him not to worry, as he was well aware of the economic condition of the village. His main goal was to keep the Sidon procurator at bay.

Father began to see that his "free" Roman citizenship certificate did not come without a price. However, accepting the position of praefect would give him the opportunity to protect the village from the harsh taxes laid upon other cities and villages in the region. Father accepted the position.

After learning what had just transpired, I suggested that Father acquire some papyrus scrolls from the garrison's office supplies in order to write occasional status reports as the new praefect. He thought that was a great idea and was able to pick up a dozen or so scrolls. However, we needed a lot more, so we later shopped around Tyre and was able to obtain a goodly number. We also picked up some spices from the spice shops along the waterfront as well as a few knickknacks requested by mother and Mary-Beth.

The trip home was uneventful. Hermes was found designing the new house. He had gained architectural experience while working as a builder in Sparta. He needed some bigger sheets of papyrus for the layout. Unfortunately, we didn't know this until after returning from our trip.

A few days later, commanders Banes and Darius showed up. They shared a chariot ride from Tyre. We put them up in the guest house. Darius handed a scroll to father. It was the official certificate assigning him as the praefect of Beth-Gebar. Banes was a heavy set jolly good fellow and had stayed with us before. Darius was short and thin in stature. He appeared to be very stern and strict in character. He tended to order people around. Banes reminded him that we were not Roman soldiers and were to be treated as Roman citizens.

Hermes wanted to bash him a good one but retained his character as a servant and slave to the household. Upon retiring for the evening and after much wine, Darius grabbed Mary-Beth by the arm and quietly asked her to join him for the night. Ragamuffin could see that she was not in a comfortable situation and reached up and grabbed Mary's arm and asked her to put her to bed. Darius didn't like the interference and went to shove Ragamuffin away with his right hand.

Ragamuffin immediately grabbed his right forearm with her left hand and bent below him while reaching behind his right knee with her right arm. A quick yank with the left hand followed by a coinciding yank with the right arm and body lift caused Darius to flip over her and land on his back. Ragamuffin did a quick roll as Kaysi had sprung to attention and leapt toward Darius. We were not sure if it was his dog's breath or the snarling teeth that kept Darius from moving. Quick intervention by Mary-Beth kept the two apart.

Father appeared on the scene and seemed to be aware of what had happened. He scolded Ragamuffin and said, "I told you time and time again not to wrestle with Roman soldiers," and sent her to her bedroom. Father apologized to Darius as Banes brushed off his uniform. Darius wanted Ragamuffin arrested for attacking a Roman officer. Banes leaned close to his ear and suggested that he shrug the whole incident off for a couple reasons. One was that if the word got out that he was beaten up by a twelve-year-old girl, he could never live it down. And besides, arresting a member of the House of Gaius without Decarus's orders would result in a good thrashing followed by a bath in boiling oil.

At that, Darius retired for the evening. Ragamuffin made up for the incident by serving him a decorative fruit plate for breakfast and some warm bread and hot tea. Darius asked Banes if there was some way the events of last night could be kept secret. Banes talked to Hermes, and Hermes assured him that it will be kept a family secret and for Darius not to worry. Darius, in an unusual mellow state, asked Ragamuffin if they could be friends, and they apologized to each. He also apologized to Mary-Beth, blaming the wine for his ill-begotten behavior. She accepted the apology and offered Darius more bread and tea.

It wasn't long after their departure when one of the Christian Jews came running toward the house. Apparently, some Jewish officials from the Sanhedrin in Jerusalem had a letter authorizing the arrest of Rabbi Zachias. The Sadducees were in control of the Sanhedrin and were at odds with the Pharisees. When word got out that Zachias had become a Christian, they demanded his arrest. As such, the Pharisees weren't in a position to protect him.

Father had Hermes and I arm ourselves and told us to mingle in with the crowd that had gathered in front of the synagogue. Hermes was to make sure that the false rumors concerning Matthias and his association with the Jewish resistance were to make their way to the guards who arrived with the Jewish officials. Meanwhile, Father made his way into the courtyard of the synagogue and approached the chief arresting officer.

After inquiring as to what was going on, the officer explained that he had a warrant for Zachias's arrest and was taking him to Jerusalem for trial. Father explained that he was the village prefect and that he honors only arrest warrants endorsed by Decarus, the procurator over the region. The arresting official objected to Father's position and asked him why he was dressed for battle. Before Father answered, one of his guards spoke into the official's ear, and the color of his face began to pale. Father mentioned that one never knows when a scoundrel might cross his path. Apparently, Hermes was successful in getting the word to one of the guards.

Father suggested that they depart for Tyre and discuss the matter with Decarus before he had to arrest the official for creating a public riot. I noticed that Hermes was off at a distance, waving his arms up and down. That was apparently a cue for the crowd to start shouting and make all kinds of commotion in the background.

The official turned to Rabbi Zachias and mentioned that he could voluntarily leave with them rather than be arrested. Father came to his defense by telling the official that Zachias was under house arrest for creating the disturbance, and that he would have to bring up this whole matter before Decarus before any judgment could be made. As prefect, he did not have the authority to judge significant matters that could potentially effect Decarus's position. The official was told to take up the matter with Decarus. At that, the official and his entourage departed for Tyre. They were not a happy lot.

It was later learned that they stopped at the Tyre garrison and explained the matter to commander Darius. Commander Darius conferred with Commander Banes given that the matter involved the praefect of Beth-Gebar and the House of Gaius. Both commanders discussed the matter with Decarus and suggested that he delay any meeting with the men until they investigated the incident with Matthias. Decarus told commander Darius to tell the Jews from Jerusalem that he would study the matter and give his decree in a week or so, knowing full well that they would not stay in Tyre for that length of time. Decarus hoped that the Sanhedrin officials would simply drop the matter. However, he knew that he would most likely get a letter from Pontius Pilate chastising him for not honoring the arrest warrant, which he himself endorsed. Nothing was heard from Pontius Pilate, and the issue was laid to rest. Pontius probably was too busy dealing with the Samarian unrest to be concerned with Sanhedrin issues, in light of the fact that he was the one who selected who was going to be the chief priest. The Sanhedrin was already on his unfavorable list of associates for forcing his hand in the crucifixion of Jesus.

During dinner that evening, someone mentioned Cleo's name. I told them that some of the soldiers who knew Cleo nicknamed him "Hop to It." Apparently, after giving orders to several centurions, Cleo would always pause before dismissing them. As they turned, Cleo would call out their names, and when they turned, he would point his finger at them and say, "Hop to it!" It wasn't long before Ragamuffin began to give this command when addressing Kaysi.

When the letters were ready to be delivered to Caesarea, Father suggested that Hermes and I deliver them. This meant another long chariot ride. The chariot was in good order by then, and Father suggested that we both should be well armed for the journey. He was not too keen on traveling the road between Tyre and Caesarea. We stopped at the garrison in Tyre for a short visit. A number of the soldiers recognized us. Commander Banes arranged for a stay at the guest house and informed Decarus of our presence.

Decarus was glad to see me. Hermes was known to be a slave of our household and was not permitted to enter the praetorian. Commander Banes kept him entertained and had the servants take good care of him. Decarus told me that the inspector general noticed that there were no taxes collected from Beth-Gebar, and that he had to address the matter. I asked him what amount of taxes he expected from a poor, impoverished village. He responded with thirty denarii.

I thought about it, and then I asked Decarus if my Father's position as praefect included a salary. He asked me what I thought a reasonable salary would befit a person of such stature in the House of Gaius. I suggested thirty denarii, and Decarus leaned back and chuckled. He asked me if I would like to be his new accountant.

I told him that we were on our way to Caesarea, and that if he had any letters to be delivered, we'd be happy to deliver them. He asked me who *we* were, and I mentioned Hermes. He was familiar with Hermes from one of his visits to our home. He had one of his servants retrieve two scrolls from his office and handed them to me. They were to be given to Flavius. He invited me to dine with him that evening and directed the servant to invite Hermes as well.

The trip to Caesarea was uneventful. We checked in at the garrison. The guards recognized me and took care of the chariot and horses. I told them that Hermes was my assistant and bodyguard. I told them I had business with Flavius and asked if he was available. One of the guards located Flavius and led us to his office. I handed him the two scrolls from his Father. He was pleased to receive them and invited us to stay in the guest house during our visit.

He mentioned that he and Patricia were attending meetings with the Christian believers, and that Cleo would sometimes show up. I told Flavius about the copied letters, and he was quite interested in reading them. We delivered the letters to the brethren and spent the evening dining with Flavius, Patricia, and Cleo. Marcus was in Jerusalem on business. Before leaving the next morning, Flavius handed me a sealed letter to be given to my Father. My curiosity was certainly aroused. He also gave me a letter to be given to his Father.

We made an overnight stop in Tyre. One of the horses started to limp just as we entered the city. Commander Banes said that the stable master would check him out. Decarus was pleased to get a letter from Flavius. Banes said that the horse had an injured leg, and that it would take several days to heal. Meanwhile, he loaned us one of their horses. The trip as a whole was tiring. I was exhausted for two days.

I gave the letter to Father. He opened it and shared the contents with Mother. After some discussion, Father shared the letter with me and asked for my opinion. Apparently, Flavius asked Father for Abigail's hand in marriage. He stated that he fell in love with her the first time that he met her, and that his Father's pressure to focus on the upper echelon of Roman military culture kept him distracted from what really matters in life. He stated that he sees no future in Caesarea and has plans of his own which he could not divulge at that time. He also stated that his occasional visits with the Christian believers have changed his mindset and influenced his way of thinking. With the believers, he saw an element of peace and joy that he had never experienced before. He promised to take excellent care of Abigail and would do his best to make sure she stays in contact with the family either directly or by letters from where they settle.

I told Father that I believe Flavius was a sincere individual, and that he would be quite acceptable as a family member. I further stated that I believed that Flavius would make an excellent brother-in-law. Father valued my opinion but wouldn't make a decision until he talked with Rabbi Zachias. Flavius was not a Jew, and it was uncertain whether he had made a decision to follow Christ. Rome was at odds with the Jews for their constant rebellion and disturbances. Flavius, being a Roman military officer, would be forced to side with Rome on any decisions concerning the Jews. That in and of itself may create family conflict.

Nevertheless, against his best wishes, Father decided to let the marriage take place as long as Abigail agreed. Father talked with Abigail for quite some time. They agreed that if Decarus approved of the marriage, then they would make it happen. Father directed me to carry a letter of acceptance to Flavius by way of Decarus. He wanted me to discuss the matter with Decarus before going on to Caesarea. I suspected the other letter from Flavius informed his Father of his intentions concerning Abigail.

Hermes was busy copying letters that we had received from Ephesus. Ragamuffin expressed interest in learning Greek and helping him. Hermes had been teaching his wife, Emma, how to read and write in Greek. Ragamuffin became his third student. Although I was quite proficient in Greek at that time, I still needed to expand my vocabulary. Hermes continued our training in self-defense and spent a lot of time teaching and writing in Greek. Father wanted me to take Hermes with me to Caesarea. I really didn't think Hermes was up to another chariot ride.

I checked with Zachias to see if he or any of his friends would be interested in traveling to Caesarea. Zachias declined but said that he would ask a couple of his students. Joseph, who was helping Zachias translate the apostle letters into Hebrew, offered to go with me. He spent his whole life in the village and wanted to see what the outside world was like. Father agreed to let him accompany me to Caesarea.

Joseph and I spent the night at the garrison in Tyre. Decarus was aware of Flavius's intentions and agreed wholeheartedly with the union. I told him that I was heading to Caesarea to give him Father's approval. He also gave me a letter that indicated his approval. He mentioned that Joseph and I could take a ship out of Tyre, as there was a military vessel leaving Tyre in the morning. With the uncertainty of a timely return trip, I declined and Joseph and I continued on in the chariot.

The trip to Caesarea was horrible. It rained the whole way. The chariot wheels kicked up mud, and the both of us were covered from head to toe. When we arrived at the garrison, one of the guards recognized me. He greeted me and laughed at our plight. We were drenched and totally caked in mud. One of the guards took care of the horses and chariot, while another guard went to inform Flavius of our arrival. Flavius was occupied at the moment, but Cleo heard of my arrival and ordered the servants to take care of us. They washed our clothes and outfitted us with clean ones from the guest house. We did a thorough rinse off before soaking in a hot bath. Joseph couldn't believe that we were being treated like royalty. He was not accustomed to hot baths and servants, and to be in a garrison among the elite of the Roman Empire seemed a bit overwhelming to him. It was more than a garrison, in that it included a palace where Pontius Pilate resided.

That evening, I gave the letters to Flavius, and he was quite pleased with both approvals. He told me that he would have to work up a schedule to travel north for the wedding, and that he would inform me some time tomorrow what it would be. Meanwhile, Joseph and I met with Flavius, Cleo, and Patricia. Sipping wine on the porch was out of the question because of the rain. We sat around the fireplace in the praetorian and chatted until late into the night. It was hard to read Patricia. I wasn't sure what her take was on Flavius's intentions for Abigail.

When Patricia disappeared for a short while, I leaned over and asked Flavius how Patricia took the news of him and Abigail. He said not to worry. Apparently, Patricia had her eye on a certain vendor down on the waterfront. They had been seeing and conversing with each other for quite some time. The problem was that the vendor was a Phoenician with no ties to Roman culture, especially to the upper echelon of society in which Patricia was bred. Patricia was keeping it a secret from her Father. Flavius sort of hinted that Marcus knew about the relationship, as he in turn secretly had her followed, more for protection than for prying into her life. Patricia didn't like body-guards following her everywhere.

That was a relief to me. I liked Patricia, and the last thing I wanted to see was for her to be hurt in any way. The vendor's name was Baldassare. He started going to the church meetings with Patricia. Neither of them has yet to accept the Lord as their Savior, but I suspect they will in short order.

After breakfast, Joseph, Patricia, and I walked the waterfront. Joseph was in awe of the different building structures. We had lunch at Peter's restaurant and later met with some of the Christian believers. Marcus invited us to dine with him that evening. It was a private gathering at his palace residence. Marcus expressed his displeasure with the political moves taking place. He saw the writing on the wall and mentioned that a request to transfer to one of the Asian cities to the north might suit him better. He preferred the Aegean Sea over the Mediterranean, and he loved making short trips to various Greek islands.

The weather did not improve for the trip home. We stopped in Tyre, and Commander Banes could not stop laughing when he saw us. The chariot was cleaned in Caesarea but looked worse upon arriving in Tyre. Banes took good care of the horses, one of which really belonged to the garrison. Our other horse never did recover from his injury. He was useless for pulling a chariot. I was still shaking from the cold when meeting with Decarus. The warm bath didn't take away the chills. Joseph seemed to recover quite well. I gave Flavius's tentative schedule to Decarus. He recommended that Father and he get together and work out the wedding details.

After spending the night at the guest house, we returned to Beth-Gebar. The rain had stopped, but the road was still muddy. Joseph had a nice swim and hot bath before eating some of mother's stew. I walked with him to the village. I was totally exhausted from the trip. I slept until noon the next day.

Father had talked to Stephanie's parents and obtained their consent. When her parents told her that they arranged for her to marry me, she teased the both of them and told them that she really had her eye on Hiram the son of a local fisherman. She knew that they despised both Hiram and his father. They considered his father a lazy good-for-nothing, and that Hiram was a chip off of the old block. The teasing shortly changed to excitement as she ran about the house doing this and that but not really accomplishing anything. She asked her mother a thousand questions but wasn't really listening to any answers and really wanted to come over to our place to share the news with Abigail. She was full of excitement when she showed up at the house. You'd think she was marrying Abigail instead of me. I did get a hug and a kiss. Mother chided in and said that those kinds of kisses are reserved for the wedding day. With that, Stephanie gave mother a hug and told her that she was so right and ran off to find Abigail before mother could say another word. Mother just shook her head and went on doing what she was doing.

Of course, Abigail already was aware of everything going on. She was in a cloud of her own with Father and Decarus arranging for her wedding. Decarus wanted the wedding held at the praetorian. Father wanted Rabbi Zachias to do the wedding, but Flavius wasn't a Jew, so at first, Zachias refused. But Father mentioned that since he was a Christian Jew, he could use the Christian side of his priesthood to do the wedding. Since Abigail was a Christian and Flavius was occasionally attending the church in Caesarea, Father convinced him to do the wedding. Rabbi Zachias's only misgiving was that Abigail and Flavius were not equally yoked, both as a Jew and a Christian. Nevertheless, Zachias's heart dominated his mind, and all was settled.

I asked father about his negotiations with Stephanie's parents, and he said that he offered them fifty denarii for Stephanie's betrothal to me. He said that her Father only took thirty denarii as he remembered that I rescued his boat awhile back. Her mother wanted one hundred denarii, but her father settled at thirty denarii. Stephanie was purchased for a bargain.

There were all kinds of arguments that arose over the wedding, everything from what dress to wear, what is the best hairstyle, what head covering makes sense, what kind of head band to wear, where to spend the wedding night, who to invite, and on and on. Abigail wanted to wear the white dress that Patricia purchased for her in Caesarea. Mother was insisting that traditional wedding dresses are to be worn below the ankles with a long train behind them. Much to mother's chagrin, Abigail won the dress argument. A train was added, but the dress was not lengthened. Other than that, mother got her way on everything else.

Cleo and Patricia were present. They ran into the same kind of weather that Joseph and I experience on our trip to Caesarea. Fortunately, her dress survived the rain and mud. Decarus's wife was most helpful, especially in helping Patricia to regain her composure after such an arduous journey. Her servants waited on Patricia hand and foot. Cleo was in uniform at the wedding.

Flavius was dressed in a sharp-looking uniform for the wedding. Abigail had her hair done up in a beautiful arrangement of braids with a light green flowery head band that looked quite elegant. One would have thought she was a Greek goddess. Patricia had purchased her some gold earrings, a gold bracelet, and gold bracelets for her ankles, all having small sparkling gems mounted in them. Patricia heard about the wedding dress issue and thought that the jewelry would make up for not having her ankles and feet covered.

Antonio showed up. He actually sailed a small fishing boat to Tyre. The whole family was there. One of Father's cousins came down from Sidon to attend. Joseph kept an eye on the home site while we were gone. It had taken several trips in the chariot to get everyone there.

The musicians played a mix of stringed instruments, mostly harps and lutes, along with a couple flutes. Trumpets were blown at the opening ceremonies. I chuckled inside upon hearing the trumpets as I had never experienced this kind of an affair. Rabbi Zachias did an excellent job in giving the wedding vows. Ragamuffin loved the music from the stringed instruments. When Patricia found out, she sent her a small harp and a lute that she purchased from her secret companion, Baldassare.

Decarus rented a villa on the coast for their wedding night. They actually spent a whole week at the villa.

The next wedding was mine. Things went rather smoothly for this wedding. The ladies modified the blue-green dress that Patricia picked out for Stephanie. The major issues were the dress color, length, and the lack of a train. Stephanie nor her mother really cared about the color. The dress was the talk of the village. Phoenicians were not as traditional as the Jews. The more colorful the event, the better. She had her hair done up in braids similar to Abigail's. The flowery head band looked nice.

Although Stephanie was of the house of Israel, living among the Phoenicians has jaded her Israeli traditional values. At first, Father preferred that I marry into the tribe of Benjamin, but one visit from Stephanie, and Father definitely wanted her as a daughter-in-law.

The wedding was held in the synagogue. Rabbi Zachias conducted an excellent ceremony. The whole village knew Stephanie, so the wedding reception was held in the village square. The villagers supplied the music and food. It was quite the affair. The villagers were awestruck with Stephanie's radiant beauty. They were familiar with her attractive figure and the beautiful smile when she talked. The dress and flowery head band was breathtaking. Cleo and Patricia for one reason or another couldn't attend. Commander Flavius and Abigail caught a Roman military ship that was heading north. They arranged for a vessel out of Tyre for the return trip. Abigail, as with most women, didn't like chariot rides. I suspect that Patricia wasn't too keen on chariot rides after her trip to Tyre for Abigail's wedding. Commander Banes showed up, not only as a representative of the garrison in Tyre, but as a close friend of the family. Decarus had business matters to attend to and declined.

As a gift, Decarus arranged for a stay at the same villa that Flavius and Abigail stayed in for their wedding. The villa and its view were beautiful. The flowers were in full bloom, and the light late afternoon breezes from the Mediterranean made for pleasant dining along the waterfront.

Chapter 8

GREECE

Silvanus, son of Matthias, son of Gaius to my descendants. Joseph joined our Greek lessons. Emma could speak Greek but was never taught how to read or write in the language. Joseph was fairly proficient in the language but needed some improvement. I suspect he was using the class as an excuse to see Mary-Beth. Ragamuffin seemed to excel in her learning and wanted Joseph to teach her how to read and write in Hebrew. Rabbi Zachias taught the children, both boys and girls, how to read and write in Hebrew and taught the boys Jewish history. He was exceptionally well versed in the Torah. In most other villages, boys would receive a formal education, while girls were taught by their mother or grandmother skills they would need to become, in time, good wives and mothers. Greek was spoken throughout the village.

Ragamuffin asked Joseph if he thought Rabbi Zachias would let her attend some of his classes. Joseph twisted Zachias's arm, and he agreed to teach her on a one-on-one basis. It wasn't long before she mastered the Hebrew Scriptures, which included the Torah, the history books, as well as the books of the prophets.

Meanwhile, Gaius, Father, and I continued to work on the new house. Money was in short supply, and the cost of material was increasing. Fewer people seemed to be traveling these days. Gaius was starting to really slow down. He was not much help on the new house. His eyes were very weak.

Caligula succeeded Tiberius as emperor. He also succeeded in making the senate powerless. No one could figure out why the military would allow him to do that. My guess was that he eliminated generals that apposed his philosophy and chose generals who agreed with him. It was rumored that Caligula was making himself a god and wanted people to worship him as such. This didn't bode well for Christians and Jews who would not bow down to him. Christian persecutions were on the rise throughout the empire. Military leaders up and down the coast were on edge. A call to Rome could mean certain death.

We hadn't heard from Abigail for over a year. Everyone really missed her. It was sad to see her move away. Kaysi has been limping lately. He doesn't seem to be doing well. The spring is barely flowing. There has been very little rain over the last few years. Father and I walked around the property praying for rain. A black cloud would show up on occasion and drop rain. It helped out the garden and trees but didn't affect the water flow in the spring. Each morning, everyone carried water to the garden and vineyard. Each had their section to water. Most of the wells in the village were dry. Villagers would walk the road and fill jugs with what little water flowed from the spring. It was a long wait, but well worth it.

We had plenty of food. However, grain was in short supply. Travelers mentioned that there was a grain shortage in Sidon and the cities to the south. Egypt and Palestine seemed to be hardest hit. Grain was plentiful in the cities on the eastern shore of the Aegean Sea. Perhaps we could arrange for the believers in Ephesus to ship us some grain. We had enough money to purchase grain for ourselves but not enough to cover the believers in Caesarea and the rest of Palestine. Father and I discussed it and decided that I and perhaps Hermes could catch a ship out of Sidon and meet with the believers in Ephesus or Troas.

One day, Antonio stopped by for a visit. Apparently, he just arrived from Caesarea on the same ship that we had sailed on together. Captain Madera found that there was more money in shipping than in fishing and decided to convert his fishing vessel back to a cargo ship. Antonio mentioned that the ship is on its last legs and probably won't make it through another storm. They were on their way to Sidon, Troas and then to Greece.

He had a shoulder bag with him that contained some letters and scrolls. He had met with Abigail, Patricia, Cleo, and Peter while in Caesarea. Abigail had given him a letter for us. Peter had copies of some of the accounts of the apostles. Apparently, some of the apostles decided to write down eyewitness accounts of their experiences with Jesus. Peter's group copied several scrolls for our use.

We immediately read the letter from Abigail. All was well with her. She was six months pregnant. Life around the garrison was not all that pleasant. Patricia was a good friend to her. They spent a lot of time on the waterfront or at the church meetings. Decarus was quite ill. Flavius requested a temporary transfer to look after him and the affairs at the garrison. It was approved, and she thought they might arrive in Tyre by ship in about three weeks.

This was great news. The bad news was that the chariot was in dire need of repairs. It would take an experienced Egyptian carpenter to fabricate one of the parts. It was a piece of wood that was pressed into shape. Father did not have the equipment to do that. I asked Antonio to let us know the next time smugglers arrive in the village. Father and I were going to ask them if they knew of any Syrian chariots that were available on their route to Damascus.

The horse acquired from the Greek traders and Syrian raiders' battle was no longer with us. We have yet to return the horse that belonged to the garrison in Tyre. We asked Antonio to check on grain availability and prices in Troas. Father gave him what little money we had and asked him to purchase some grain for us on their way back from Greece. That's if they make it back. I asked him to check in on the brethren in Troas and see if they could provide some grain for the believers in Palestine. Antonio said that he would do whatever he could.

Marcus requested a transfer to Troas. Rome has yet to approve it. Troas is a major seaport on the Aegean Sea. There was lots of turmoil in Rome with Caligula killing several senators and threatening to move the capital of the empire to Egypt. Roman law prohibited senators from traveling to Egypt. Probably a carryover from the Cleopatra, Mark Antony, and Julius Caesar conflict.

Hermes had two children, a boy and a girl. He had very little money himself. The ladies outfitted the children with clothes left over from our childhood. We didn't throw anything away. Hermes and I talked about ways to make money. He came up with the idea of riding with Antonio to Greece and looking up his old trading partners. We were hoping to make some money helping crewing the ship with Antonio and then working on a return vessel from Greece.

Father thought that it was a good idea. I immediately ran down to the village to locate Antonio. Antonio talked to the captain, and he agreed to bring us on as crew members but would only pay us if the cargo reaches the next three ports. That was fine with us. We packed a second set of clothes and some food and gave some bread and wine to the captain as a gift.

Antonio gave me the money that Father had given him. That way, he wouldn't have to be responsible for acquiring grain for us. We stopped in Sidon for a couple of days. While there, I visited with Father's cousins. His two uncles, Joseph and Demitrius, had passed away some time ago. The families were partnered together as marketeers. Coming from a family of traders, they were able to set up a distribution center for shipments coming into Sidon. I suggested that they talk with our captain, and maybe they could work a deal with him. I told them why I was aboard the ship and they offered some financial help. I declined for the moment. I asked them what goods they would like to see from Greece. They wanted lots of grain and other food items that were hard to get because of the drought. I got a feel for the prices they were willing to pay and mentioned it to Captain Madera.

As we sailed to Troas, the captain and I discussed how we could prosper from a shipment of grain. One thing I noticed was that the ship didn't do well with the weight of the onboard cargo. The ship still leaked and a lot of time was spent pumping and bailing water. I had time to meet with the brethren in Troas after unloading the cargo meant for that port. The brethren said that they were buying grain at a decent price from villages north of Troas. I mentioned the plight of the Palestinians, and they were willing to work something out. I gave them what money I had and told them to buy grain for my family, and that we would somehow pick it up on a return trip.

The trip to Thessalonica was a bit rough. The ship was light on cargo and was able to withstand the high wind and seas. Upon arriving in port, Hermes worked a deal with the captain to give him time to locate his old trading partners in hopes of picking up a load in Thessalonica.

I located some Christians in Thessalonica. They were excited to see me. We shared news of what was going on in the Christian community. We talked about letters that they received from the apostles, and I mentioned the scrolls that Antonio acquired in Caesarea. We agreed to trade copies, and they handed me what copies they had.

I asked them about the availability of grain for shipping to the south. They said that grain from the Black Sea area was being shipped out of Neapolis, just east of Philippi. Hermes talked with some friends in port and found out that a couple of his old partners were actually working out of Neapolis. After we finished unloading the ship, we all decided to sail to Neapolis. The captain did well financially and paid us quite well for our help. He said that the ship was probably good for one more run south before putting it up for sale.

The port in Neapolis was quite busy. Hermes didn't find his friends, but he did find local businessmen who knew them. He found a grain trader who still had lots of grain in his warehouse. Hermes negotiated a deal for the captain. There wasn't enough money for a full cargo load, but it was enough to make a nice profit if sold in Sidon. We loaded the ship and headed to Troas, praying that the seas would be kind to us. We had quartering winds and seas the whole way. The wind was light, and the leaks were manageable. The Christian brethren in Troas came through with the grain we requested. It topped off the ship's cargo. We requested that the brethren pray continually for sailing mercies as we left port.

The wind and seas were much calmer going south. The journey was slow and the sun was hot. Combined with the balmy weather, we were sweating profusely. We all stripped off our clothes, and when the wind stopped, we took in an occasional swim. The captain didn't fill the water jugs before leaving port. We were drinking a lot of water in the hot weather. To our chagrin, we had to ration water until we reached Sidon. The captain picked up some fruit in Thessalonica. That helped, but the fruit ran out before reaching port.

Father's cousins were glad to see us. They purchased the whole cargo except for the grain loaded in Troas. The captain paid us well. The trip to Beth-Gebar was short. The family was excited to get the grain. Antonio and Joseph helped deliver the grain to our home. Father was in awe of the money we made on the trip. The captain was more than generous to us. Hermes was more than happy with his wages. Things were looking up again.

Mary-Beth mentioned that they buried Kaysi while I was gone. Ragamuffin took it pretty hard. I found Ragamuffin on top of the hill. She had her writing material with her, but she was sitting there looking toward the Mediterranean. I gave her a good hug and did my best to console her. We sat and talked for quite a while. I told her about the letters from Thessalonica, and that the brethren wanted copies of the apostle accounts. She said that she had made several copies of the gospel writings received from Peter. She said that she wanted to go with me when the copies were to be delivered to the believers in Thessalonica. I told her that I would talk with Father and try to work something out. This lifted her spirits as she continued copying Christian literature.

During the evening meal, Father and I discussed how we were going to deliver grain to the believers in Palestine. Hermes thought he heard the captain mention selling the ship to a prospective buyer in Joppa, and perhaps he would be willing to stop in Caesarea to drop off the grain with Peter. Peter could be trusted to get the grain safely to Galilee and Jerusalem with some help from Cleo and Patricia.

Captain Madera agreed, and several days later, I was on the way to Caesarea. I had no idea how I was going to return home. Antonio and Joseph sailed with me. The cargo was light and presented no problem in the seas encountered on the way. We docked at the commercial pier but didn't unload the ship until Antonio and I located Cleo. Cleo would arrange for no import taxes. Peter and the brethren helped to unload the vessel and store the grain at his restaurant.

Captain Madera sailed south to Joppa the next day. Antonio and Joseph went with him. They were going to figure out a way back to Caesarea and perhaps catch a ship headed toward Tyre or Sidon for the trip home. It was a long walk home, but if we had to, we would have done it.

I met Abigail and Flavius. It was exciting to see them. She was due in a month or so. Maybe less. They arranged for a military cargo ship to deliver them and their goods to Tyre. The ship was loaded with linen and cotton cloth from Alexandria and some silk imported from the east. There were a few prisoners on board. The ship was destined for Italy but were ordered to drop Flavius and Abigail off at Tyre. I asked if I could catch a ride with them, and Flavius made the arrangements.

I did ask him if he needed his favorite chariot to be delivered to Tyre, and if so, I would be more than happy to deliver it for him. He laughed and asked how the old rickety chariot that my Father had was working. I told him the sad story about it needing way too much fixing, not to mention that we no longer had horses to pull it. He smiled and recommended that I catch the ship with him and Abigail.

I met with Peter and told him to tell Antonio and Joseph that I had caught a ride to Tyre with Flavius. I mentioned our trip to Thessalonica and promised him copies of the new letters, as he handed me some copies of the gospels that he gave me on an earlier trip.

Soldiers carefully loaded commander Flavius's goods. The soldiers treated me with a lot of respect. My several visits to the garrison and meeting with Marcus and the commanders made them think that I was someone special. I took advantage of that status but made it a point to mingle with the soldiers and crew in order to make as many friends as possible. One never knows when having these kinds of contacts might come in handy.

We sailed in the morning and arrived the next day. After spending the night, Commander Banes arranged for a chariot ride home. The driver enjoyed our hospitality, and we gave him a good send off the next morning. He was happy to get away from the garrison.

I wondered when Joseph and Antonio were going to return. The captain knew a lot of traders and other ship captains. Catching a ride north shouldn't have been a problem.

Father was busy fixing our small grain mill. One of the brethren owned a fairly large mill and ground some of the wheat for us. The women really liked that, as a good portion of the day was spent grinding grain. When Ragamuffin got older, she and Mary would work as a team on the small grinding mill. They both had strong arms. However, they rejoiced when Father would have Hiram in the village grind the wheat for us. Hiram took a small portion of the flour for his efforts. The drought meant that there was little wheat to grind this year, so Hiram welcomed the business.

Ragamuffin was happy to see me. She loved talking, and I was the only one patient enough to sit and listen to her. She used to talk to Kaysi a lot. I wondered if getting her another dog would be a nice gift. She was wondering if people should really call her by her real name, Rachael. Ragamuffin was getting to the age where she was thinking about boyfriends and future marriage. She observed Joseph and Mary-Beth talking a lot. I suspected that whoever married Ragamuffin would be talked to death. I didn't tell her that, but Mother always said that Ragamuffin would someday drive someone crazy with her constant talking. I told her that I would start calling her by her real name. She said that it was all right to call her Ragamuffin, but when guests show up, she wanted to be introduced as Rachael. I had a feeling that when she was introduced to the soldier who drove me home, she was a bit embarrassed by us calling her Ragamuffin. He was young and handsome, and they did talk a lot, but she was still too young to be getting attached to boyfriends. Mother wanted to marry off the oldest remaining daughter first. Mary-Beth and Joseph seemed like a good match.

Ragamuffin did have some exciting news. Rabbi Zachias had shared a passage in the book of Daniel that appeared to be a prophetic passage that pointed to Jesus as being the Messiah. She had showed the passage to father, and when she compared the accounts of the apostles concerning Jesus with the passage, she couldn't but believe that Jesus was indeed the Messiah.

I asked her if she had the scripture available, and she reached into her shoulder bag and pulled out a scroll containing words from the prophet Daniel that Rabbi Zachias had lent her. I read the following:

> Seventy weeks are determined for your people and for your holy city, to finish the transgressions, to make an end of sins, to make reconciliation for iniquity, to bring in everlasting righteousness, to seal up vision and prophecy, and to anoint the Most Holy. Know therefore and understand, that from the going forth of the command to restore and build Jerusalem until Messiah the Prince, there shall be seven weeks and sixty-two weeks ... And after the sixty-two weeks Messiah shall be cut off, but not for himself; and the people of the prince who is to come shall destroy the city and the sanctuary.

She said that Rabbi Zachias and she were concerned about the part that said that the city and the sanctuary would be destroyed. If the crucifixion meant that the Messiah was cut off, then one would expect that the city and sanctuary would soon be destroyed. She and Rabbi Zachias felt that the Jews and Christians in Palestine needed to be warned of the eminent destruction.

I felt that the Christians would listen, but the Jews who did not believe that Jesus was the Messiah would not. Even if both Christians and Jews believed the prophecy, it is difficult for most people to get up and move. The people were entrenched in their environment. When the Jews were permitted to leave Babylon, many stayed behind because they had assimilated into the culture of the Babylonians. Nevertheless, we decided that all of us must spread the warning wherever we go.

A week had gone by and there was no sign of Joseph, Antonio, or Captain Madera. We were beginning to worry about their welfare. Ragamuffin came running down the hill and said that she thought she saw the Captain's ship on the horizon. We walked back up the hill and watched for quite some time. Sure enough, it was his ship. The waterline was fairly high, which meant that it was carrying a full cargo.

We walked to the village waterfront and waited for the ship to anchor. The pier was no longer useful. The last set of big waves finished it off. Villagers in a couple small boats rowed out to the ship. Captain Madera, Joseph, and Antonio came ashore. It turns out that the captain sold the ship to Ptolemy in Joppa. Ptolemy gave him a good price for it, and in turn asked him to continue as the ship's captain. The captain agreed for at least one roundtrip voyage.

Ptolemy sailed with them to Alexandria and picked up a load of linen and cotton cloth. The plan was to send half the load to Damascus and the other half was to go to Athens. The ship was leaking like a sieve when they pulled into port. They had to lighten the load in short order. The captain hired some local fishermen to off load half the cargo. A place was needed to store the bundles of cloth. I suggested that if it was temporary storage, the bundles could be stored in the new house that we were constructing. For a minor fee of course.

The captain agreed and mentioned that a caravan would arrive within a week or so to pick up the goods. The caravan would come from the east, the usual smuggling route. Father suspected that the cargo would be sold on the black market in Damascus. The captain paid Father a handsome fee and asked that he keep the bundles out of the rain. Father asked no questions.

Meanwhile, the captain was making arrangements to ship the rest of the cargo to Athens per Ptolemy's instructions. Knowing that the captain paid his crew well, I suggested that Hermes and I would be interested in serving as part of his crew. Antonio agreed to join us.

When Ragamuffin found out that the ship was going to Athens, she asked me to convince Father to let her go on the trip. Father said that cargo ships were not a place for women. They were not designed to accommodate females. I did not argue with father on that point. However, I wanted to see if there was an open door for her to sail with us. I discussed her desire with the captain. At first, he restated what Father said. However, he was quite adventurous and said that having a girl on board would probably liven up the trip. A few modifications would have to be made to the cabin area to allow for privacy of the opposite sex. The captain said that sea voyages were dangerous, and that I would have to take full responsibility for her safety.

I talked to Hermes about the situation and asked him to come up with some sort of scheme to get Ragamuffin onboard the ship. Ragamuffin insisted that she be allowed to share the gospel and to warn Jews and Christians alike of the impending destruction of Jerusalem. Hermes said that he would work on it. Hermes talked with Rabbi Zachias about Ragamuffin's desire to go to Athens with us. Zachias mentioned that women aren't allowed to enter the inner court of the sanctuary, and if they were, they would not be permitted to speak. Perhaps if she entered the women's court of the synagogue, she could probably speak, but her audience would be quite limited. Zachias also mentioned that Ragamuffin would most likely be accepted in the Christian churches as a speaker, but if the church is made up of Jews who have turned to Christ, tradition may prevent her from speaking to the congregation. Girls did not receive education in the Holy Scriptures. If a woman wanted to know something concerning the scriptures, they were to ask their husbands who were educated when they were young.

Be that as it may, Rabbi Zachias did say that Ragamuffin knew the Jewish Scriptures and the Christian writings quite well and could provide a convincing argument for not only showing that Jesus is the Christ but also warn the Jews of an impending destruction of Jerusalem by the Romans. His closing comment made a lot of sense, in that preventing one of God's servants from spreading the glad tidings of Jesus was probably not a good thing.

Rabbi Zachias presented his opinion on the matter to Father, and with a lot of arm twisting, Father relented and gave Ragamuffin permission to go on the ship. Hermes and I were directed to be with her at all times. Meanwhile, Father and the local believers agreed to keep us in constant prayer until we returned.

Captain Madera and Antonio made modifications to the cabin to accommodate Ragamuffin. We convinced Joseph to sail with us. It was fair weather all the way to Troas. While there, we picked up supplies and a paying passenger. Ragamuffin brought life and laughter to the crew and helped out where she could. She prayed for villages and cities that she saw along the way. She would ask the Lord to flood the area with the Holy Spirit and to send forth the Word of God.

The winds were contrary, and the seas were rough most of the way to Athens. Ragamuffin and Joseph had a tough time in those kinds of seas. Everybody went out of their way to look after Ragamuffin. The captain, who normally radiated a disgusting air of rough and toughness, was her best servant. When she was cold, he put a blanket around her. When she wanted something to eat, she got the best of the bread or fruit. When she needed privacy, the captain guarded the cabin doorway. When she was sleeping, nobody was allowed to speak above a whisper.

The port in Athens was quite crowded. The captain knew which pier to go to, but the pier was full of ships. We had to anchor for three days while we waited for one of the ships to move. Then, it was difficult to dock, as the wind was not in the right direction. A small boat with a couple of sailors dragged our ropes to the pier. The dock handlers did well in handling our ropes as we eased into the pier. The fee to use the pier was a bit high.

The captain left Antonio in charge of the ship as he went to locate the merchantman who was to receive the goods. The plan was to stay in port for four or five days. The rest of us set out to find Christians within the city. Ragamuffin marveled at the large buildings and architecture. It took several hours before getting directions to a possible Christian group, and it took as long to get to the area that they described. We were totally exhausted. The heat and humidity took its toll on us. Finally, we encountered someone who knew where the believers met.

A Christian brother, Anatolios, greeted us and led us to his home, which was used as a church. It was a sizeable home with a huge atrium. He had a couple of servants who washed our feet and gave us clean sandals to wear. We were in desperate need of a bath and a set of clean clothes. Water was not too plentiful, so we opted for washing the best way we could. We men were provided with robes. Anatolios's wife took care of Ragamuffin.

The evening meal was sumptuous. The Greeks really know how to dine. Lots of vegetables, grapes, fish, and a variety of breads were served. The wine was most excellent. Ragamuffin didn't drink any wine, even though we told her that we would keep it a secret from Father. She wanted a clear head in the event she had a chance to speak to the believers concerning the gospel of Jesus.

Ragamuffin gave copies of the apostles' written accounts and letters from Ephesus to Anatolios. He was really excited to receive written accounts of the events surrounding Jesus. Anatolios invited her to speak to the brethren who were meeting that night at his house.

The meeting began with singing and praising God. We didn't know the songs but did the best we could to sing along with them. Ragamuffin was introduced as Rachael, and she did a great job preaching the simple gospel of repentance and remission of sins. She read passages from the Jewish scriptures that pointed to the Messiah and told them of the impending destruction of Jerusalem. They marveled that a woman, and a young woman at that, could read and speak fluent Hebrew and Greek. She demonstrated both knowledge and understanding of the scriptures.

She told them that sin was no longer a hindrance to entering the kingdom of heaven because of the cross, and that all that anybody had to do to enter the kingdom was to repent, that is, reject the world and decide on a new and better way of life through Jesus.

We continued to praise and worship late into the evening. Ragamuffin laid hands on the sick. The Spirit seemed to be on her that evening, as several people were healed of various sicknesses. A lady was deaf in one ear, and when Ragamuffin prayed over her, hearing returned in that ear. Several people received Jesus as their Savior that evening.

The servants cleaned our clothes, and in the next morning, Anatolios arranged with a friend to show us the city. He had a business to run and couldn't spare the time. We all marveled at the sites. All except Hermes who had visited the city several times when he was young. The Parthenon was our favorite structure. The Greeks seemed to worship a number of gods. We were familiar with many of them, as Greek culture pervaded wherever the Greeks had conquered prior to the Romans. Hellenism was still strong along the eastern Mediterranean shores and in Egypt. The Greeks still had controlling interests in Egypt.

The cafés made for excellent rest stops. Anatolios prepared a late meal for us. There were no plans to meet with the believers that evening. Some people heard about the miraculous healings the night before and brought a couple of sick children by for prayer. We all prayed and laid hands on the children for healing. One of the children seemed to recover, while the other child remained ill. Anatolios thought that the child had a demon, and that it would take a traveling apostle to drive it out. We had a long discussion on spiritual deliverance and concluded that we needed help in this area.

We thanked the brethren for their hospitality. Anatolios had taken up a collection and gave us some money to help us on our way. I told him that we had sufficient funds, but he insisted that we take the offering and use it to support our ministry. We again thanked him and headed back to the ship. It was another long walk.

The captain was glad to see us. He was a bit worried about our welfare. The cargo was unloaded, and he had received payment. He said Ptolemy will be quite happy with the proceeds from the sale of his goods. Hermes, thinking of our need for additional funds to finish the house construction, casually mentioned to the captain that we should purchase more grain in Neapolis and sell it in Sidon for a decent profit.

The captain at first shook his head and said that the ship wouldn't handle another load. However, greed clouded his thinking, and he finally agreed. We outfitted the ship with the necessary supplies and began our journey north. I recalled promising the believers in Thessalonica that we would deliver some copied Christian literature. I asked the captain if he would stop in Thessalonica, and he agreed. He needed some pitch and some cloth for caulking in the event we should encounter leaks, and he knew where to get it for a reasonable price in Thessalonica.

The voyage was slow but steady. We had little trouble docking in Thessalonica. We did hit the pier a little harder than the captain would have liked, but there appeared to be no damage. The docking fee was reasonable. While the captain shopped for supplies, we all, accept for Antonio, located the Christian brethren and gave them literature similar to what was given in Athens. We prayed and worshipped with them, and Ragamuffin gave a most excellent sermon. She seemed to be gaining more confidence and strength in her dissertations, despite the fact that there was an argument over whether she, being a woman, should be preaching to learned men. Her overwhelming mastery of Hebrew and Greek scriptures and a clear presentation of the saving gospel of Jesus Christ settled the argument. The presence of the Holy Spirit filled the room as she spoke.

She invited the unsaved to repent and develop within themselves the mind of Christ. Several people did so. Most of them were women. She laid hands on the blind and deaf. For some reason, the deaf could hear, but the blind continued to be blind. It seems like her gifting had its limitations. Although, we all knew that the healing power of the Holy Spirit had no limitations. We debated this issue late into the evening.

The late night trip to the ship was difficult as it was dark and the two lamps given to us were dim at best. However, the brother who guided us knew the way quite well and warned us of any hazards along the way. He cautioned us about robbers lurking in the alley ways. We didn't encounter any, but Hermes kept his hand on his sword.

We were all exhausted when reaching the ship. Captain Madera and Antonio were fast asleep. The mosquitoes were a nuisance that night. So none of us slept well. We got underway early and were glad to escape the pesky bugs. Antonio and I took turns manning the rudder. Hermes handled the sails. Joseph slept a lot. So did Ragamuffin. A storm kicked up halfway to Neapolis. I thought the ship was going to roll over at one point. The captain was good at playing the wind and seas. We tacked back and forth and made very slow progress.

Every once in a while, the seas and wind would combine, and the ship would take a big roll and sometimes a huge wall of water would splash over the bow and make its way to the back deck. Needless to say, Ragamuffin and Joseph weren't feeling very well. Ragamuffin said that she was never going to sail again.

It was another day before we reached Neapolis. We had to anchor one more day before the wind cooperated with us and allowed us to dock the ship. We did the usual and searched for Christians in the city. There were no Christian churches, and the Jews wanted nothing to do with Christians. Despite their hostility, we prayed over the city and returned to the ship.

The captain located the same grain merchant that we used before and negotiated a fair deal for the grain. He used some of the money that he owed Ptolemy but expected to get it back plus more in Sidon. The captain figured that if the ship sank and all was lost, then it didn't matter whether he owed anybody money.

The grain was loaded within two days. The waterline was a bit high, and we prayed for decent weather on the return trip. The wind was light and steady, and the sea swells were small. The pitch and rolls of the ship rocked us asleep. During my watch, I noticed a two-masted ship trailing behind us at quite a distance. A few hours later, it was fairly visible. It was riding high on the water, which indicated that it was not carrying any cargo. We figured that it was headed to Troas.

We had no navigator. The captain did well using the sun, moon, and North Star as his navigational aids. If it was a cloudy day and there was no shadow, he would look at the swell direction and assume it was from the west and steered according to that. Antonio was always saying that we were lost, and that it will take three years before we would get home. Ragamuffin would half believe him. She would ask several times if I thought he was right. I told her not to worry, and that if the sun or stars were visible, all we had to do was head east, and we would eventually hit land. If all else fails, follow another ship, and you'll hit a port somewhere. Of course, if the blind leads the blind, they will both fall off of the edge of the earth. Ragamuffin had a good sense of humor.

The captain got a bit edgy as the other ship neared us. I noticed Hermes and the captain were conversing with each other and keeping an eye on the other ship as it got closer. Hermes came over to me and mentioned that the trailing vessel could be a pirate ship. Octavian made a special effort to rid the Mediterranean of pirate ships. His success attributed to the relative peace along the Mediterranean shores during his reign as Augustus Caesar. However, there were still rogue ships roaming the high seas.

Hermes and I had our swords and knives. The captain had a sword but had never really used it in training or battle. He had a small cross bow with a few darts and a long bow with a quiver of arrows. Hermes gathered us together and explained to everyone that there was a possibility that the ship following us was indeed a pirate ship, and that we needed to develop a plan to defend ourselves in the event of an attack.

Unbeknownst to us, Hermes heard rumors of a pirate ship roaming in the area and made a couple of purchases while in Thessalonica. One was the purchase of three special arrows for the long bow. The other was a mace, an iron ball connected with a chain to an iron handle. He kept the knowledge of pirates and the purchases secret so as to not worry the crew.

I observed Hermes leaning on the back rail and couldn't help think that Hermes was developing a plan to defend ourselves. Everyone seemed tense except for Hermes. It was almost like Hermes was itching for a fight. When he and the captain both concluded that they were pirates, Hermes gathered us together again and gave us his plan. He said that the pirates will probably maneuver close to our ship and toss ropes with hooks on them to grab and pull the two ships together. Once the ships are next to each other, the pirates will attempt to board our ship.

Hermes told the captain to turn to port immediately as the hooks are set and bump the other vessel. As the two ships touch, Hermes and I would board the other ship on the bow and attack the nearest pirates. This will catch them off guard as they will not expect that move. He told Antonio and Joseph to grab the hooks while the ropes temporarily slackened and toss them away from the ship. Any hooks that were still anchored were to be cut with the captain's sword.

Hermes prepared three hollow arrows by filling them with oil. They had three small holes along one side. The arrows were laid flat with the holes up. He instructed Ragamuffin to dip the tip of the arrows in burning oil and to shoot them toward the top of each sail. The idea was that if the arrow stuck in the canvas, the oil in the arrow would leak and keep the flame burning and hopefully set the sail on fire.

Ragamuffin was skilled in the use of small crossbows and darts. She was to use them if anyone tried to board the ship. We emptied our shoulder bags and poured some salt into them. Hermes said to throw salt into the eyes of the first pirate that approached me. He said that the first two pirates should be easy kills. As soon as possible, we were to cut ropes connected to the sails. The main goal was the foresail. As soon as the sail fluttered in the wind, captain Madera was to bump the ship again so that we could jump back onto our ship. Hermes handed the mace to Antonio and told him to use it wherever and whenever he could. He told Joseph to stay with the captain at the rudder and to relieve the captain whenever the captain saw need for something to do.

It seemed like a good plan. The pirate ship paralleled us and a goodly number of men began screaming as it immediately turned toward us. Just as Hermes suspected, they threw the hooks. Some connected, while others fell into the sea. Our captain did as instructed, and he bumped the other ship. That opened the opportunity for Hermes and me to jump aboard and attack the nearest two pirates who were in the process of righting themselves after the bump.

Ragamuffin did her trick with the arrows. Two hit their mark and stuck. The other bounced off and fell to the deck. Antonio tossed the remaining hooks into the sea. The first two pirates were easy kills. I didn't use the salt on them. As the others approached, we tossed salt at their faces. Hermes made short order of his opponent. He fought like a madman. My second opponent was a bit tough. He knew how to use his sword despite having salt thrown into his eyes. I felt pain in my left arm and realized that Hermes had cut me with his sword.

Close quarters fighting was not fun. As I caught my opponent with a nice straight thrust, Hermes yelled for me to kick him. I gave him a solid thrust kick and sent him back toward the other approaching pirates. This created enough delay for me to cut a couple of ropes. I had no idea what the ropes were connected to. I just simply whacked at ropes tied to anything above me.

Hermes immediately yelled for us to abandon ship. Our captain tried to time the bump but missed by a few seconds. I made it to our ship, but Hermes landed in the water. I felt pain in my right shoulder. As I turned to look, I saw a small arrow sticking out of me. I was shot as I jumped ship.

Realizing that Hermes was in the water, our captain immediately turned starboard and loosened the sail. As we floundered in the sea, Hermes swam toward our ship. Antonio and Joseph helped him aboard. They had a difficult time as Hermes seemed to weigh about a thousand talents of silver being wet and having no strength to pull himself aboard. They finally got him over the rail, only to land on Ragamuffin's leg. Apparently, Ragamuffin fell during the last bump of the ship.

Captain Madera let the ship flounder for a while as the other ship was still under sail and moving away from us. They had to turn and come back around us to make another attack. Floundering gave us time to recover and decide what to do next.

Antonio told the captain that there were leaks on the port bow. The two bumps caused serious damage. The captain grabbed his cloth, pitch, and some tools and ran forward to caulk the seams that were leaking. Hermes was coughing up sea water, and I was sitting on the deck holding the wound on my left arm. It was high, next to the shoulder. I told Joseph to pull out the arrow in my right shoulder. It was lodged into the bone. He rocked the arrow as he tried to pull it out and broke the arrow, leaving the blade in the shoulder. Hermes came over and figured out a way to get the blade out.

Ragamuffin came close to me and put pressure on the wound on my left shoulder to stop the bleeding. I bled all over the right side of her undergarment. She generally took off her dress because of the humidity and heat. Her undergarment looked like a dress anyway, and no one really minded as long as Mother didn't find out. I looked at her and told her that it wasn't appropriate for her to be wearing an undergarment during battle, and that it was against the rules of warfare. She laughed and began to cry. She leaned on my shoulder and said that it hurt. I told her that it really didn't hurt that bad. She said in a low voice that she meant that she was hurting.

I asked her where she was injured, and she said that she fell when the captain bumped the other ship for the second time, and she hurt her right shoulder, elbow, and wrist. As if that wasn't enough, Hermes landed on her right leg and hurt her ankle when they got him aboard. I reached over with my left hand and sort of gave her a hug. I tried not to grimace in pain as I did so. I kissed her forehead, and as I pulled away, I noticed that her right ear was bleeding a little. I mentioned that to her, and she said that she caught it with the bow string.

Antonio picked her up and carried her to her bed. It was really the captain's bed as he wanted her to have the best of accommodations while traveling with us. Antonio placed a blanket under each side of her to help keep her immobilized while the ship was rolling in the seas.

Hermes kept an eye on the other ship, and when it was parallel to us heading in the opposite direction, he ordered Joseph to man the rudder as he set the sail. Antonio was pumping water from the bilge. I was useless because of my wounds. Once the sail was set and we were underway again, Hermes looked for something to suture my wounds. The captain had some fishhooks, but they were too big to use. I remember Gaius telling me about the fishhook needles that he designed for use during the Arabian conflicts.

Ragamuffin asked Hermes what he was looking for when he entered the cabin. She told him to look in her leather bag where she kept her clothes. He found a needle and some thread. Hermes told her that having a lady on board was a good move. He kissed her on the forehead and left.

He did his best to stitch the wounds, although he drank most of the wine that he used for cleansing them. I told him to put some honey on the stitches before wrapping them. I didn't want the wounds to get infected. He place a few sacks of grain on the deck and made me as comfortable as possible.

The captain stopped the leaks but used up all of his cloth and pitch in doing so. Joseph helped Antonio empty the water out of the bilge. They kept an eye on the pirate ship. It kept pace with us. The captain figured that they had some issues of their own. The mainsail appeared to be undamaged. It had a black spot on it from the flaming arrow, but no hole could be seen. They appeared to be repairing the foresail. It was floundering for quite some time. There was a hole at the top from the fire, but not big enough to make the sail useless.

Hermes and the captain decided to change course and head more in an easterly direction. They didn't think they could outrun the pirates and make it to Troas. They figured that they had a better chance of escaping them if they were to beach the ship anywhere along the coast. The pirates caught up with us but stayed a fair distance off our starboard side.

I told Hermes to dump the cargo. With a lighter ship, we could gain more speed, and if the pirates attacked again, we could maneuver the ship quicker and make it more difficult for them to board us. Also, if the pirates saw us dump the cargo, they really had no reason to attack us.

He discussed it with the captain, but greed and stubbornness ruled the hour. They decided that dumping the cargo would be the last resort. As the sun was disappearing over the horizon, Hermes gathered what weapons he could find. We still had the mace. Hermes lost his sword and knife when he went overboard. I offered him my knife and sword. Ragamuffin had expended all the long arrows. The captain said that a couple of them hit their mark, or something worth hitting, not necessarily who or what she was aiming at. She was not use to shooting arrows on a moving platform.

There were a few darts available for the small crossbow, but they were only good for short ranges. Joseph found a couple of arrows stuck in the skins covering the grain sacks. He said that several of them flew over the ship. The captain didn't think that the pirates would attack at night. If anything, they would make their move in the morning.

It was a long night. Antonio notice layers of fog forming. He suggested that when the silhouette of the pirate ship disappeared from view they couldn't see us and suggested that we turn to port and distance ourselves from them in hopes of them not finding us in the morning. Captain Madera liked the idea, but time was of the essence because it took time to get enough distance away so that they could not see us at twilight. At the right moment, Captain Madera gave the command, and we turned to port. There was hardly any wind and our speed was very slow.

I checked on Ragamuffin. She couldn't sleep because of the pain. I kissed her on the forehead and told her to pray for wind. She smiled and reached for my hand. We prayed together. I laid hands on her wounds and asked God to reach down with His healing hand and quickly take away the pain and heal her wounds. I kissed her forehead again and left.

The captain and Hermes decided to come about and sail behind the pirate ship in a southerly direction. We kept the ship as dark as possible. The night was balmy and cool, but we all seemed to be sweating as we slowly moved south. We lost total sight of the other ship and hoped they lost total sight of us. At first light, there were small patches of fog and no sight of the other ship. The captain said that they could appear behind us at any time.

As time went on, Antonio's scheme seemed to work. Eventually, the wind picked up, and we were again making good headway. We didn't change course to the east until late afternoon. The captain recognized the mountains of Troy and knew which direction to sail toward Troas. Antonio and the captain did a nice job docking the ship. Ragamuffin was somewhat mobile. Her ankle still hurt, but her arm was much better. Her shoulder was still sore, but she could move her elbow a lot more. Her wrist was stiff and sore. The injury to her ear was scabbing over. Her undergarment was stained from my blood. I told her to change into her dress if she could.

My wounds were still bleeding, so I decided to go to the garrison and find a military surgeon. Hermes went with me. We dropped a few names to get their attention. Marcus was well known and respected by most of the commanders. We reported the incident to one of the commanders before finding the surgeon. The surgeon looked at the stitches and decided to replace them. He had finer needles and thread. I asked one of the commanders who took down the information on the incident if he could provide us with some arrows and a sword for protection on our remaining journey. He declined on the sword but gave us a number of arrows. I went back to the ship on my own, as Hermes went shopping.

Joseph took the remaining Christian literature to the local church. They were happy to receive them. They treated Joseph quite well after hearing his tale of the pirates. He was their hero of the day. They gave him some fresh fruit and bread for the ship's crew and walked with him to the ship.

The captain picked up some more cloth and pitch. There was a steady leak where the ships bumped each other. Antonio's arm was wearing out keeping the bilge from filling with water. He didn't want the grain to get wet. Hermes showed up with a package. He took it into the cabin without telling us what it was. It turned out that he purchased a new undergarment for Ragamuffin. He felt embarrassed buying women's clothes especially an undergarment. When we found out, we kidded him half way back to Sidon. Hermes had a great sense of humor, although he did threaten to throw us all overboard at one point.

As we departed Troas, we noticed a Roman galley leaving the harbor. The oars were moving at the beat of a drum, and when they caught the wind, the oars were retrieved as they headed northwest. I was surprised that it didn't have a full set of sails as most other ships had. I suspected that they were headed out to look for the pirates. A pirate ship could not outrun that vessel with both oars and sails at work.

The rest of the voyage was uneventful. The seas were rough but manageable. Most of our efforts were spent pumping and bailing water. We were most happy when we docked in Sidon. Father's cousins met us and purchased our grain for a decent price. We lost seven sacks due to water damage. As usual, the captain paid us well, including Ragamuffin.

The voyage to Beth-Gebar was short. The family was most glad to see us. Hermes carried Ragamuffin all the way from the beach to within sight of our home. She didn't want Father to know that she is injured and did her best to walk the rest of the way. Father eventually found out from the tales spoken around the fire ring. Everyone waited hand and foot on Ragamuffin. Even the villagers brought food and gifts to her when they found out from the captain what she and the rest of us went through. I'm most certain that the captain embellished the tale a bit. It was as if Ragamuffin fought the whole battle herself, and we just stood by watching her do so. We all took it in good stride. After that, Ragamuffin could never do anything wrong.

We gave Father most of our earnings. The household was again flush with money. Gaius was failing and bedridden. Father whispered into my ear and told me to follow him. We went down to the stable, and there it was, a Roman chariot. Apparently, two soldiers in separate chariots pulled up to the gate. One of the soldiers entered and told Father that one of the chariots was his and was not to ask any questions. The soldier hopped onto the other chariot, and they returned southward. They would not stay for a meal and didn't want to be seen at the house any longer than was necessary. Father was told to modify it so as not to be identified as a Roman chariot. Father knew what to do and thanked them for the gift. I suspected Flavius had his hand in this.

Stephanie was really excited to see me. Despite smelling terrible from the trip, I was given a good hug and a kiss. I felt that she had something to tell me but was keeping it back. That evening, Mary-Beth poured us a hot bath at the spa. She even laid out towels and our robes on the ledge. While soaking in the spa, Stephanie leaned over and whispered in my ear that she was pregnant. That was exciting news. We hugged and kissed a couple of times over the news. I fell asleep with her holding me close. It would have been the other way around, but both my shoulders still hurt from the wounds. She and Mary-Beth served me a nice breakfast the next morning. I think Mary-Beth was even more excited than Stephanie.

Chapter 9

J E R U S A L E M

Silvanus, son of Matthias, son of Gaius, to my descendants. The spring was flowing at a trickle. Hermes and the girls watered the garden and trees from the pool. Very little water reached the road. The pool would partially fill at night. Writing is painful. The wounds bothered me for several weeks. The stitches were out, but the healing was slow. The shoulder that took the arrow hurt for several months. Rabbi Zachias continued with our studies of the Hebrew Scriptures. His main students were Joseph and Ragamuffin. Antonio occasionally showed up and joined them. They would spend half the time at the synagogue and the other half either at the top of the hill or at the dining table. Antonio usually showed up about the time Mary-Beth's bread came out of the oven. He would always sit next to Ragamuffin. The first thing he would do was to grab the ankle that was injured and give the ankle and foot a good massage. Ragamuffin always volunteered the other foot as well. He was the only guy that could get away with it. Otherwise, he would be beaten most severely by mother with a wooden spoon. Everyone let Antonio be Antonio. He was full of life and brought a lot of laughter into the family.

The captain had yet to leave for Joppa. He was in no hurry to get Ptolemy's money to him. Besides, he couldn't find a crew to go with him. The ship still has a couple of small leaks. He rowed out daily to empty out the bilge.

Mary-Beth was glad to see Joseph. The two seemed to be getting along quite well. However, you could see by Mary's eyes that she was jealous of Ragamuffin. Joseph was spending way too much time with Ragamuffin. There were times when she wouldn't speak to Ragamuffin at the grain mill.

Antonio worked with Father on the newly acquired chariot. The rule was to make it look the least Roman as possible. Antonio took the leatherworks off and replaced it with a different design set. He took off the quiver and bow holder and replaced them with a sheath designed to fit a standard sword.

Commander Flavius and Abigail were at the garrison in Tyre. Father and Mother would take the chariot for short visits. Shopping on the waterfront in Tyre was a whole new world. This kind of life was quite a change for her. Most people never traveled. What they knew of the outside world was from the occasional traveler who visited the village. Both of them were treated quite well by Decarus and Commander Flavius. Abigail's baby was due very shortly.

Occasionally, Father would take Mary-Beth to Tyre. Mary was afraid of the big city. She always held Father close wherever they walked. Mary liked to sample the bread at the bakeries along the waterfront. She loved talking to the women who sold and baked bread. It wasn't long before she was baking bread with different ingredients, texture, and shapes. Antonio was her taster.

Joseph seemed to be quite jealous of him. I talked to Ragamuffin when Joseph wasn't around and told her to help Mary-Beth out a little bit and suggested that she associate less with Joseph. She said that she had slight feelings for Joseph but didn't really love him and didn't realize that Mary was that upset over her being with Joseph. Ragamuffin could see where I was coming from and volunteered to work with me. She made sure Joseph sat next to Mary at the dinner table and not next to her, and let Mary wash Joseph's feet when he arrived and not her. She stopped serving Joseph bread that Mary had just made. These little things seemed to make life better for both Mary and Ragamuffin. Personally, I think Joseph was a better match for Ragamuffin, and that Antonio was a better match for Mary-Beth.

Ragamuffin was still concerned about the destruction of Jerusalem as prophesied by the Prophet Daniel. Rabbi Zachias said that the best way to check it out would be to visit with the chief scribe and historian in Jerusalem. Around the time of Ezra, scribes seemed to be getting better organized. They tracked history through some of the tougher times. Israel was at the crossroads of Egyptian wars with the Babylonians, Greeks, and Romans.

Rabbi Zachias and Father were most likely not welcomed in Jerusalem. The priests at the Sanhedrin had Rabbi Zachias on their wanted list. Given that Father prevented his arrest, he would also be at risk for an arrest. Father wasn't too concerned as he felt protected as a Roman citizen and assigned as the prefect of Beth-Gebar. Zachias suggested that Joseph could go and do the research. Ragamuffin wanted to go with him. Zachias said that women do not serve as scribes and would not be welcome at the main synagogue library. However, she insisted and asked Father if she could go. With the usual arm twisting, he relented, and I ended up having to go to look after their welfare.

Joppa was closer to Jerusalem then Caesarea. It was a long chariot ride regardless of the distance. After some discussion, we decided to ask Captain Madera if he would take us to Joppa. He had to take the ship there anyway, and we would be his crew. From Joppa, we opted to walk to Jerusalem and figured that we could do it in three or four days. From Jerusalem, we could walk back to Joppa and catch a ship to Tyre, and hopefully, Flavius could arrange a chariot ride home.

The captain was excited to have a crew and immediately set out to provision the ship for the voyage. We packed some of Mary's bread, some water skins, and other items needed for the journey. Father handed us a jug of wine for the captain. We took enough money to stay in an inn several times if necessary.

We had to wait a few days for the weather to clear up. The captain preferred a nice offshore wind before getting underway. It made for an easy departure. The ship rode high with no cargo. The seas were rough the whole way. Ragamuffin forgot about her seasickness on the previous journey. She remained in the cabin the whole time. The leaks didn't get worse, which kept our work load to a minimum. Docking the ship in Joppa was not going to be easy. We had to anchor for two days until the wind died down enough for us to make it to the pier.

The captain wanted to locate Ptolemy before we began our walk to Jerusalem. When the two of them appeared, we bid them farewell and headed for the eastern road. The captain knew our schedule, and said that he may wait for and catch the same ship to Tyre.

We purchased bread and fruit in Joppa. The walk was difficult. It was hot and dry. We made it to Lydda by sundown and found an inn. The local café had good food and wine. The people were pleasant and quite inquisitive. Lydda was a major stopover for travelers heading to or from Jerusalem. We all complained about sore feet and wished we were at home soaking in the spa.

After a good breakfast and purchasing more bread and fruit, we continued on our journey. The inns in Emmaus were full. However, we were able to stay in a bed and breakfast place. The family was most enjoyable to be with, and we agreed to stay with them on the return trip. We pushed hard to make Jerusalem the next day. We had a limited amount of funds. The inns were more expensive than we had planned.

Jerusalem was a beautiful sight. We stayed in an inn just outside the main gate. On the next day, we searched for the synagogue described by Rabbi Zachias and looked for a scribe whose name was Levi. It wasn't long before we found him. Rabbi Levi was a pleasant fellow. He inquired of Rabbi Zachias's welfare and was happy that he was doing well. We described why we were there, and Levi was excited to help us. His daily routine seemed to revolve around Sadducees from the Sanhedrin wanting to know about this law and that law and what was recorded when and by who. The rest of his time was spent overseeing scribes copying the Holy Scriptures.

He easily found the writings of Daniel, and Ragamuffin located the prophetic scripture that pointed to the Messiah and the destruction of Jerusalem. She read it aloud:

> Seventy weeks are determined for your people and for your holy city, to finish the transgression, to make an end of sins, to make reconciliation for iniquity, to bring in everlasting righteousness, to seal up vision and prophecy, and to anoint the Most Holy. Know therefore and understand, that from the going forth of the command to restore and build Jerusalem until Messiah the Prince, there shall be seven weeks and sixty-two weeks; the street shall be built again, and the wall, even in troublesome times. And after the sixty-two weeks Messiah shall be cut off, but not for Himself; and the people of the prince who is to come shall destroy the city and the sanctuary. The end of it shall be with a flood, and till the end of the war desolations are determined. Then he shall confirm a covenant with many for one week; but in the middle of the week He shall bring an end to sacrifice and offering. And on the wing of abominations shall be one who makes desolate, even until the consummation which is determined, is poured out on the desolate.

Rabbi Levi mentioned that the high priests and scores of priests from the Sanhedrin have studied this scripture during the time of John the Baptist and Jesus and continued to do so after the crucifixion. He further stated that the decree which most correctly addresses the "command to restore and build Jerusalem" was the decree of Artaxerxes to Ezra. Levi said that their best understanding was that the seven weeks referred to forty-nine days, each day representing one year, and that the forty-nine years most likely referred to the Jewish Jubilee. In the fiftieth year, the trumpet of the jubilee was sounded. It proclaimed liberty to all Israelites who were in bondage to any of their countrymen, and the return of their ancestral possessions to any who had been compelled through poverty to sell them. The fiftieth year occurred after seven times seven years had been counted from the institution of the festival or from the last jubilee. Rabbi Levi suspected that the first jubilee after the captivity was important in that it prevented any injustice relative to land ownership as the city was being rebuilt.

Rabbi Levi further mentioned that the seven sevens and the sixty-two sevens represented a period of four hundred and eighty-three years and stated that the command to go forth and rebuild Jerusalem was made during the seventh year of Artaxerxes I's reign as king of Persia as mentioned in the book of Ezra. Levi was aware of John the Baptist and knew about when he began his preaching as well as when the first news arrived about Jesus and His teachings. He showed us scrolls of history that were labeled with different time spans. He counted back to the scroll that fit the four hundred and eighty-three year period, which would account for the seven sevens and sixty-two sevens. It was the year that Artaxerxes I was the reigning king of Persia. It was in his seventh year as king when he wrote a letter or decree that allowed the Jewish captives to return to Israel. The temple was already finished by that time. King Cyrus permitted the rebuilding of the temple at the request of Ezra the scribe.

Rabbi Levi then stated that the beginning of the seventieth week coincided with the beginning of Jesus's ministry, and it was during this week that He was cut off, that is, crucified. Also, sometime after the beginning of His ministry, Jerusalem and the sanctuary will be destroyed. The rest of the prophecy was a bit cloudy. It appeared that a seven-year covenant of some sort will be established and that halfway through the seven-year period, sacrifices and offerings will cease. This indicates that the destruction of the temple takes place sometime after that. One keyword that indicates the amount of time before the final destruction was the word *flood*. It rained forty days and forty nights during the great flood. Perhaps wars and desolations take place over a forty-year period before the final destruction. In any case, when one hears of the sacrifices and offerings coming to an end, within three and a half years, Jerusalem and the temple will most likely be destroyed.

Rabbi Levi concluded that a goodly number of the priests agreed that Jesus was indeed the Messiah. He stated that some members of the Sanhedrin secretly believe that Jesus was the Messiah, and that a number of prophesies support their positions on that.

Ragamuffin wanted to know why the priests supported the crucifixion of Jesus when they were fairly certain that He was the Messiah. Levi gave two words—*power* and *corruption*. Then he asked Ragamuffin a question, "Who appoints the high priests and lords it over them?"

As they exited the library, Rabbi Levi marveled at Ragmuffin's knowledge of the Hebrew Scriptures and asked her who taught her these things. She responded with Rabbi Zachias's name. He said that Rabbi Zachias was always rebellious that way. Levi said that usually only boys were taught the things that she knew. He said that next Rabbi Zachias will be asking the chief priest if a woman could become a priest and laughed.

Ragamuffin borrowed some ink and papyrus and wrote it all down. Levi took note that she could write as well as read Hebrew. I told Levi that Ragamuffin was quite proficient in reading and writing in both, Hebrew and Greek. Levi, needless to say, was quite impressed.

Rabbi Levi invited us to his home for an evening meal and found us a place to stay with one of his relatives. He had a nice family. As we were leaving the next day, Rabbi Levi slipped me a goodly amount of denarii to help us along the journey. He closed my hand so that I couldn't open it and refuse the gift. I thanked him and told him that he and his family would be in our prayers. As we left, Ragamuffin turned toward Levi and said, "Remember, Rabbi Levi … forty years!" Zachias smiled as he turned and headed toward the synagogue.

We stayed at the same bed and breakfast in Emmaus. The nice couple was glad to see us back. Ragamuffin asked if we could spend a few days there. Sometimes, we forget that Ragamuffin was maturing as a girl, and sometimes, Ragamuffin forgets that she is a girl. While she rested at the home, Joseph and I searched for Christian churches in the area. There were a couple churches meeting in homes. We were welcomed in both of them. Both homes were also restaurants that connected to the main street. The owners sat with us as we ate. We talked politics and news concerning the spread of Christianity and were invited to their meetings. The restaurants stayed open until late evening, except on the Sabbath. We prayed and worshipped at one place in the morning and another place in the evening on the Sabbath. I was invited to speak. The churches were eager for a fresh word. They possessed written gospel accounts, but I preached on repentance and remission of sins anyway. It was the same message that I heard Ragamuffin preach in Greece. I also preached on Daniel's prophecy and warned them of the impending destruction of Jerusalem.

There were Roman soldiers at one meeting. They were among the gentiles who were turning to Christ. I talked with them after the service. They were concerned as to what they would have to do if ordered to be part of the destruction of Jerusalem. On one hand, they had to obey orders as Roman soldiers. On the other hand, they are also soldiers for Christ. I agreed that it was difficult to serve two masters. You begin to love one and hate the other. I told them that the destruction would most likely take place forty years after the beginning of Jesus's ministry based on our research in Jerusalem, and that they would not have to worry about making a decision on who to obey. I told them that the smart thing would be to warn others of the impending destruction, not just Christian Jews, but all Jews.

We noticed the lack of variety in food, and the poor quality wine that was served. The drought over the years seemed to be affecting the quality of life in the region. The Lord has been good to us in Beth-Gebar, although the village itself was dying. The older people were staying, but the younger people were relocating to either Sidon or Tyre for work and a better way of life.

When Ragamuffin was ready to travel, we were quite anxious to get home. The journey to Lydda was hot and dry. We stayed at the same inn as before. The journey to Joppa seemed to take forever. Fortunately, we did not encounter any robbers along the way. I'm sure the brethren were praying for us.

When we reached Joppa, we looked for the captain and the ship. We didn't see either of them, and so we searched the waterfront for Ptolemy. A soldier recognized and called out to me. He was one of the guards at the garrison in Caesarea. We talked for a while. Apparently, Marcus was in Joppa on business. He mentioned that Marcus and his family were transferring to the garrison in Troas, except for Cleo. He was staying in Caesarea. Cleo was the only commander whom they really liked. They did miss Flavius, however. I asked him to greet Marcus and Patricia for me, and that I wish them well at Troas.

We were exhausted and weather worn from the journey and walking the waterfront. Joseph suggested finding an inn. We did so, but it was rather unkempt. The next morning, we found Ptolemy. He said that he hired the captain to pick up some cargo in Alexandria, and that the ship was two days overdue. I told him to tell the captain that we were going to try and catch a ship north to Tyre. He knew of a ship heading to Sidon and offered to make arrangements for us to travel with them. He said that the only drawback was they don't like to have women onboard, but he knew the ship's captain, and he probably could persuade the captain to make an exception.

The ship was leaving the next day. Ptolemy seemed to know everyone on the waterfront. It seemed like no one refused a request from him. Ptolemy said that he appreciated us helping to deliver his cargo in Beth-Gebar and Greece. Apparently, we and Father were well spoken of by the captain. I'm certain that captain Madera embellished some of the events we encountered to save Ptolemy's ship.

We traveled at no cost to Sidon. The ship's captain and crew were quite accommodating. We slept and ate in one area on the deck and helped out when and where we could. We shared sailing stories with the crew. They were excited to hear about our encounter with the pirates. We became heroes in their mind and were not treated as sand crabs who had never been to sea before.

When one of the crew members heard that we were of the House of Gaius, he asked us about a girl of that house who beat up a Roman centurion. He had heard a rumor that the girl was an Amazon and a descendent of Alexander the Great. I marveled about how the incident with Commander Darius became quite an embellished tale. I told him that the girl was protecting her sister, and that commander Darius wasn't hurt that badly. The crew member then responded with, "Then it's a true story?" I left it at that and wondered where the tale would go from there. Unbeknownst to them, the girl mentioned in the tale was on their very ship. I told Ragamuffin about the tall tale. She chuckled at the thought of being an Amazon from one of the Greek islands and a descendent of Alexander the Great.

When we reached Sidon, we looked up Father's cousins. They fed us and gave us a place to stay for the night. The walk to Beth-Gebar was relatively short. A few hours of walking, and we were home. Stephanie was worried about us. Father and Hermes kept reassuring her that we were safe and would return soon. We allowed Ragamuffin to be the first to use the spa. The pool level was too low to swim in. Stephanie went with her carrying a clean robe, a towel, and a clean pair of sandals.

Joseph sat with Mary-Beth and told her everything about our journey. Mary washed and massaged his feet and fed him some of his favorite bread and wine. I filled Father and Mother in on our experiences and findings in Jerusalem. All was well at home, except that Gaius wasn't doing well. That evening, Stephanie and I spent time in the spa together before retiring for the evening. Hermes had heated the water for us and brought us bread, cheese, and wine. She didn't mind having him around as long as it was dark. Most of us sat in the spa without any clothes on. A lit candle on the table next to the spa was the only light. Mother and Mary-Beth had been taking good care of Stephanie and the baby. The baby was due in six months or so.

Rabbi Zachias was excited to hear about the results of our research in Jerusalem. He was equally happy that Rabbi Levi took good care of us. He mentioned that his well was going dry, and that he had to make several journeys with his donkey to get water from our spring. He said that Mary-Beth fed him bread and wine every time he showed up. Apparently, Mary was trying new bread recipes on him.

Chapter 10

THE SHIPPING TRADE

Silvanus, son of Matthias, son of Gaius, to my descendants. It's been a couple of years, and there was still no sign of the captain. Word has it that his ship, or should I say, Ptolemy's ship, sank off the Egyptian coast during a storm, and that he and his crew were rescued after a few days in the sea. They were clinging to debris and floating cargo from the ship. The captain was supposedly still working for Ptolemy and sailing cargo ships along the coast.

Stephanie and I moved into the new house after the baby was born. The baby boy is doing quite well. We named him Gaius. Grandfather Gaius passed away about a year ago. We buried him next to Priscilla in a plot near the saddle northeast of the hill.

Abigail and her daughter had to move in with us. Apparently, threats were made against her in Tyre because she—a Jew—married a Roman centurion. She and commander Flavius were living near the garrison. Flavius was approved as the temporary procurator of Tyre, as Decarus's health had considerably deteriorated. Now that his position is official, he is moving into the housing section near the praetorian. Abigail and their child will be safe there.

Mary-Beth and Joseph finally got married. Rabbi Zachias was quite happy for the two of them. The wedding was held at the synagogue, and the reception held in the village was wonderful. Mary-Beth is an excellent wife for Joseph. Father and I are thinking about building them a house on the east side of the hill.

Hermes's and Emma's two children are growing like weeds. Mary-Beth spent a lot of time helping to take care of their children along with Abigail's child when she was visiting Flavius. Ragamuffin continued to study the Holy Scriptures and is quite knowledgeable in them. She wanted to travel to Galilee and Jerusalem to share the Word with Christians in the area, mostly in hopes of hearing from some of the apostles themselves who were with Jesus during His ministry. Father is considering to escort her but preferred that either Hermes or I go with her. Stephanie and Emma both rebelled at that suggestion. I stayed out of the middle of that battle.

My parents moved into Gaius's bedroom. This allowed for us to expand the kitchen and dining area. Money was in short supply again. Flavius has been sending us money to take care of Abigail, and a sack of grain always seemed to arrive at the right time.

News from the garrison was that Caligula was assassinated, and that Claudius succeeded him. The hope was that the senate would regain control in Rome. Claudius worked quite well with the senate, except when they debated his proposed new laws. Claudius maintained tight control and kept the army at his side through bribery. Decarus said that Claudius was a good administrator and was an ambitious builder throughout the empire. Fortunately, he did not focus on persecution of Christians. That was left to the local procurators. Our friendships with Marcus and Decarus had its benefits in protecting Christians under their authority. It seems that Jewish influence with local procurators was the biggest threat to Christians.

Marcus is serving as procurator of Troas. Patricia is there with him. She sent a couple of stringed instruments to Ragamuffin—a small harp and a lute. A merchant traveling from Caesarea was paid to deliver them. He spent the night with us. Apparently, she gave the instruments to him over a year ago. He just got around to making his trip north. Mary-Beth and Ragamuffin spent time with village women who taught them how to play the musical instruments.

The economy in the area was deteriorating. The younger people were going north to Sidon or south to Tyre for work. The mines were controlled by the Romans who used slave labor. Most of the laborers involved in construction projects were slaves. Welfare seemed to be centered on trade. Shipping was the most lucrative business. People in the village seemed to get what they needed through bartering rather than using money, as money was in short supply.

We talked about planting wheat in the field to the south. So far, the field serves as hay for the horses. A man from the north stopped by the other day. He was selling coal. He usually traveled as far as needed to sell the coal. During this trip, few people purchased his coal. His destination was Tyre. There was a metal smith there who would normally purchase any remaining coal in his cart. Father saw him and purchased what coal was left. He needed it for working with metal, either reshaping iron or smelting gold and silver.

The man slept on the ground at night. His clothes were dirty, and his hands were black from handling coal. Father invited him in for an evening meal. He enjoyed bathing in the pool. Mother and Emma washed his clothes. He didn't look too bad once cleaned up. It turned out that he was from Antioch and attended the local Christian church.

When he found out that my name was Silvanus, he became excited and rushed to his cart and pulled a scroll out of one of his sacks and showed it to me. The scroll was titled, "The Writings of Silvanus." He said that he reads from it every day as he travels. Ragamuffin and I read portions of it and wished we had a copy. Silvanus was a Christian brother who preached with the apostle Paul and Timothy. The man promised to give us a copy on his next southern journey.

He prayed and worshiped with us that night. Mary-Beth and Ragamuffin played the stringed instruments while we sang and danced. He was very grateful for our hospitality. We gave him bread and fruit for his journey home. Ragamuffin gave him copies of some of the Christian literature that she had.

The young children kept the women busy. That created more work for Father, Hermes, and I. Ragamuffin was never around. Mother wanted her to get married before she turned into an old woman. Father and I drew straws to see who was to accompany Ragamuffin to Galilee to locate and visit with Christians. He lost. It was probably better for him to go with her as he and Rabbi Zachias were quite familiar with the territory as they had traveled the route to see Jesus and John the Baptist.

They took the chariot, which was a bit overloaded with food, a change of clothes, and a few weapons. Father was not a trained swordsman. Ragamuffin was good at using a bow but had no real desire to use it. They visited with Flavius in Tyre. They found out that Commander Banes married a local Phoenician woman. Decarus was not doing well. They prayed with him during the evening and left early in the morning.

They stayed at inns along the way and visited most of the villages around the Sea of Galilee. Ragamuffin listened to many accounts concerning Jesus. She would spend the evening writing them down. In some cases, she was able to obtain copies of written accounts of the life of Jesus and the apostles. She shared what she knew and warned them of the impending destruction of Jerusalem. They all marveled at her knowledge and understanding of the Holy Scriptures. They also marveled at her ability to read and speak both Hebrew and Greek.

Most evenings involved prayer and worship, and hands were laid on for the sick. She had a knack for healing the deaf. There was something about her when she spoke. Father said that he thought he saw a faint glow of light around her when she preached. I witnessed that when she preached in Greece. Father and Ragamuffin listened to powerful speakers while on their journey. They noticed that various Christian groups celebrated the crucifixion and resurrection of Jesus with bread and wine. They referred to this practice as communion to remember the body of Christ that was broken for us, and the blood that was shed for the remission of our sins. It was a practice that we eventually instituted on the Sabbath. We were all glad when they returned. The family tends to worry a lot when one or more members are gone.

One night, Father, Hermes, and I sat around the fire ring discussing ways to improve our financial condition. We all came to the conclusion that buying grain in Greece and selling it in the drought-stricken cities along the eastern Mediterranean coast was a lucrative form of business. Father and Hermes thought that it would be wise to consult with Father's cousins in Sidon. The family has been in the trading business for several generations. Our financial problems could be solved if Father could purchase and ship grain from the north and sell it in Sidon.

Hermes mentioned that his former business partners were still operating in the northern areas of Greece. Perhaps they could connect with them and set up some sort of partnership where they could purchase grain or other cargo and crew a ship to deliver the goods.

Father and Hermes took the chariot to Sidon the next morning and met with Father's cousins. They agreed to buy grain and other food items from them at prevailing prices and gave them names of shipping agents along the coast of Greece. They said that the shipping agents know which ships and which ships' captains can be relied on to make it to port in a timely fashion. That meant that Father and Hermes would have to travel to Greece.

After returning home, they discussed it with the family, and a couple of days later, I gave them a chariot ride to Sidon to catch a ship to Greece. The cousins knew most of the sea captains and shipping agents operating out of the port of Sidon. In about a week, they were able to sail on a ship to Thessalonica. There was no cost to do so. The shippers did a lot of business with the cousins, and doing them a favor had long-term business benefits.

The weather was very kind to them as winter was approaching. Thessalonica was a welcome sight. Hermes and Father walked the waterfront and found out that his former partners were still in Neapolis, and it was believed that they did some shipping agent work as well as crew cargo ships.

Neapolis was quite a distance to walk. They were able to catch a ship a few days later for a reasonable fee. They arrived in Neapolis the next day and were able to find family members of some of his former business partners. They said that his former partners were crewing a cargo ship to Athens, and that they should be returning any day. Apparently, they served as shipping agents, and when they had cargo to deliver, they would arrange for a ship and served as part of the crew to insure that the shipment made it to its destination.

They were the Macedonians who fought the Syrian raiders in the valley to the north of us. It was the battle in which Hermes was severely injured. On their return north, they sailed their repaired ship out of Sidon and hit a fairly large storm. They were sailing close to the shore because they didn't trust their ship to make it back to Thessalonica. The ship hit a rock outcropping and broke up and sank. The only thing they salvaged was the money they made from selling their goods in Sidon and Tyre.

In the process of finding their way north to Troas, they were beset by robbers and lost everything. They couldn't fight them off because their weapons went down with the ship. The robbers took their money and any jewelry they had on them. It took them a long time to recover from their losses. However, their current business seemed to be doing quite well.

Father and Hermes stayed with the family members until the Macedonians returned from Athens. They were quite excited to see Hermes. Several days were spent swapping sea stories and renewing friendships. They were more than happy to take on Father and Hermes as business partners. The Macedonians were quite busy shipping goods along the Grecian coast and could use help in shipping goods to and from cities along the eastern Mediterranean such as Sidon, Tyre, Caesarea, Joppa, and even as far away as Alexandria. Shipping out of Joppa and Alexandria was known to be difficult, as it was controlled by powerful families, Ptolemy probably being one of them.

Their operation was quite inefficient. As shipping agents, they arranged to ship someone's goods for a price, then sail with the cargo ship to insure delivery and collect money from the sale of the goods. While they were gone, no one was arranging for the next shipment. They needed a full time shipping agent to have cargo ready as soon as their ship returned and not wait for the next shipment. Father explained that to them, and they had already realized that but had never taken action.

Father and Hermes suggested loading a ship with grain, then they would serve as part of the crew and sell the grain to Father's cousins in Sidon and provide them with the proceeds of sale on the return trip. Winter was closing in, and there was time for one more trip before the ships would spend the remaining winter in their home ports.

The Macedonians knew of extra grain being stored in the city and purchased enough to make it worthwhile to ship it to Sidon. It was about two-thirds of the normal cargo size for the ship that they hired. Hermes suggested well arming the crew based on his previous encounter with pirates.

They set sail a few days later and stopped in Troas to see if there was any grain to be purchased to round off the load. Unfortunately, there was no grain or any food products available for shipment. The trip to Sidon was uneventful. Father's cousins purchased the grain for a reasonable price.

His cousins had some Egyptian cloth, both cotton and linen, that was purchased at a very low price. It was suggested that the cloth should bring a good price in Neapolis. Father and Hermes discussed it and decided to take a chance and hope the Macedonians would approve of the purchase. It wasn't a full load, and the ship rode high enough to take advantage of the wind and make good speed on the trip to Neapolis.

The Macedonians applauded the cloth deal and said that they could easily sell the cloth to those who traded in the northern cities of Greece and Macedonia. Father and Hermes were paid quite well. The only problem was returning to Beth-Gebar. The weather was getting to be quite chilly, and the northern winds were unpredictable. There was a ship leaving for Troas loaded with apples and pears. Father and Hermes offered to serve as crew members at no cost to the ship's owner. Hermes sold himself as a warrior with experience in dealing with pirates. He was convincing enough to get them free food and passage to Troas.

Upon arrival in Troas, they visited with Marcus and Patricia while they waited for another opportunity to sail south to either Sidon or Tyre. Marcus let them stay at the garrison's guest quarters. Patricia wanted all the news she could get about the family. Apparently, she and Marcus really liked Troas. Marcus had a few successes in battling pirates which made him look good in the eyes of the leadership in Rome. Patricia was seeing a man who sold goods along the waterfront. She missed her friend in Caesarea, but her new friend, David, seemed to be the one whom she would marry if he could be convinced to do so.

Father met the gentleman while accompanying Patricia on a shopping trip. She still had the tendency to overspend her father's money. David was quite handsome, very kind, and cordial. He was very businesslike and had the air of being very successful and wealthy. She introduced Father and Hermes as wealthy traders and close friends of her father, Marcus. It was obvious that Patricia had our business interest at heart. Many times, it's not what you know that makes one successful, but who you know.

Patricia gave Father letters and small gifts for my family as well as for Flavius and Abigail. Hermes was able to locate a ship heading south to Tyre for a reasonable cost. The ship was in route to winter in Alexandria via Joppa. There were several passengers on board. The ship was empty of cargo, and the weather was quite bad during most of the journey. They were both glad to reach Tyre. They visited with Flavius and Abigail and gave them the letters and gifts from Patricia. Flavius arranged for a chariot ride to Beth-Gebar.

They were gone for a fairly long time, and the family was extremely happy to see them again. Many nights were spent around the fire ring listening to their adventures on the high seas and visits while in port.

Chapter 11

HERMES MOVES TO NEAPOLIS

Silvanus, son of Matthias, son of Gaius, to my descendants. While in Neapolis, Hermes's former partners offered him a position in their shipping business. Hermes discussed the offer with Emma. Emma wasn't too keen on relocating as she grew up in Beth-Gebar and would miss her family and friends. However, she realized that the village was dying in that the younger villagers were leaving for one reason or another. Larger villages such as Sidon and Tyre were full of life and presented numerous opportunities for employment that led to a higher standard of living.

Ragamuffin joined in on the conversations and was wondering if Hermes' friends could use her as a shipping agent. If Hermes and his family moved to Neapolis, Ragamuffin thought that she could live with them while working for his former partners. She also mentioned that the city seemed to lack a Christian church, and that would give her an opportunity to evangelize the community. Ragamuffin said that she would be good company for Emma and the children while Hermes was at sea.

Father and Mother weren't happy about Ragamuffin's desires. They would prefer that she got married and settled down with the rest of the family. However, they knew that she was a bit headstrong and would get her way in the end. Father considered moving to either Thessalonica or Neapolis himself. Hermes suggested that he and Emma could test the waters and see how things worked out. If all went well, he would inform Father and anyone else that wanted to join him and Emma in Neapolis.

These discussions went on throughout the winter months, and finally in the spring, Hermes and Emma made the bold decision to move to Neapolis. Antonio heard that Hermes was going to Neapolis and offered to go with him in search of work. The two of them caught a ship out of Sidon, and after weathering a couple of storms and a few port stops, they made it to Neapolis. Father's cousins told Antonio that if things didn't work out, that they could arrange to get him hired on as a crew member on one of the ships that did business with them. I believe that Antonio preferred to remain with family and friends, although the cousins were becoming closer as a family as well as being quite friendly to anyone who associated with us. There was a close connection between family, trust, and profit when it came to business relationships.

Prior to leaving Sidon, Hermes met Captain Madera. He was still working for Ptolemy. They were trying to get an early jump on the spring shipping season. Lots of goods were waiting at ports along the Egyptian coast for shipments north to Greece and westward to Italy and Spain. Captain Madera offered Antonio a job as his lead crew member if things didn't work out in Neapolis. The captain was as gruff and tough as usual, but when away from his crew, he reverted to his usual jovial self and was quite fun to be with.

Hermes found his friend, Arion. He and his two partners, Geordie and Kosmo, were working on their one and only cargo ship. They were happy to see Hermes and agreed to bring him and Antonio into the business. Hermes mentioned Ragamuffin to Arion and his wife, Rosa. Rosa said that she could stay in the guest room of their home. Arion said that there were not enough funds to pay

Ragamuffin a salary of any sort until the end of the shipping season, but they had enough to take care of her while living with them.

Kosmo mentioned that it would be at least another month before shipping activity would be in full swing. It would be several months before goods such as olive oil and grain would be ready to ship. Spices didn't make their way westward until late summer. Items such as alabaster figurines or glassworks that were made during the winter months were available for shipment. The Italians favored these items along with artistic clay jars and urns. The Greeks had a knack for artistic painting. Greek influence in Italy was still very strong.

Arion suggested that Antonio could stay in the guest house until Hermes showed up with his family, and that he could help ready the ship for a short run to Athens. They had a small order of glassworks to ship. The order would eventually be combined with other shipments to make one big shipment to one or more ports in the western Mediterranean. Antonio was excited to get started. Meanwhile, Hermes searched for a ship heading south to either Sidon or Tyre. Kosmo recommended that he either wait until their ship sets sail for Athens, catch a fishing boat to Thessalonica, or perhaps walk to Thessalonica. The wait would be a minimum two weeks in Neapolis, and the probability of catching a ship out of Athens would be much better.

Hermes ended up walking to Philippi. A local fisherman who was delivering some goods to Thessalonica offered Hermes a ride. While searching for transportation along the waterfront in Thessalonica, he had a chance meeting with Captain Madera. The captain had off loaded his cargo and was heading back to Alexandria by way of Neapolis. He wanted to pick up any grain that was in storage and sell it in Sidon, making a profit without Ptolemy finding out. Hermes mentioned that there was no grain in storage in Neapolis. He heard that there was grain in storage in Byzantium, however, at a hefty price. The distance to Byzantium was quite lengthy and not all that safe during that time of the year. If Captain Madera could weather the storms as he transited the Dardanelles, then he might be able to make something happen.

Captain Madera decided that heading back to Alexandria would be his best option. Hermes asked him if he was stopping anywhere along the eastern Mediterranean on his way, and the captain asked him where he wanted to be dropped off, knowing very well that Beth-Gebar would be the ultimate choice. Hermes suggested the House of Gaius, and the captain laughed. Captain Madera had some family remaining in Beth-Gebar and decided to make that his next port of call. Hermes told the captain that he didn't want to be responsible for getting him into trouble with Ptolemy. The captain said that all sea captains worth their salt were thick-skinned, and that Ptolemy would chew him up one side and down the other if he found out. On the other hand, Ptolemy couldn't find a better ship captain along the whole eastern Mediterranean. Handling ships was in the Phoenician blood, and besides, Captain Madera doesn't question the legitimacy of any cargo shipped out of Egypt.

The weather seemed unseasonably cold as Madera's ship headed south. The winds were fairly steady, and they encountered a considerable amount of rain. Captain Madera picked up a couple of passengers before leaving port. One of them was going to Rhodes and the other to Ephesus. Paying passengers was money in his pocket. The trip to Beth-Gebar was a fair distance out of his way. The captain was hoping to pick up more passengers. He picked up a Roman centurion in Rhodes. His destination was Caesarea. The centurion missed a Roman war ship due to sickness and had been waiting several weeks to catch another one.

The trip east was uneventful. Captain Madera decided that it was less risky to drop Hermes off in Sidon. The cousins had some left over honey and some wine that needed to be shipped to Caesarea. The captain was more than happy to accommodate them. The centurion was happy in that he didn't have to walk to Caesarea. Having a centurion on board usually meant docking in Caesarea without paying a docking fee, and if the captain's song and dance was just right, he would avoid taxes on the goods that he was carrying for the cousins.

Hermes asked the captain if he would be heading north soon, hoping to catch a ride for him and his family to Neapolis. Madera

said that he would stop by on the way north, but said that his shipment would probably limit how much of Hermes's household goods
that he could carry. Hermes offered to pay him well for going out of
his way to do so. Madera just laughed as he boarded his ship.

The walk south to Beth-Gebar took several hours. The spring
flowers were in bloom, and the cool weather was refreshing. The
family was excited to see him. Emma was in the village visiting
friends. Joseph and Mary-Beth walked to the village to find her. They
saw Zachias tending a fruit tree outside the synagogue. They told
him that Hermes had returned. Emma was sitting under a shade
tree drinking tea with a couple of women. They were laughing and
having a good time. When she was told that Hermes had returned,
Emma jumped up with excitement and immediately bid her friends
a good-bye. Zachias joined them as they walked back to the house.

Hermes was returning from the pool as they arrived. The cool
water was quite refreshing. A good hug from Emma brought more
life into him. Ragamuffin gave him a good neck massage while he
ate some of Mother's good cooking and related all that he experienced along his journey. She asked about Antonio. He mentioned
that Antonio was working with his partners. Hermes told her that if
she still wanted to go to Neapolis, that she could stay with Arion and
Rosa, and that she could work as a shipping agent, but not to expect
much in the way of payment until the end of the summer.

It was several weeks before the captain returned. He anchored
just off shore. Ptolemy wanted some cargo to go to Damascus by way
of the mountains. Father agreed to store what he could on our property. The villagers were happy to see him. The captain paid well to off
load the cargo. Money was a welcome sight. The mayor accepted the
usual bribe to keep things quiet.

Captain Madera spent the evening around the fire ring. His tall
tales kept everyone laughing. Hermes and the captain worked out a
deal to transport his family to Neapolis. Madera's planned last port
of call was Troas. He told Ragamuffin and Emma that they could
use his cabin along with Hermes two children. Madera said that he
would rough it with the crew.

Ragamuffin and I walked up to the top of the hill. It was a clear night, and the stars were shining rather brightly. I told her that I would miss her greatly and wished her well on her journey. On one hand, she was excited to go. On the other hand, she wept on my shoulder knowing that she would miss the family and the property that she grew up in. She said that she wanted to serve the Lord and do great things. I mentioned that Stephanie and I would probably be joining her in the near future. Tyre seemed to be of interest to Stephanie. It was a nice place to live and not too far from family in Beth-Gebar. I suggested that she stop by and visit Patricia while in Troas. She agreed, and we prayed together for quite some time before retiring for the evening.

The captain slept in the guest house and had a good breakfast before returning to the ship. Rabbi Zachias arranged for a few people to help load Hermes household goods. They left most of the furniture behind. Mary-Beth and Joseph were happy for that as they didn't have much in the way of furniture and other household items. Mother wept as she hugged Ragamuffin and wished her well. She begged Ragamuffin to write and visit as often as she could. We were all in tears as she and Hermes's family got underway. The walk back to the house was slow. We were all sad to see Ragamuffin leave. Mother had fallen in love with Hermes's children. They would be sorely missed.

The wind and seas were quite accommodating during the trip to Troas. Ragamuffin and one of the girls were quite seasick. As usual, Ragamuffin said that she would never sail again. For some reason, she seemed to forget that she gets seasick. Madera said that it would take several days to off load the cargo.

Ragamuffin located Patricia at the palace. Patricia's eyes lit up when she saw her. Patricia arranged for her to sleep in her bedroom. They had excellent meals at the praetorian and shared numerous stories. Patricia took her shopping along the waterfront. They stopped by to see David. At Ragamuffin's request, Patricia introduced her as Rachael.

David showed her his warehouse. He was dealing mostly in carpets this time of year. Different tribes brought their carpets to Troas to sell. They would weave the carpets during the winter months. He showed her the different colors and patterns associated with each tribal region. The patterns identified the tribe and the colors dictated where they were located, as the dyes were unique to the vegetables grown in the region. David mentioned that the tribes could get a better price in Troas as opposed to Byzantium, in that the Romans tended to tax the northern tribes quite heavily. Also, the merchants in Byzantium were quite greedy.

David mentioned that some of the caravans carrying Persian carpets would trade with him rather than deal with the merchants in Byzantium. David shipped his carpets to Greece and Italy. The Italians preferred the Persian carpets. They were a status symbol. Although the wool was slightly better, there wasn't a whole lot of difference between the quality of carpets from the north and those from Persia. Persian carpets that incorporated silk to add a sheen to them were in high demand in Italy. Because of their practical mindset, the Greeks tended to purchase carpets made from the northern tribes.

Rachael took in all this information and thanked David for the education. She and Patricia had lunch with David. On the way back to the praetorian, Rachael asked Patricia if the two of them were going to get married. Patricia smiled and said that she and David were planning a wedding. Marcus was not too keen on her marrying a Jew. He preferred that she marry into the upper echelon of Roman leadership. However, Marcus' heart softened and decided that marrying a wealthy Jew was acceptable as long as Patricia really loved him.

Rachael told Patricia to invite Stephanie and me to the wedding as well as Flavius and Abigail. She understood the difficulty of attending the wedding due to the distance. However, she mentioned that Captain Madera could always be persuaded to provide transportation if the timing was right. Patricia said that she would do whatever could be done but wouldn't make any promises.

The two of them walked to the ship to meet Hermes and his family. Patricia had met Emma at Abigail's wedding. Captain Madera was checking with shipping agents to see if anyone needed goods shipped to Neapolis or other Greek ports. He returned while the ladies were sitting around a table at a nearby café. Madera emoted his "woe is me" act as he couldn't strike up any business. Patricia patted him on the shoulder to console him and told him that she felt real bad for him. He could tell that she was just kidding him.

Patricia recommended that he talk with David, as David might have a few carpets ready to ship to Greece. She told him to use her name, and that he was a friend of Rachael the daughter of wealthy trader known as Matthias of the House of Gaius. She had introduced Father to David as a wealthy trader on a previous port visit. Madera was quite excited over the possible venture. Patricia offered to go with him to meet David. He accepted, and as the two of them walked off, Rachael decided to tag along with them.

Patricia introduced Captain Madera to her friends who she met along the waterfront. All the vendors knew her. Patricia gave the captain a tour of David's warehouse. They met David while he was talking to a carpet trader from the Phrygia region, just east of Troas. David liked the dyes and patterns from that area.

David was actually excited to talk with captain Madera about a possible shipment to Athens. Patricia could see that she gained a few points by helping David with his business. Patricia pulled Rachael aside and whispered into her ear, asking her to make sure that the captain made good on the delivery. Rachael assured her that the captain was a close family friend, not to mention that she was the captain's best friend. Captain Madera treated her like she was his favorite niece.

Rachael asked David how he transacted payments, and he explained how he worked through shipping agents, and that funds eventually owed him were received by way of cargo ships that served a dual purpose as money transports. David said that he received some payments almost a year later. He said that there was a lot of trust involved in foreign business transactions. Rachael asked David if he wanted captain Madera to collect on the carpet transaction while in Athens, and David said that if she trusted the captain, then he would pay the usual percentage that he paid his shipping agents for handling the money. David mentioned that it would be nice to get his payments in a more timely fashion.

The carpets were loaded the next day. Patricia was at the dock to watch the activities. She, Rachael, Emma, and the children spent time at the café while Hermes supervised the loading. Patricia gave Rachael a few drachmas to help her get situated in Neapolis. Rachael tried to refuse, but Patricia held her hand and would not let her return the gift. Patricia told Rachael that her friendship was worth more than what money could buy.

They got underway the next morning. Patricia and David saw them off. The captain decided to head to Neapolis first, as the children were getting to be pests. Besides, Hermes partners might have a partial shipment available to round out his cargo to Athens. Ptolemy would probably flog the captain silly if he knew that the captain was using the ship for his personal welfare. Ptolemy most likely knew what was going on as he had contacts in just about every port. Ptolemy would always scream and yell at the captain when he found out about the misuse of his ship. However, when no one was within earshot, he would pull the captain aside and ask him to deliver certain cargo and not to tell anyone about it. They had what one may call a symbiotic relationship.

Ragamuffin occasionally witnessed to the captain when they were alone. She spent a lot of time sleeping due to seasickness but would occasionally walk around the deck and talk to the ship's crew. Everyone liked her. One of the crew members accepted Christ on the way to Neapolis. The captain was slowly softening. She figured that it wouldn't be long before he would give in. He already was changing his ways, such as cursing less and treating his crew with respect. Perhaps that's why the crew liked her.

Ragamuffin asked the captain to introduce and address her as Rachael around business associates, and that it was okay to call her Ragamuffin around the crew and with her friends. The captain agreed and thanked her for helping him with the extra business. He said that the House of Gaius has been quite profitable for him.

Captain Madera leaned close to her and, in a quiet voice, told her that if anything ever happened to him, she was to contact Markos in Athens. He said that he operates a ship building company called Markos Marine. She asked him what his relationship was with Markos, and he said that it was best that she didn't know at that time.

Neapolis looked beautiful as they entered the harbor. A lot of people put a fresh coat of paint on their houses during the spring months. Freshly painted houses surrounded with flowers made for a nice atmosphere. Geordie and Kosmos were at sea delivering cargo. Arion arranged for transporting Hermes's household goods to the two-bedroom house in back of his home. Antonio was evicted, not unexpected of course. He was at sea with Arion's partners. Geordie had a place for him to stay. Ragamuffin moved in with Arion and Rosa. Her room was small, but clean and comfortable.

Ragamuffin offered to pay Rosa rent for the room, but she declined. Ragamuffin wanted to take a bath, but all that was available was a wash basin with a washcloth and towel. She missed the spa and the pool at home. Water was a valued commodity in Neapolis. However, there were bath houses along the river. Rosa showed her the best places to go. For safety reasons, she recommended that they go together. In general, women were safe in the city, but being a port city, vermin had a way of mixing with the population. Most crime was committed by foreigners.

Ragamuffin decided that a bath would be nice and offered to pay for Rosa and herself to go for a late afternoon bath. Rosa thought that it was a great idea and already was beginning to like Ragamuffin. Rosa needed companionship. She didn't like going out into the city by herself. The captain stopped by and joined us for the evening meal. The setting was under the stars with several burning oil lamps. Ragamuffin asked the captain if he needed help in transacting business in Athens. Arion suggested that she introduce herself to his point of contact in Athens since she was going to be his shipping agent. Ragamuffin was getting seasick just thinking about getting back on board the ship.

Arion asked the captain if his ship could handle large sealed urns of olive oil. The captain said that he didn't have the framework to contain the urns. A special framework was needed to keep the load from shifting as the ship rocked and rolled in the waves. Arion said that he could build the framework, and if the captain was interested, he could deliver olive oil to Alexandria, as the continuing drought had placed a large demand on imported olive oil. The oil was of a poor grade due to sitting around all winter but was good for feeding oil lamps. The captain agreed.

Since he was returning to Neapolis, Ragamuffin decided to sail with him to Athens. The world was becoming quite adventurous for her. She slept until midmorning and made it to the ship by noon time. The captain was pacing the deck waiting for her. The crew helped with her luggage as she boarded. His demeanor changed as they got underway.

It was slow going most of the way to Athens. Ragamuffin and the captain quickly located David's shipping agent. The cargo was unloaded and delivered immediately to the warehouse. Rachael showed the agent the paperwork from David that allowed her to collect payment for the cargo. Rachael collected the fee for sending the funds to David as they were bypassing the normal route. Captain Madera told her to hold on to the money and keep the transaction fee for herself. It was her first income for doing business.

Madera wanted Rachael to meet Markos and arranged for them to stay at a local inn. He took care of the expenses, which included time at a bath house. The next morning, they walked quite a distance to Markos's home. It was a luxurious home on a hillside overlooking his shipyard. The painted columns on the porch were beautiful, and the atrium was filled with flowers of all kinds.

To her surprise, Markos was introduced as Madera's brother. That explained the remarkable resemblance between Markos's looks and that of Captain Madera. A servant washed and massaged their feet. Rachael wore a nice dress, but it looked too common for being in what appears to be a palace owned by well to do people. Her hair was braided down her back, and when she saw Markos's wife, she felt uncomfortable as she saw the beautiful dress and hairstyle that she was wearing. Her name was Rhodora. As odd as it may seem, Rachael realized that Stephanie's wedding dress would have been perfect for this occasion.

Food was spread out on a long table. The table cloth was pure white, and the silverware, plates, and food dishes were methodically arranged from one end to the other. Markos's son, Stephanos, arrived while they sipped on fruit juices and shared one story after another. Stephanos was tall and very handsome. His hair was dark, and he was well tanned. He was quite cordial and businesslike and reminded her of Patricia's fiancé, David. His conversations and demeanor indicated that he held a position of power and control.

The captain dominated the storytelling. Stephanos told Rachael that he heard about her adventure with the pirates and how she defeated them single handedly. Rachael blushed and said that the captain did more than his share of the fighting, and that his skill in handling the ship was what saved the day. Captain Madera enjoyed the accolades but insisted that Rachael was an Amazon warrior in disguise. Rhodora leaned toward Rachael, and as she placed her hand on her shoulder, she said that rumors abounded about her beating up a Roman centurion. She said that she thought that those rumors were fairy tales knowing that they came from the captain but was taken aback when Rachael said that she flipped him onto the ground and only slightly hurt him. The fact that she actually did that to a centurion caused their mouths to drop. It was totally unheard of for a woman to experience such events in her life.

Rhodora led Rachael off to her bedroom and found a beautiful, light dress for her to wear. There were servants everywhere. Other guests showed up, mostly neighbors who wanted to meet the captain and his friend. Rachael was in awe over the difference in lifestyles of the two brothers. The captain was treated as if there were no difference. The neighbors held the captain in as high esteem as Markos. Stephanos kept looking in her direction as they sat at the table. He listened to every word that she spoke.

Rhodora asked her if she would like to spend the night. Captain Madera said that they would be delighted to do so. Rhodora poked him in the ribs and said that she was asking her, not him. Rachael said that she would love to stay an extra day to just take in the view of the beautiful bay and surroundings. Stephanos offered to give her a tour of the shipyard. Rachael accepted the invitation.

She was exhausted from the trip and asked to retire early in the evening. Rhodora offered her some wine, but Rachael refused.

Rachael always avoided strong drinks. She wanted a clear head when interacting with people.

Breakfast was spread out along the same table as lunch. There were covered dishes of various hot foods along with fruit and breads of several kinds. She wore the same dress that Rhodora gave her the day before. The captain said that he had some business to take care of and would meet her for lunch. One of the servants led her to the shipyard where she met Stephanos.

He walked Rachael through the whole shipbuilding process. Rachael was quite impressed. She noticed that Stephanos inspected each stage of development as they walked. He provided quick answers to workers who pulled him aside with work related questions. There were a few times that he would study a diagram that was handed to him and he would provide a lengthy explanation on how something was to be built or rebuilt. The passageways were clean as if they knew that a visitor was coming through. The workers would glance at her when Stephanos wasn't looking. Rachael became quite attractive as she matured into a young lady. She began to realize this when men stared in her direction. The beautiful dress probably added to it. She felt that something had to be done with her hair but felt helpless in that area. She only had her hair done up nice when she attended weddings, and her sisters helped her with that.

Lunch was the usual spread of fine food. Rachael wondered if they ate that way every day or did they do this to impress her. Rachael remembered the conversation she had with the captain while aboard the ship. If something was to happen to him, he wanted her to contact Markos.

On the way the way back to the ship, she asked the captain about that. The captain leaned toward her and said in a soft voice, "Stephanos is my son. His mother died in child birth, and I couldn't raise him on my own. My brother, Markos, offered to adopt and raise him as his own. Stephanos knows of the adoption. He loves me as much as my brother and Rhodora. I visit them whenever I'm in Athens. I tell them about you, Hermes, and Silvanus. They love to hear about my adventures. Although, I have to admit, the tales are a bit embellished."

Rachael smiled as she put her hand on his shoulder.

Rhodora told her to keep the dress and added a couple more to the sack that the captain was carrying. She had a sack of her own. It included a few gifts from Stephanos such as perfumes from Arabia and silk scarfs. Rhodora included some soft under garments and silk pajamas.

After spending the night aboard the ship, they sailed to Neapolis. Rachael was getting used to the sea. She had very little seasickness during the voyage. The sea breeze was steady. It had an early summer warmth to it. She said that if it wasn't for the men on board, she would have stripped off her clothes and basked in the sun for a while. She missed the spa rooftop at home. The girls would go topless and soak up sun on hot days. The high walls kept the boys and men from seeing them. Mother would shake her head when she found out what they were doing. She considered it very unlady like, even though she knew that they swam topless in the pool.

The captain tied up next to Arion's ship in Neapolis. The pier was full of ships ready to begin the summer long shipping activity. Hermes and Antonio were performing maintenance aboard the *Diana*. The ship was named after the goddess Diana. They figured that such a name would bring them good luck. This spurred Ragamuffin to start a church to rid the city of idolatry and such. Everyone met at Arion's place for a late night dinner and swapped stories about their latest adventures. Antonio wanted to know more about Stephanos. Ragamuffin could sense a bit of jealousy.

Chapter 12

AMPHORAS

Silvanus, son of Matthias, son of Gaius, to my descendants. On the morning of the Sabbath, Rachael walked to the synagogue. The building was small as there were very few Jews in the city. The synagogue was clean and neat, and the grounds were well taken care of. There were men sitting in the courtyard. A priest was among them. Their conversations seem to center around politics, and in particular, Roman rule.

As Rachael approached them, she overheard them berating Jews who became members of the Christian cult. They were surprised that a woman would be walking in the courtyard, especially by herself. The priest went over to her and asked if he could help her. Rachael explained in Hebrew that she was out for a walk in the cool of the morning. Recognizing that she was a Jew and not being of his synagogue, he inquired as to whom she was and where she came from. Rachel gave a short history of why she was in the city.

One of the men spoke to her in Greek, and she responded in fluent Greek. She had worn one of Rhodora's dresses, and she looked quite attractive in the early morning sunlight. The men moved closer to her and began to ask her a lot of questions, mostly about her family and her Jewish background. They marveled about her command of both languages.

Then Rachael asked them a question. "Was the man, called Jesus, whom was crucified in Jerusalem, the promised Messiah?" The men looked at each other and were surprised that she asked the question. The priest mentioned that there has been much discussion concerning the crucifixion, so much so, that he inquired with Jerusalem on the matter. The response from the high priest was an emphatic no.

Seizing on the opportunity, Rachael asked the priest about the prophecy in Daniel that pointed to when the Messiah was to appear and that the timeline agreed with the time that Jesus was teaching and performing miracles in Jerusalem. Rachael quoted the scripture found in Daniel and pointed out that the timeline for the scripture began with Artaxerxes I when he permitted the Jews to rebuild Jerusalem, and that the sixty-nine weeks lined up with the beginning of Jesus's ministry. She also mentioned that He was crucified halfway through the seventieth week, which also agreed with prophecy.

The men looked at each other and were amazed that she was so well versed in the Hebrew Scriptures. Rachael arose, and as she left, she turned toward the group of men and told them that they should research the matter as it could very well be that the Jews in Jerusalem were instrumental in arranging for the death of their Messiah. The men were left speechless as she walked away.

The smell of a late morning breakfast was wonderful. Rosa was a great cook. Arion was setting the table as Rachael arrived. Emma and the children had settled in. Emma helped with the cooking. The men were sitting around the table discussing their next business opportunity. There wasn't a whole lot to discuss as there appeared to be no opportunity available. It was still a bit early in the shipping season.

Rachael suggested that they sail along the Dardanelles and along the east side of the Sea of Marmara and purchase carpets from the small villages and resell them in Greece. She said that it was early enough in the season that they could purchase the carpets before they make their way to Byzantium on the Bosporus Strait or to Troas. There were two advantages to doing this. One was that it employed the shipping company, and second, the middle man would get cut out of their profits.

Byzantium seemed to control the carpet trade from Asia to the west. Rachael figured that Arion could pay the villagers more than they usually get for their carpets, yet get them cheaper than purchasing them in Byzantium, as well as shipping them at a lower cost than transporting them by way of land routes or trade routes to the west. Aside from bad weather, it was safer to ship the carpets by way of the Aegean and Mediterranean Seas than to use the land route through Thrace which was a rather hostile environment. Tribes along the trade routes were quite rebellious due to Roman taxes on everything from crops to livestock. Traders had to pay extra to have their goods guarded from raiders and robbers of all sorts. The Romans found it was easier to rid the Mediterranean of pirates than dealing with the numerous barbarian tribes of the north.

Arion liked the idea with one exception; they didn't have the funds to purchase the carpets. Rachael suggested using the money that she had collected for David in Athens. David wasn't expecting his money for quite some time and wouldn't miss it. The venture was risky but very appetizing.

Arion discussed the idea with Hermes, Geordie, and Kosmo. They all decided to make a go of it. However, they were not experienced in the carpet trade and needed someone who could not only select decent carpets but knows who to sell them to. Rachael said that David showed her what to look for when purchasing carpets and her dealings in Athens was a good start as for finding a vendor. That meant that Rachael would have to sail with them.

Rachael hated sailing and told them that their ship was not set up to accommodate females. Arion said that he could make the necessary accommodations aboard his ship. The *Diana* was larger than captain Madera's ship and had enough space in the cabin for two people. Rachael refused to sleep with the crew, even though most of the crew were Arion's partners.

After loading the olive oil on board captain Madera's ship, they bid him farewell and began outfitting the Diana for a trip north. Before leaving, Rachael asked Madera if he would cover the carpet venture in the event David's money was lost. She promised to pay him back on any loan made. He agreed with a wave of the hand and a chuckle or two as he turned and left. Arion figured at least three days before being ready to sail.

Rachael loved to stroll down the waterfront wearing the dresses that Rhodora had given her. The dresses were light and cool to walk in. On the morning after the Sabbath, she decided to stop by the synagogue again. It was a work day, and only a few men, mostly elderly men, were sitting in the courtyard. The rabbi was not present. Rachael greeted them, and they just looked at her for a moment and then told her that women weren't allowed in the courtyard. Rachael apologized and asked them where the women's courtyard was. They said that there wasn't one. She asked why, and the response was that the property was too small to add one; however, they said that women generally sat on the steps leading up from the street. Rachael took the hint and walked away but stopped and decided to sit on the wall at the side of the steps and pray as she took in the view of the Aegean Sea with the beautiful harbor and boats.

It wasn't long before the rabbi showed up and sat next to her. He leaned toward her and asked in a low voice, "How did you know when Artaxerxes I wrote the decree that permitted the Jews to rebuild Jerusalem?" Rachael smiled and told him the story about our trip to Jerusalem and the meeting with Rabbi Levi at the library. He asked her what Rabbi Levi's thoughts were concerning Jesus. Rachael told him that Rabbi Levi believed that Jesus was the Messiah, but not only he but others as well. They were more concerned about their positions rather than vocally airing their beliefs.

Rachael suggested that he travel to Jerusalem and discover things for himself. She said that Rabbi Levi would be more than happy to accommodate him, and that all he had to do was mention our names. She also said that if he was to stop by and visit Rabbi Zachias in Beth-Gebar, Zachias would be a good reference, as he and Rabbi Levi were close friends.

The rabbi then asked Rachael where she received her education, as Jewish girls were not educated at the synagogues as were the boys. She told him about her relationship with Rabbi Zachias, and he was impressed, to say the least. He apologized for the way the elderly men treated her. He said that they were of the old school where women weren't allowed to speak in the synagogue, primarily because of their lack of education. It was expected that women would ask their husbands on matters of religion. He told her that when he was present, she was welcome in the courtyard, and that because of her education, she in a sense has become like a man and could speak as freely as she wished to.

Rachael smiled and told him that he reminded her of Rabbi Zachias. She then asked him if it was possible for a woman to become a rabbi. He smiled and said, "Don't push it." As he walked away, he turned and asked, "Was that Rabbi Zachias in Beth-Gebar whom you mentioned?" Rachael nodded as she began walking down the steps.

That afternoon, she and Emma decided to gather that evening and hold a worship service. Hermes joined them, and the three of them sang songs as Rachael played the harp. Rosa sat nearby, and when the opportunity came, she began to ask many questions concerning Rachael's belief in Christianity. Rosa tended to play homage to several Greek gods but didn't visit the temples because she didn't want to be labeled with the kind of women that frequented there. Arion was listening to Rachael but kept his distance, pretending to be busy with other things.

Rachael packed a nice dress for the journey and decided to wear old clothes while on the ship's deck. The weather was already turning warm. The Aegean was calm with a slight breeze as they got underway. The villages along the Dardanelles were small and few in number. The shoreline exhibited grassy plains with short scrubby trees sparsely laid out in the landscape. The lack of water was probably what limited the number of villages.

Arion anchored as close to the villages as possible. The currents were swift and unpredictable due to the narrow strait. Kosmo and Antonio would take the small boat and row to the nearest beach. The first few villages had nothing to offer. This discouraged the crew to the point that most of them wanted to turn back to Neapolis. Rachael and Arion insisted that they continue into the Sea of Marmara before making any decision on returning.

The last village along the eastern side of the strait offered some hope. It had the appearance of a trading center. Kosmo and Antonio scouted out the village and returned with good news. There were several carpet merchants. Rachael was excited as Kosmo rowed her ashore and escorted her through the village. The first carpet merchant showed her some carpets from Bithynia and Galatia. The designs were nice, but the weaves were thick and judging from the size of the knots made at the bottom, the material was too thick, indicating poor quality. Kosmo asked her where she got her carpet knowledge. She said that David explained the differences in carpets as she toured his warehouse.

To her surprise, there were some carpets that had a sheen to them. Upon close examination, the sheen came from silk woven in with the fine wool. The fine weave, small knots, and silk indicated that it was a Persian carpet. She wondered how Persian carpets ended up at this location. Kosmo theorized that they might be stolen goods as caravans from Persia were subject to robbers. The trade routes to the east are the least protected. Rachael asked the merchant how he ended up with Persian carpets, and his response was that many caravans stopped in the village and had their goods shipped to Byzantium using the Sea of Marmara. Shipping them was less expensive, quicker, and safer than the land routes. Kosmo was partially right in his judgment, assuming that she could believe the merchant.

Rachael wanted to see the other carpets in the village before negotiating any purchases. The carpets at the second shop were obviously of poor grade and not worth looking at. The third shop had nicely made carpets with attractive designs. The coloring appeared to be from various vegetable dyes slightly different than what she had seen before. The merchant said that they came from a small village in the western area of Galatia, not far from Phrygia.

Rachael was able to negotiate a reasonable price for ten of the carpets. She had a good feel for prices from talking with David as well as the merchants in Athens. The Persian carpets were a bit pricy, but the costs were still well below those sold in Athens. The merchant who sold them the Persian carpets had a brother who owned a fishing boat and offered to transport the carpets to the *Diana* for a small fee. Using Arion's small row boat meant several trips, not to mention getting the carpets wet with sea water.

The fifteen carpets used up half of their money. Arion decided to sail along the eastern side of the Sea of Marmara as he knew of two major trade centers a fair distance up the coast. Rachael worked similar deals with the merchants in the next port. With a total of thirty-one carpets, Arion set sail for Athens with the hope that Rachael could work a deal with her contacts there.

Upon exiting the strait, they headed directly to Athens. Neapolis was too far out of their way. With the exception of one day, the weather was kind to them. The port in Athens was quite busy. Arion's experience got them a spot at one of the larger piers. As usual, the docking fees were quite expensive. While visiting the Markos family on an earlier trip to Athens, Rachael noticed some vacant piers near the shipyard and wondered if it wouldn't be less expensive to dock there. However, one had to take into consideration the cost to transport the goods into the main part of the city. A short visit with Stephanos might answer the question. Besides, Rachael wanted to visit with his family before heading back to Neapolis.

Rachael and Kosmo found the merchant who purchased David's carpets. He refused to walk down to the ship and look at her carpets. He didn't want to waste his time with someone who he didn't know in the carpet business. She suspected that being a woman had its drawbacks. Being a bit dismayed, she decided to locate other merchants who might be interested in the ship's cargo.

She found another carpet merchant near the grand bazaar. He showed interest and was willing to examine the carpets. He took his time looking over all the carpets and was quite impressed with their quality. They returned to his shop, and after talking with his brother, the merchant made an offer for the carpets. The offer was quite low and unreasonable. Rachael knew what they were worth and offered them at a price reasonably below market value. He hesitated and said no to her offer. It was obvious that Rachael lacked the art of negotiation when it came to dealing with commercial goods. Kosmo stepped in and suggested that we check with a couple of other places before accepting any offers. The merchant was about to come back with a higher offer, but before doing so, Rachael asked him if he knew of a short route to the Markos Shipyard. Kosmo asked her why she was interested in the shipyard. She told him that she wanted to stop by and visit with Markos and Stephanos.

Upon hearing this, the merchant wanted to know what her relationship was with the Markos family. Rachael mentioned that she was close friends of the family and was planning on spending the night there. The merchant walked over to his brother, and after a lengthy discussion, they decided to offer Rachael her asking price for the carpets. Kosmo and Rachael looked at each other with puzzled looks and closed the deal. Kosmo worked with the merchant to off-load the cargo. Meanwhile, Rachael headed toward the shipyard. If she found the shipyard, she would know where the house was.

Rhodora was surprised to see her and directed one of the servants to wash and massage her feet. She told one of the servants to run to the shipyard and notify Stephanos that Rachael was at the house. Rachael felt a bit uneasy stopping in unannounced, but Rhodora was not disturbed the least by her unexpected visit. One of the servant girls helped her freshen up before relaxing on the porch that overlooked the shipyard and the Aegean Sea. She and Rhodora were served tea as they talked. Rhodora wanted to know all about her latest adventures, especially if they involved pirates and beating up Roman centurions. They both had some good laughs.

Rachael mentioned her carpet transaction with the local merchant and his response after mentioning Markos's name. Rhodora laughed and said that she and her friends had been buying carpets from those old buzzards for many years. She told Rachael that if they didn't treat her right, that she would personally pay them a visit and give them a thrashing that they would never forget. Apparently, the merchant and his brother were regular guests at their family festivities.

Stephanos returned early and invited Rachael to an evening at a local café. Rhodora said that she and Markos would join them later. Rhodora found a clean dress and some jewelry for Rachael to wear. She told Rachael that she must do something about her hair, and said that she would take care of that in the morning. Rachael wasn't sure what that meant.

The café was quite busy and filled with what appeared to be wealthy patrons. Stephanos seemed to attract everyone's attention, especially the women. Rachael felt out of place, especially with her hair. Stephanos cordially introduced her as he walked through the café. His left arm never left her side. He made her feel welcomed with everyone he talked to. It was a social atmosphere filled with small talk and laughter. She noticed that he never talked business in front of the ladies. Business discussions were only conducted off to the side with the men. She noticed that Stephanos was in total command.

When alone, some of the women asked her how she met Stephanos and how she was connected to the family. Her response was that she was into shipping, and that his uncle was a close business partner. Most of them didn't know he had an uncle involved in the shipping trade. Rachael had a small sip of wine here and there but preferred fruit juice when she could get it. The waiters made sure that she was well taken care of. Rachael enjoyed the attention. However, in the back of her mind, she was concerned about her hair. She loved the way the other ladies did up their hair. Her braided pony tail didn't quite fit in.

She and Stephanos talked about everything from religion to politics. He was particularly interested in her Christian beliefs. She told him about the Jewish prophecies and how they pointed to the arrival of the Jewish Messiah who was crucified by the Romans. Stephanos, as well as his companions, had nothing good to say about the Romans. They all wished Alexander the Great would rise from his grave and straighten things out.

On the way back to the house, Stephanos told her that he was going to name his next ship after her. She said that Rachael was not a good name for a Greek ship. He said that she was probably right but said that he would name the ship Ragamuffin. Rachael laughed and asked why that name. Stephanos said that her nickname has been part of family conversations since the day Captain Madera began telling tall tales about her. Rachael wanted Stephanos to tell her everything that Madera told him about her.

Rhodora never did show up at the café. Apparently, Markos wanted the two of them left alone. Rachael slept in late. Upon wakening, she decided to hustle back to the bazaar. Rhodora would have none of that. She had to have a good breakfast and then have her hair done up in proper fashion. Rachael was shocked to see herself in the mirror. Rhodora had her put on a nice flowing dress. With that, she had one of the servants escort her to the bazaar.

The merchantmen couldn't believe that it was the same lady. They recognized the servant and talked to him while they arranged for payment for the carpets. The servant escorted her to the ship as she was carrying quite a bit of money. The crew did a double take as she strolled up the pier with a fancy dress and her hair done up. Arion greeted her at the gangplank and asked her if she knew the whereabouts of Ragamuffin, knowing full well that it was her.

Rachael was a bit embarrassed as she walked on board. She told Arion that when dealing with merchants, one should have a professional look about herself. Arion and the crew were glad to see her. They were worried about getting paid for the carpets. Rachael thanked the servant and offered him a tip for his services. He refused as he placed some drachmas in her hand and closed the hand tightly so that she couldn't refuse them. He said that they were from Stephanos for her journey home. She thanked him as he made a quick departure.

The sea swells were fairly high on the voyage to Neapolis. The *Diana* made heavy rolls as the wind picked up. Rachael had changed into her old clothes and did her best to not mess up her hair. She forgot to return a necklace to Rhodora and hoped that Rhodora didn't think that she stole it. She thought about it and decided to use the necklace as an excuse to return to the Markos household and perhaps see Stephanos again. Antonio asked her where she got the dress. Rachael told him that Rhodora gave her the dress and arranged to have her hair done up that morning. She didn't mention the night out with Stephanos.

Rachael gave Arion his share of the profits. The money left over belonged to David. They sailed that day, and upon reaching Neapolis, they had to anchor in the harbor, as the pier was full. Antonio carefully rowed her ashore. She decided to wear a nice dress as she strolled along the waterfront and up the street to Arion's place. Rosa took careful note of her looks and commented on her hairstyle. Rachael was very tired and wanted to sleep. Curiosity drove Rosa to have tea with her before her nap. She wanted to know everything, especially her encounter with Stephanos.

It was a relaxing evening. Some of the crew members stopped by for some wine and cheese. Arion and Kosmo were plotting their next adventure. Geordie suggested finding items that are in demand for shipping, such as amphoras used to ship wine and olive oil. Geordie noticed that amphoras that were used to ship items to such places as Egypt or Italy were never returned. Shippers were constantly looking for items and material in which to ship their goods. Kosmo said that he saw amphoras being sold in the first small village they encountered along the Dardanelle Strait. Arion said that amphoras and other pottery items were made all along the coast and sold in the major market places. Kosmo added that the cost to make pottery was insignificant compared to the cost to deliver them over land routes. He also said that it would be nice to have one size and shape to make them more efficient to store them in the hold of the ship.

Rachael suggested that purchasing them from one source would make it easier to get consistent sizes and shapes, and that having them made in the poorer regions meant lower manufacturing costs. She also suggested that since amphoras and other pottery items weren't returned, one could put exterior designs on them to make them sale-able on the open market. She said the container would add value to the item being shipped.

Arion liked the idea but asked how to get started. Rachael suggested talking with the villagers that made the pottery and get them to agree with their plan. Also, she said that her father, Matthias, was skilled in working with clay and could help them develop a manufacturing process that would produce high quality pottery with consistent size and shape. Once the process was complete, Rachael could talk with Markos and have him design his cargo ships to handle their shape and size amphoras. When ships come in for repair and upgrades, Markos could use our designs. Standardization would not only facilitate ship building designs but facilitate the shipping industry as a whole.

Rachael had it in her mind to corner the market on amphoras. Kosmo really liked the idea. Arion and Geordie were a bit hesitant but decided to go for it. Rachael suggested revisiting the village on the strait to see if they were willing to do business with us and at the same time purchase more carpets to pay for the trip. Meanwhile, Rachael's plans were to travel to Beth-Gebar to see if Father was willing to help her out. She also needed to give David the money she owed him.

Rosa told Arion that the payment for the olive oil shipment arrived while he was gone. She said the money came from Philippi. They surmised that Captain Madera was probably doing business in Philippi and couldn't make a stop in Neapolis. Rachael wanted to go to Philippi on the chance of meeting Madera. Hermes offered to walk there, even though it was a fair distance. Arion said that there was a lot of work to be done to prepare the *Diana* for her next voyage. Two of the ship's seams had minor leaks in them and had to be caulked.

The next morning, Rachael walked the waterfront looking for a ship heading to Troas or one of the cities near Beth-Gebar. She had no success and decided to stroll by the synagogue. Rabbi Uzziah saw her and invited her into the courtyard. The other men were surprised that he did so. He introduced her to the others, some who had met her before. He said that because of her knowledge of the Holy Scriptures, she qualified to be in the courtyard of men, even though she was a woman.

They wanted to know more about her family history and how she was educated. She told them one story after another. They were impressed to say the least. Rachael finished her conversation by explaining the gospel of salvation for the Jews as well as the gentiles. The men conversed with each other and wanted to discuss the matter with Rabbi Uzziah privately.

Meanwhile, Rachael pulled the rabbi aside and asked him if he would like to sail with her to Beth-Gebar. While there, he could meet Rabbi Zachias, and that I might escort him to Jerusalem to meet Rabbi Levi at the library. Uzziah said that he would give it some thought. Rachael figured that having Rabbi Uzziah traveling with her would make for an excellent escort and, perhaps, have better influence with any Jewish sea captains heading south from Neapolis. Another advantage would be that if the rabbi was convinced that Jesus was the Messiah as foretold in the Scriptures after meeting with Rabbis Zachias and Levi, then she could possibly add Jews to the small home church currently being held at Arion's home.

A week had passed with no success. A neighbor lady heard about Rachael's healing ministry and brought her sick child by for prayer and healing. Rachael and Emma prayed over the child. The results were not immediate, but a short time later, the mother returned with exciting news that her child was well again and was playing with other children. She became the second convert in their little church. Rachael and Emma decided to call their little church The Church at Neapolis.

Emma had written a couple of simple Christian songs in Greek. Rachael put the songs to music using her small harp. She wished that she had a bigger harp, as the tones seemed louder, crisper, and fresher.

Another week went by with no success in finding a ship. It had rained all week. The *Diana* was at sea, and Rachael hoped that their quests were successful. The ladies were sitting around a warm fire when a knock came to the door. It was Captain Madera. He had made a delivery to Athens and decided to stop by Neapolis in search of cargo for his southern journey. Neapolis was quite a bit out of his way, but Rachael surmised that he just wanted to stop by and see her. He probably met with Markos and family while in Athens and heard about her visit with them.

Rachael was excited to see him. She didn't know of any cargo waiting to be shipped. The two of them checked the warehouses along the waterfront. The best that they could do was ten amphoras of last year's olive oil and some glassware that wasn't earmarked for other Greek cities or Italy. The captain offered to deliver the olive oil and glassware to Alexandria. He figured Ptolemy would purchase them and sell them either in Alexandria or Cairo. The Egyptians liked

Grecian glassware. The warehouse vendors agreed to work through Rachael as their shipping agent given her connection with Arion.

Rachael asked the captain if he would be willing to stop by Troas on the way south, and perhaps Beth-Gebar. Madera said that he could not refuse a request from Ragamuffin. Rachael asked the captain if she and possibly Rabbi Uzziah could travel with him. It meant that captain Madera would have to give up his cabin again. He gave the usual nod followed by a low grumble.

After a hot bowl of Rosa's stew, the captain went to his ship and arranged to load the olive oil and glassware. Fortunately, he didn't discard the structure that was installed to handle the previous set of amphoras that contained olive oil.

Rachael stopped by the synagogue and found Rabbi Uzziah. She asked him if he was still interested in traveling to Beth-Gebar. He said yes, and Rachael told him that the ship was most likely sailing early the following day.

It was still raining when they departed for Troas. The Aegean Sea was quite choppy, but Rachael seemed to handle the ship motion better than usual. Rachael discussed her plan to corner the amphora market with Captain Madera. He thought it was a most excellent idea and wished her well in the venture. The ship made good time and docking in Troas was uneventful.

Rachael and Captain Madera stopped by David's warehouse and handed him the money that she owed him. David was pleased. Apparently, he hadn't heard about her trying to sell carpets to one of his merchants in Athens. Captain Madera asked him if he needed any shipments to go to Alexandria. David said that the Egyptians were spoiled with Persian carpets delivered by land routes from the east, and that there was no market for locally made carpets. However, if the captain stopped by on the way north, he probably would have some more carpets to ship to Athens and possibly Italy. The captain said that he doesn't sail to Italy but would be happy to deliver carpets to Athens.

Before getting underway for Beth-Gebar, they visited Patricia at the palace. As usual, Patricia was excited to see her and wanted to know everything that she was doing. She told Rachael not to tell

David about her carpet exploits. Patricia said that he will probably find out, but it would be better after they got married. Apparently, she was getting married in about four weeks. Rachael promised to attend the wedding if the timing was right on her return trip to Neapolis. She told Patricia this as her hand was resting on captain Madera's shoulder. After a couple of taps on the shoulder, you could hear a low grumble in his voice. Deep down inside, Madera was really happy to accommodate any of Rachael's wishes. He considered her to be his favorite niece. Rachael would often refer to him as her uncle. It always drew a smile and melted away any sense of gruffness in his attitude.

The rain had let up during part of the trip to Beth-Gebar. The captain anchored for enough time to have Rachael and Rabbi Uzziah rowed to shore. One of the villagers saw the ship and two of them rowed out to meet the captain. The captain always enjoyed paying them a small fee for doing so. Any money gained for the villagers was acceptable. Captain Madera was their local hero.

One of the villagers offered to carry some of their luggage. Rachael introduced Rabbi Uzziah to Rabbi Zachias. Rabbi Uzziah was invited to stay at the synagogue. They both escorted Rachael to her home. There was the usual great excitement when they arrived. Lots of hugs and kisses. I built a fire in the fire ring as father retrieved some wine from the cave. Mother and Mary-Beth began fixing a meal fit for a king. Joseph joined us after a while. He had been watering the garden and the vineyard. The rain encountered on the way south hadn't hit the area. The drought seemed to be continuing another year.

Chapter 13

MY SECOND TRIP TO JERUSALEM

Silvanus, son of Matthias, son of Gaius, to my descendants. Captain Madera decided to remain in Beth-Gebar for a few days. There was always a room available at his cousin's house in the village. He was invited for dinner that evening as we celebrated Ragamuffin's arrival. She was excited to hear that Abigail was pregnant with her second child and that Mary-Beth was expecting as well.

Ragamuffin talked with Father about her amphora project and wondered if he could build a potter's wheel capable of producing amphoras that were the same size and shape. Father thought about it for a minute or two and told her that it could be done. He recommended an iron rod bent to the shape of the amphora and the use of a piece of metal to ride up and down the rod to shape the clay. Father said that in order to make them all the same, a number of rods needed to be made to the exact shape of the first one.

Ragamuffin was excited to hear that. Father said that he could borrow a potter's wheel from the village, and that he had enough metal to make one rod. He needed to know the height and maximum diameter of the amphora.

Father said that a lot of money would be needed to fabricate a number of the units. He had no iron to speak of and recommended that she hire the metal smith in Tyre to make the iron rods. Father knew of a carpenter in Zarephath who made potter's wheels. He said that with the right funds, he could fabricate a dozen or so units for her to take back with her to Neapolis.

That evening, the captain pulled me aside and handed me a mixed bag of silver and gold coins. He told me to hand it to Ragamuffin after he departed for the village. I knew what the money was for and thanked him for his generosity. I promised to pay him back as soon as we could. Captain Madera laughed and waved his hand as he walked away.

Ragamuffin walked to the top of the hill. I joined her after a while and found her silently praying. I placed the bag of money on the small table in front of her. She wanted to know what it was for and where it came from. I didn't have to say anything. She knew where the money came from and what it was for.

She spent the rest of the evening going over all the details of her adventures since leaving home. I was amazed at what she was able to accomplish in such a short time. She asked me to guide the rabbis to Jerusalem so that they could meet up with Rabbi Levi. I told her that I would do that. Ragamuffin wanted to stay behind and work with father on the amphora making device.

That morning, I searched for the captain in the village. He was at one of the cafés sipping tea and telling seafaring stories that captured the attention of all the patrons. I believe that half of the stories were made up, and that the villagers felt the same way. In any case, they loved to hear his stories and laugh to their hearts' content.

Captain Madera agreed to drop the rabbis and me off in Joppa on his way south. With that, I hustled over to the synagogue to let the rabbis know. They had one day to prepare for the journey. Mary-Beth baked some bread for us, and Father provided the usual jug of wine for the captain. Rabbi Zachias had sufficient funds to pay our way.

Stephanie, Ragamuffin, Joseph, and Mary-Beth walked with me to the beach. After some hugs and kisses, a couple of villagers rowed us out to the ship. The winds were light, and the offshore breeze eased us out of the harbor and set us on our way to the south. It seemed to take forever as the wind died on us several times. The air became dry and hot, and as we approached Joppa, the winds picked up from the east. The captain referred to them as the ill winds and feared the worst. With a bit of a struggle, we docked in Joppa. The winds were getting worse, and the captain felt that his ship was not sheltered enough in the harbor. He wanted to find better shelter on the lee side of the cliffs just south of the city. He would anchor there until he felt safe enough to continue on to Alexandria.

After picking up food for our journey to Jerusalem, we headed to our first rest stop. Rabbi Uzziah walked with a slow pace, and we didn't reach Lydda until sundown. Rabbi Zachias arranged for us to spend the night at the synagogue. The servants took excellent care of us. The road to Emmaus was a difficult walk. We faced the ill winds the whole way. I recommended that we stay at the bed and breakfast place that I had stayed in on the previous journey. The owners were excited to see me again and were delighted to have us stay with them.

The winds continued unabated the next day. I wondered if Captain Madera had an opportunity to weigh anchor and set sail to Alexandria. The winds were ferocious. We were dead tired upon reaching Jerusalem and spent the night at a local inn. We found Rabbi Levi at the library early the next morning. He was very excited to see Rabbi Zachias. Zachias cautioned him on letting others know of his arrival in fear of being arrested. Rabbi Levi fed us and found places for us to stay.

Rabbi Levi mentioned that I, Joseph, and Rachael caused quite a stir during our previous visit to Jerusalem. Apparently, the Sanhedrin became aware of our visit and had inquired as to why we were there and why Rabbi Levi allowed a woman into the library. When it was learned that we were investigating whether Jesus was the Messiah or not, we had opened some old wounds in the priesthood. Even Pilate became aware of our inquisition. The Sadducees were in control of the Sanhedrin. It was rumored that the Pharisees, seeing an opportunity to regain a foothold in the Sanhedrin, found a way to inform Pilate about our visit. Pilate was still quite irritated with the Jews over his involvement with the crucifixion of Jesus. When Pilate had our visit investigated, the only thing that he could find out was that we were of the House of Gaius, and that's where the issue seemed to rest. Rabbi Levi said that he almost lost his position as head scribe over the event of our visit.

Cuspius Fadus was the current procurator of Judea. Pilate was called to Rome several years ago. It's rumored that Tiberius Alexander was in line to replace Cuspius. We spent the rest of the day in the library, researching prophesies and getting involved in lengthy discussions concerning John the Baptist and Jesus. All agreed that Jesus had to be the Messiah as foretold in the Holy Scriptures. Rabbi Levi's wife along with a few friends prepared a great feast for us that evening.

Early the next morning, Rabbi Levi was warned that officers from the Sanhedrin were headed his way. For our safety, he had one of his sons lead us out of the city in darkness. Our bags were full of bread and fruit for our return journey. Rabbi Levi pulled me aside and placed a bag of money in my hand. He told me to take good care of Rabbis Uzziah and Zachias. He knew that I could be trusted. I would have loved to be a fly on the wall when the officers showed up at his house.

We stayed at the bed and breakfast place in Emmaus. The rabbis found us accommodations at the synagogue in Lydda. As we approached Joppa, we were overtaken by a contingent of Roman soldiers on horseback. After inquiring who we were, they arrested us. One of the riders was a servant of the high priest. I asked him why we were under arrest, and the servant said that we were accused of disturbing the peace and plotting against Rome. I told the centurion that I was the son of a Roman citizen, and that I was a close friend to the procurators of Tyre and Troas and that these accusations were false. Because of the lack of proof in what I said, he said that the matter will be handled in Jerusalem.

The centurion ordered the soldiers to tie our hands and march us to the praetorian in Joppa. He and the remaining soldiers rode to Joppa to arrange for extra horses to take us back to Jerusalem. When we arrived at the praetorian, one of the guards noticed me and asked why I and the rabbis were being led as prisoners. I didn't recognize him at first, but it turned out that he was one of the Christian soldiers whom I had met during my last visit to Jerusalem. I explained that the soldiers from Jerusalem didn't know who I was and suggested that he inform the procurator of my predicament. I informed him that I was a close friend of the procurators of Tyre and Troas, and that my sister, Abigail, was married to Flavius, the procurator of Tyre. The soldier said that he knew Abigail and Patricia as he was assigned to look after them while serving in Caesarea.

After informing his commanding officer, the soldier arranged for the prison guards to take good care of the rabbis and myself. We were unchained in an unlocked cell and given a decent meal. The rabbis and I gave our food to the prisoners in the adjoining cell. The kind gesture was much appreciated.

Meanwhile, the procurator didn't have time to deal with the matter and requested that a visiting centurion from Caesarea handle the issue as he was familiar with who's who in that region. The visiting centurion was Cuspius's administrative assistant. The visiting centurion asked for the names of those arrested. An officer had our soldier friend inquire as to our names and quickly informed the visiting centurion. Upon hearing the names, the centurion smiled and ordered the prisoners and the centurion from Jerusalem along with the servant of the high priest to appear before him immediately.

The administrative assistant had his back turned toward us as the centurion and high priest appeared. As the assistant turned and sat down, Rabbi Zachias and I looked at each other and at the same time said, "Cleo?" The figure sitting in the large marble chair looked down at us and yelled, "Silence!" as his eyes slowly scanned from the rabbis to the servant of the high priest, to whom he cast an evil eye.

Cleo looked at the centurion from Jerusalem and asked why he has arrested a member of the House of Gaius, which had close ties to Rome and was a friend of the emperor himself. Before the centurion could speak, Cleo ordered the guard to remove our chains. With a dropped jaw and stuttering, the centurion said that the arrest was at the order of the high priest. Cleo interrupted and asked, "Since when do Romans take orders from the Jews?" Cleo further stated that if Cuspius finds out about this, he would boil him in oil and feed him to the dogs. Before that happens, he said that the centurion and the high servant would both be flogged and boiled in oil. He further stated that this matter was closed and at the interest of all involved, not a word should reach Cuspius.

The centurion and the high priest nodded as Cleo motioned for me to approach his seat. The centurion was seen grabbing the garment of the servant to the high priest and shaking him as they departed the praetorian. The centurion was obviously in a foul mood when addressing the servant. With that, they immediately departed from Joppa the next morning. Cleo invited me for dinner that evening and let me stay in the guest house. The rabbis stayed at a local synagogue. I suspected that Rabbi Uzziah will return to Neapolis with an astonishing tale.

During the evening meal, I leaned over and reminded Cleo that there was an arena in Rome that was full of man eating lions, and that if word got out that he misrepresented the emperor's name by falsely associating the House of Gaius with Rome, he would become a tasty morsel for some hungry felines. Cleo told me not to worry as Cuspius couldn't function without him. I smiled and told him that his father Marcus and his sister Patricia would be proud of his actions today. We both smiled as we tapped our wine cups together.

Cleo mentioned that some of the Christians who attended Peter's church were arrested by Jews from Jerusalem. When Cleo got wind of it, he intervened and sent the Jews home empty-handed. He suspected the high priest in Jerusalem will complain to Cuspius, but Cleo wasn't concerned. He said that Pilate wanted his support while serving as the procurator of the northern kingdoms, and that Cuspius keeps stalling the transfer. The family often joked about Cleo becoming a tribune in Rome, or even the emperor. With a strategic mindset and maintaining a low profile, Cleo just might succeed in one of those roles.

Three days later, we caught a ship to Tyre. The air was still dry, and it seemed that we were always out of water. I stayed a couple of days at the praetorian at the invitation of commander Flavius, or should I say, procurator Flavius. His father, Decarus, had passed away from his illness. Abigail was excited to see me. Commander Banes arranged to give the rabbis a chariot ride to Beth-Gebar. Rabbi Uzziah was impressed that a Roman soldier would accommodate two rabbis in a Roman chariot. Rabbi Zachias smiled and told him that the House of Gaius was well connected with Rome. It was a stretch of the truth, but such rumors seem to have its benefits.

Chapter 14

AMPHORA PRODUCTION

Silvanus, son of Matthias, son of Gaius, to my descendants. Rachael spent a great deal of her time working with Alex the potter. Father showed her and Alex where the clay deposit was. The potter said that it would take a lot of work just to dig out the clay, and if they were to go into production on the amphoras, it would take someone two or three days a week just to dig, transport, and process the clay. He also said that he would have to expand his building to house more workers and store the clay.

Rachael and I dug the first few blocks of clay and carried them down to the potter's house. We would come home with clay on our arms and face. Our clothes were just as dirty. She definitely was living up to her name, Ragamuffin. The potter liked the clay better than the clay he was getting along the wadi just east of the village. There was less rocks and debris in the clay, which made for easier processing before kneading it into shape.

Father and I made regular visits to the metal smith in Tyre and the carpenter in Zarephath to check on their progress in making parts for the potter's wheels. He and the potter made several practice runs, and with a few modifications, the potter produced several amphoras that were the same size and shape. The potter painted the amphoras with various designs before firing them in the kiln.

Several weeks passed before Captain Madera showed up. His load was destined for Athens, and he had no desire to stop and pick up Rachael as it was quite out of his way. Also, he didn't want to give up his cabin again. He appeared in a foul mood. However, a day with Ragamuffin, and his demeanor changed. She and mother made a bedroll for her to use while aboard ship. With that and a pillow, she offered to sleep on the deck. The captain would have none of that, but she insisted on sleeping on the deck when the weather was good. Captain Madera knew that arguing with her was a waste of his time. He did say that sleeping in his own bed was a nicety.

Several amphoras were placed on board, and they departed in a timely manner. The seas were rough, but the winds were just right for making good time. The port in Athens was as busy as ever. Ragamuffin remained aboard ship while the captain arranged for offloading the cargo. She needed to get the amphoras delivered to Markos and found someone recommended by one of the shipping agents. They were mounted on a donkey, and she feared that they would fall and break before making it to the shipyard.

Stephanos met her as she arrived. One of the workmen spotted her as she approached the front gate. Stephanos was pleased to see her and the amphoras. They talked business for quite some time and agreed to use the amphoras as a standard in his shipbuilding plans. He told her that to make it work, she would have to market her amphoras in every major port along the Aegean and eastern Mediterranean coasts.

It was a major undertaking, but Rachael committed to making it happen. Stephanos invited her to stay at the house and said that his mother would be excited to see her. He had a workman carry her backpack and shoulder bag, and said that he would be there shortly.

As expected, Rhodora was pleased to see her and immediately arranged for the servants to look after her. Rachael handed her the necklace that she accidentally walked away with on her last visit. Rhodora laughed and said that she never missed it and told her to keep it. She wanted to know if Captain Madera was going to show up. Rachael told her that he would drop by when his ship is unloaded, perhaps tomorrow or the next day.

Rachael took the braids out of her hair and combed it straight. She wore a headband to hold it in place. She anticipated that Stephanos would take her out for the evening and wanted to look her best. There was no time to have a hair dresser do up her hair. Rhodora had tea served on the porch, and as they sat and enjoyed the view of the Aegean, Rhodora asked many questions about her latest adventures.

She told Rhodora all about her venture into the amphoras business and told her that she didn't know how it was going to go without some capital investment. Rachael told her that she was going to start small and work her way up, and fortunately, Captain Madera has been quite accommodating in providing transport from port to port.

Rhodora said that Captain Madera began to like her when she held his hand while Gaius stitched his ankle wound. Rhodora said that from that point on, Rachael became like a daughter to him and often referred to her as his niece. The bond was solidified when one time during a voyage Rachael called him Uncle Madera.

Rhodora said that she found a real nice dress for her and wanted her to try it on. The dress fit nicely, and Rhodora suggested that she wear it when she went out with Stephanos that evening. Rhodora said that her headband was a bit plain and wrapped a string of flowers around it. She looked beautiful when she departed with Stephanos.

She and Stephanos had dinner on the veranda of a local restaurant, overlooking the sea. The restaurant was part of a home. Patrons basically walked through the kitchen, and the cook showed them what was being prepared, and they pointed at what they wished to be served. It was a family-run business. It was obvious that Stephanos ate there often, given the way he was greeted and treated by the owners.

The food was delicious. Stephanos talked about the ship building trade, and Rachael talked about her amphora venture. Stephanos shared some business advice and offered to front some money to help her get started. He also knew some vendors in the city who would sell her amphoras and said that he would talk with them sometime during the week. Stephanos said that the Romans wanted him to design bigger and faster warships, galleys with three levels of rowers. That meant expanding his shipyard. Stephanos was well known in Rome for the quality of his ships.

Rachael asked him what he did with his profits, in other words, where does a person safely store their wealth. Stephanos said that it was a problem at first, but he said that Markos and a number of large business owners formed a consortium to lend money to each other and to invest in interesting new ventures. A fee was charged for each transaction, and interest was charged to the borrowers. For example, when Stephanos gets a contract to build a ship, he may need funds to tool up for it. The revenue from building the ship usually covered the upfront fees and interest charged on the loan. He said that if the Romans want him to build a warship, they would have to put money up front to get things started.

Stephanos said that he keeps thousands of drachmas at his shipyard and that paying for security was very expensive. He said that in general, most Greeks can be trusted, and that most crimes are caused by foreigners. He said that he left a bag of money at a restaurant in the city, and when the owner discovered it, he sent one of his workers to his home to deliver it. Not a coin was missing from the bag. The worker was rewarded for his honesty and effort.

Markos and Rhodora showed up a couple hours later. They talked for another two hours. Markos was interested in Rachael's latest adventures and wanted to know how many pirates she killed since her last visit. She told him that she lost count.

Markos commented on the amphoras. He suggested painting the designs above and below the widest point because the sides will wear a bit while being transported. He also suggested making the neck and spout smaller as it will require less wax when sealing the tops and suggested making the handles narrower than the width of the body because any shift in the amphora during transport may result in the handles hitting the sides of the container and breaking off. Markos had a lot of experience transporting goods throughout the Aegean and Mediterranean before getting involved in shipbuilding.

He said that based on her design, he should be able to load about 2400 amphoras using his latest ship design. Rachael mentioned that captain Madera told her that a ship loaded with about 4000 amphoras sank near Byzantium because it was overloaded. Markos said that the ship was top heavy and took a nasty roll when taking a broadside hit from the first big wave just as they exited the Bosporous Strait. He said that the higher the center of gravity, the bigger the chance of rolling the ship in a storm.

Rachael woke up with a headache the next morning. She wished that she hadn't drank so much wine the night before. Captain Madera showed up for a late breakfast. He was happy to find out that he didn't have to sail to Neapolis. He said that he was loading Grecian pottery for transport to Alexandria and told her that to minimize cargo damage, he needed to travel straight to Alexandria. He promised to stop by Beth-Gebar on the next trip north. Rachael did not want to travel that distance at sea but felt that it was important to have her father redesign the potter's wheel before fabricating too many amphoras. Be that as it may, she agreed to sail with the captain. He told her that she could stay in his cabin full time knowing that she got seasick. Rachael told him that she didn't mind sleeping on the deck as long as it wasn't raining. With that, Captain Madera decided to head back to the ship and said that he planned on sailing in a couple of days.

Rhodora told the captain that she and Rachael were going into the city, and that if he waited a few minutes, he could ride with them. She had arranged with Horace to take them into the city. Rhodora gave each of them a pillow, as the cart ride was a little rough on the body. The cart barely fit the three of them, and the horse seemed to find every hole in the road. Captain Madera was dropped off at the waterfront, and the ladies headed for the hair dresser.

Rhodora introduced Rachael as her niece at all the shops. Rachael looked lovely with her hair done up, along with a flowing dress and new sandals. Horace stopped and waited for them at every shop. Rhodora asked the pottery vendors to consider Rachael's amphoras when she began to make them. The vendors agreed; however, they preferred to deal with men on business matters. I suspect Rachael's good looks and smiles along with knowing Rhodora made a big difference.

After a nap from a busy day of shopping, Rachael spent the evening at the café with Stephanos. She began to suspect that Rhodora was performing a little matchmaking. Stephanos paraded her around as if she was his fiancé. She was introduced to some wealthy Romans. Rachael realized that the upper echelon of society associated at the café, and not just anyone was allowed to enter. He introduced Rachael as a close friend of the family and as a wealthy business lady who traded in Phoenician amphoras. The Romans spoke Greek in front of Stephanos, but when apart, she noticed that they spoke Latin. She would have loved to hear what they were saying to one another.

Rhodora arranged for Horace to give Rachael a ride to the ship. She told Horace not to accept any money from her. Horace helped her with her backpack, and shoulder bag and as usual, money was place in her hands.

The trip to Alexandria was uneventful except for the high seas. The winds were perfect for maximizing ship's speed without causing damage to the cargo of pottery. Rachael still found it difficult to handle ship's motion. The captain let her sleep in his bed during the day. At night, she slept on the deck. The stars seemed to help her seasickness. When it rained at night, she would sleep on the floor in the cabin. Many mornings, she would awaken and find an extra blanket covering her. She knew where to return the blanket, except for a few times she had to find a crew member that it belonged to. The night watch kept a close eye on her.

Ptolemy was happy to see them when they arrived in Alexandria and arranged for them to stay at his villa overlooking the sea. An Ethiopian slave looked after Rachael. Her name was Shayla. Shayla was all smiles and wore a beautiful dress. She spoke Egyptian, and it was awhile before Rachael realized that she not only spoke her native tongue but also spoke an older dialect of Hebrew. It was probably a dialect spoken by the Jews prior to their captivity in Babylon.

Shayla, along with a male escort, showed Rachael the city. Egyptian architecture was quite different from what she had seen in Palestine and Greece. She did see Grecian influence in the sports arena and the library. Shayla paid for her meals and some gifts. When their escort saw Rachael look at something for any length of time, he purchased the item for her whether she wanted it or not.

While dining with Ptolemy and Captain Madera, Rachael mentioned how nice Shayla treated her. Ptolemy mentioned that he purchased her for a good price, and that Shayla ran the household when he was away in Joppa or Caesarea. He chuckled and said that in all reality, when he returned to Alexandria, he felt like he's the slave, and Shayla was the master. Ptolemy said that he often threatens to send her back to Ethiopia if she doesn't behave, and Shayla just walked away and laughed.

The city mayor heard that Rachael was visiting and invited her and Ptolemy for an evening meal. Some of captain Madera's embellished tales concerning Rachael had spread throughout the city.

The mayor and his Roman counterpart were enamored with her beauty and charm and were astonished when she nonchalantly acknowledged some of the myths and legends perpetrated by Captain Madera as he frequented various social events in the city.

Three days later, the ship was loaded with Egyptian cotton cloth and linen dresses. Ptolemy wanted the goods shipped to Damascus, which meant stopping in Beth-Gebar and waiting for a caravan to take them over the coastal range.

Rachael thanked Ptolemy for his hospitality and gifts and thanked Shayla for her company and taking care of her. Ptolemy seemed delighted to have taken care of her.

Rachael's hair began to unravel, and she began to look like the old Ragamuffin again. The crew preferred her natural scruffy look. The wind and seas were the same; however, she seemed to weather them much better on the trip to Beth-Gebar. She even helped steer the ship and work the rigging along with the men.

Beth-Gebar was a sight for sore eyes. Rabbi Zachias saw the ship arrive and walked down to greet them. He helped carry her backpack and shoulder bag. Father immediately set out to redesign the potter's wheel based on Rachael's instructions. The family, as usual, celebrated her return that evening. After unloading the cargo, Captain Madera returned to Alexandria.

Chapter 15

THE MARKET PLACE

Silvanus, son of Matthias, son of Gaius, to my descendants. While Rachael waited for Captain Madera to show up, she decided to go to Sidon and see if Father's cousins would be interested in purchasing some of her amphoras. She asked me to walk with her. We left early the next morning. It was a long walk, but the weather was cool, and we stopped a few times to drink water and have some bread and cheese. We had some good talks on the way and were glad to reach the cousins' place of business.

They were glad to see us and spent time discussing Rachael's amphora business. They offered to purchase twenty-four amphoras and would have purchased more, but they had a goodly number in stock. We spent the evening dining with them, and after an excellent breakfast, we walked back to our home.

Rachael wanted me to deliver the amphoras to Sidon, while she convinced Father to walk with her to Tyre. She wanted to find vendors in Tyre to sell her amphoras. Father wished that he had a couple of good horses to pull the chariot. I arranged with Alex to use his donkey and cart to deliver amphoras to Sidon. Alex needed a couple more days to finish the last lot of twelve. Rachael was certainly making good use of the family to promote her business. She did pay me for my efforts. Stephanie liked that, as our money supply was fast dwindling.

Rachael and Father visited with Flavius and Abigail while in Tyre. The days were getting hotter as midsummer approached. Commander Banes took care of the donkey for the night and had him ready for Rachael as she walked the waterfront and talked with several potential vendors. Father did some shopping and visited with the metal smith who was making Rachael's iron parts for the potter's wheel. He had him adjust the shapes to meet her new standards.

A couple of vendors agreed to purchase her amphoras as their inventory dwindled. They liked the artwork and the smoothness of the clay. They could see that the amphora was fired at a good temperature. They wanted strong amphoras that would not break while being transported.

With Abigail in Tyre, Hermes's family in Neapolis, Ragamuffin always on the move, and Grandfather Gaius having passed away, Joseph, Father, and I kept fairly busy on the property. Stephanie focused her attention on our newborn, Priscilla. The baby was named after her grandmother. Little Gaius follows me wherever I go. I gave him small chores to do. I'm thinking about getting him a pet dog. He needed a companion. A dog would be good for protecting him against snakes.

Our biggest project was to move the outhouses. We will probably move them further away from the house. There really isn't another option other than cleaning out the area where they are now. No one wants to do that.

When Ragamuffin returned from Tyre, she invited Alex the potter and his family over for an evening meal. She asked me if I would handle the Tyre and Sidon amphora deliveries. I told her that I would help out as much as I could. A few denarii every once in a while was good for our finances.

During the evening meal, Hermes and Antonio made a surprise visit. Apparently, they found some excess grain along the Dardenelles and shipped it to Sidon. Antonio mentioned that he was getting homesick and decided to return to Beth-Gebar. He said that he missed having Rachael around. Hermes said that Arion and the cousins were working a deal to ship some goods to Athens. He also said that the villagers in Akim along the Dardonelles were willing to make her amphoras. The clay was of a different composition and would look lighter than the ones made by Alex but would provide a variety to her inventory, not to mention lower cost. Hermes said that he would provide the potter wheels in the near future.

Father said that he would have a half dozen available in about a week, and that Hermes could take what he had if they couldn't wait that long. Hermes said that a week would be fine. Alex offered up his potter wheels if necessary. Rachael said that if they had room on the ship, she could load a few amphoras on board and market them in Athens. Hermes said that they could easily make room. Alex said that he would get right on it and said that he could make a half dozen amphoras by then.

Rachael asked Antonio if he would go to work for Alex and paint the designs on the amphoras and teach others how to do it. Antonio was excited to do it, as he loved art, and it was a way to have his work shown throughout the eastern Mediterranean and Aegean Sea areas. Rachael told Hermes that she was sailing with him to Athens and told Father to tell Captain Madera that she would probably see him next in Neapolis. Hermes left for Sidon a couple days later, and I escorted Ragamuffin and the six amphoras to the ship.

Captain Madera showed up a couple of weeks later. He said that he had to return to Alexandria for another shipment of cotton cloth. He also said that Ptolemy would purchase a hundred amphoras when they were ready. Alex, Antonio, and I were excited about that, as was Joseph, because we needed him to help dig clay and deliver it to the potter. I told the captain that Ragamuffin would most likely see him next in Neapolis. He said that he would eventually make it there, probably toward the end of summer when grain was readily available.

Captain Madera kept the wood for the lattice setup for storing amphoras aboard his ship. We had moved it from his cousin's place to the potter's place for safekeeping. He said that the lattice could hold over a hundred amphoras, if need be. We used the girls' room and the guest house to store the captain's latest cargo. As usual, he paid us well and said that Ptolemy showed his appreciation for our help by influencing merchants in Alexandria to purchase Ragamuffin's amphoras. The captain said that Ptolemy took a liking to Rachael and said that he may be able to help her sales in Joppa and Caesarea as well.

Rachael had no problem selling her amphoras in Athens. She and Stephanos spent a lot of time together. He told her that his next cargo ship should be launched later that summer. They had been working on it for two years. He said that it should be able to hold 2400 amphoras. Rachael said that he could test it out by loading her amphoras at Akim and delivering them to her vendors along the Grecian coast. She said that she would pay the shipping charge, and he could make some money before delivering the ship to his customer. Stephanos agreed to go along with the idea.

I had a feeling that she and Stephanos were probably going to get married someday. Antonio realized the same thing, and I noticed that he was seeing a young lady in the village. All the young men in the village had left for work in Sidon and Tyre, which left several lovely girls looking for husbands. I told Antonio that when he made his choice, to let me know as I told him that I was thinking about another wife. Stephanie leaned on my shoulder with her elbow and told me not to even think about it. I'm glad she has a sense of humor.

The *Diana* ported in Thessalonica for a few days before heading to Neapolis. Rachael met with the Christian brethren and preached a sermon to the local Christians at the amphitheater. She spoke out against worshipping idols and told them that they became like the god they worshipped. She told them that Jesus was the way, the truth, and the life, and that He was the only way to Father God. The philosophers questioned why her God was better than the ones worshiped in Greece.

The Jews were quite interested in hearing about the Messiah. However, they, as well as the Christian brethren, questioned whether a woman should be preaching to them. After witnessing her knowledge of the Holy Scriptures and the eloquence of her speech, they quieted down. The gentiles lacked Jewish background and training. It seemed that her only answer to the philosophers were the healing miracles that they witnessed following her messages. Several lame people were healed along with a couple who were deaf. One person had sight restored in one of his weak eyes. She tried her best to convince everyone that there was a better way of life through the cross of Jesus and spoke a great deal on repentance and the kingdom of heaven. Many accepted the new way of life, and Rachael laid on hands for the receiving of the Holy Spirit. Hermes said that one could see the excitement in the eyes of those who received the Spirit.

There were those in the city who complained about her denouncing the gods. They were the ones who fabricated the idols and sold them in the marketplace. They told the city governor, Mercaius, that such preaching was offensive to Rome where the emperor himself promoted idol worship. Although, Claudius did not promote himself as a god as did Caligula, some still thought that they had to worship the emperor as a god.

Mercaius ordered his commander to look into the matter and have Rachael arrested. It turned out that Darius, the former commander under Decarus in Tyre, was the new commander in charge of the Roman troops in Thessalonica.

On the second night of her preaching, Darius approached the amphitheater with a couple of his guards. He recognized Hermes standing in the background and had one of the guards get his attention. They greeted each other, and Darius wanted to know why he, as a slave, was in the city. Hermes explained that he was never a slave of the House of Gaius, and that he just pretended to be one. He gave a short history of his involvement with our family. Darius got a chuckle out of it.

Commander Darius asked if he knew anything about the woman speaking in the amphitheater. Hermes said that she was Rachael of the House of Gaius. Darius was awestruck by his response and asked if he had met her when visiting the family while stationed in Tyre. Hermes asked him if he remembered the little girl that flipped him on his back one evening during a visit. Darius's mouth dropped upon hearing that and began to laugh as he put his arm on Hermes shoulder. He couldn't believe that the little girl who had caused him so much trouble was this beautiful lady speaking to a large crowd and still causing him trouble.

Darius told Hermes that he was ordered to arrest her, but now that he knows who he was arresting, he had second thoughts. He asked Hermes if she would peacefully come to the palace after she finished her speech. Hermes said that he would personally take care of it but requested that no harm come to her. Darius gave his word and left.

Commander Darius met with the governor and told him that Rachael would be showing up soon. Mercaius questioned why he didn't bring her himself, and he told the governor that she was of the House of Gaius, which was well connected to Rome, and that her father was a Roman citizen. Mercaius reminded commander Darius that disobeying orders was grounds for a good flogging. Darius, being rather thick-skinned, told him that he fully understood and emoted the usual begging for forgiveness routine.

Mercaius wanted to know why she was stirring up the people if she was of Roman heritage. Darius mentioned that she was a Christian Jew and was preaching the gospel of Christ. Mercaius wanted her arrested, as Christians, especially Jews, were considered enemies of Rome, and that the Jewish rebellion in Palestine speaks for itself.

Darius told Mercaius that he was told by a commander from Tyre that if anyone harmed a member of the House of Gaius, he would most likely be flogged and boiled in oil. Given that, Mercaius said that perhaps a simple conversation with her would be adequate. He told commander Darius to find out who her Roman connections were. One of the guards overheard them speaking and asked permission to speak. Mercaius slowly looked his way and granted him permission to speak.

The guard mentioned that he saw members of the House of Gaius on one of his northern sea trips aboard a Roman cargo ship. He said that they associated with Flavius of Tyre and Marcus and perhaps Pilate in Caesarea. He also heard rumors that one of the women of the House of Gaius was considered to be an Amazon who had defeated some pirates off the coast of Troy.

Mercaius was quite intrigued by what he heard and couldn't wait to see Rachael. It wasn't long before she showed up with Hermes. He was awestruck by her beauty. She was wearing one of Rhodora's dresses, and her hair was done up in a most attractive way. He greeted her and asked her why she was stirring up the city with her religious speeches. She basically said that she was a Christian evangelist and was sharing her beliefs with those who had interest.

Mercaius asked her if she knew Flavius and Marcus, the current governors of Tyre and Troas. She said that her sister was married to Flavius, and that she and Marcus were very good friends. With that, Mercaius was able to verify her connection with Rome and dared not ask too many questions as he didn't want anything negative to reach Rome through her connections.

Mercaius told her that she was putting him in a bad way with Rome with her speeches against idolatry. Rachael told him not to worry, and that if he had concerns, she would talk to Emperor Claudius himself. His fear-struck eyes told her that it would not be necessary and told her that she could leave and asked her not to cause any more trouble in the city. She told him that she was leaving in the morning and bade him farewell. Before she could turn, Mercaius asked her one more question. He wanted to know if she had defeated any pirates while at sea, and how was she as a woman allowed on Roman as well as other ships.

She told him that she did not defeat the pirates by herself, and that sea captains very seldom refused to let her sail on their ships. The mere fact that she was involved in fighting pirates indicated that the rumor about her as possibly being the Amazon spoken of by the guard was true. With that, he was intrigued, yet troubled by her presence.

As they walked back to the ship, Hermes mentioned that Commander Darius had informed him of Mercaius' intentions and that he helped save the day. Hermes told her that Darius pulled him aside before leaving and said that Mercaius was having someone keep him informed of your activities.

The *Diana* sailed to Neapolis the next morning. Rachael was glad to be back on land in safe territory. She slept a lot over the next two days. Her next goal was to have potter wheels delivered to Akim along the Dardenelles. She figured grain would be about ready to be shipped, and that Arion could kill two birds with one stone by delivering the potter wheels and shipping grain to Sidon for a nice profit. At the same time, he could pick up more potter wheels to be shipped to Akim. Outfitting the Markos Marine ship with 2400 amphoras meant a huge demand on production.

The church in Neapolis was growing. There was a small amphitheater near the town square. Rachael preached on the evil work of Satan and contrasted the mind of Satan with the mind of Christ. She told them that the character of Christ was that of eternal life, salvation, love, peace, truth, order, mercy, and compassion, and that the character of Satan was murder, torment, torture, hate, chaos, deception, lying, and such. She told them that if any religion promoted these characteristics, then their god was Satan. She even spoke out against the gods that promoted sexual immorality such as prostitution, and that their temples should be destroyed. With that statement, she put many in the city at odds, so much so, that the mayor had to take some action.

Arion had good connections with the authorities and agreed that Rachael wouldn't address the public from the amphitheater. He suggested that the brethren acquire their own meeting place and stay away from open air speeches for a while. Nevertheless, the church grew and stood out in the community. Even Rabbi Uzziah and some of the Jews attended the meetings.

Captain Madera showed up in Neapolis. He told Rachael that Stephanos will purchase 2400 amphoras and wanted them delivered to certain warehouses owned by the consortium in all major ports along the Grecian coast. He also said that Stephanos would pay him and Arion to deliver the amphoras from Akim and Beth-Gebar. He also said that the ship being built to handle the amphoras was delayed and probably won't be launched until the following spring along with its sister ship. Stephanos also said that he may order an additional 2400 amphoras and to be prepared in the event that should happen.

Captain Madera had enough money to cover one-third of the purchase price. Arion said that it would take several trips to handle that many amphoras as his ship was designed to handle 300 empty amphoras at a time. Captain Madera said that he could handle about 230 and would take care of the Beth-Gebar cargo, if Arion would take care of the Akim cargo. They agreed on what ports they each would take care of, and Captain Madera gave Arion a list of shipping agents that he was to deal with.

Rachael was obviously excited to receive such a large order and wondered why Stephanos changed his mind about doing a test run with the new ship. She suspected that the delay in delivering the ship to the customer had something to do with it.

Captain Madera talked the mayor of Beth-Gebar into building a new quay wall and pier to handle the business. He convinced the mayor that it was good for the local economy. Father was enlisted to design and oversee the construction efforts.

Antonio was teaching others on how to make decent artistic designs on the amphoras and even experimented on using different colored minerals in his paint mixture. Even Penelope got involved. Antonio taught her how to paint floras. She was happy to do so as she liked flowers.

Rachael was concerned about the artistic look of the amphoras made in Akim and sent Antonio there for a time to teach and oversee the production efforts. Everyone was getting paid quite well for their efforts. Orders were increasing in Tyre, and Captain Madera would make an occasional trip to Alexandria, and for some reason, Ptolemy was hoarding the amphoras that he was ordering.

Both production facilities were busy throughout the winter, although the cold weather slowed down productivity. Father was thinking about building a large enclosed structure to better shelter the workers from the wind and harsh winter environment. Alex agreed to wait and see if the huge demand for amphoras was to continue into the next year.

Rachael, Hermes, and Antonio arrived from Akim by way of Neapolis. Arion picked up a load of grain in Akim to cover the cost of the trip to Sidon. Antonio said that the potter in Akim needed more wheels in order to keep up with production demands. Father had several more units lying around and used Alex's donkey cart to take them to Sidon.

Rachael appeared exhausted from her sea trips, and Father encouraged her to spend a few weeks at home to rejuvenate herself. She agreed, and with occasional visits with Abigail, the family seemed back together for a while. Antonio broke the news that he was getting married to a local Phoenician girl. Rachael had mixed feelings when she heard the news. While praying together at the top of the hill, she mentioned that she felt obliged to Antonio for his help and caring when she needed it, but on the other hand, her true feelings seemed to be toward Stephanos. We spent long evenings talking and looking at the stars. Some evenings, we agreed not to leave until we saw at least three good shooting stars.

I would later write everything down and store the scrolls in the secret room in the cave. When the air was dry, I would put the scrolls in a clay jar and seal it with wax. I hoped to preserve the writings for future generations to read.

One evening, Rachael and I discussed the rumors about her being an Amazon who defeated pirates on the high seas and beat up Roman commanders whenever she pleased. She wanted people to see her as a real person, as a Christian evangelist, and as a respectable business lady. She was afraid that when the false rumors about her dissipate, and people find out that she was not connected to Rome in any strong way, the Roman authorities wouldn't think twice about arresting her when she spoke in public places concerning the message of the cross.

She said that Stephanos told her that if anyone wanted to be recognized in Rome, they should send a gift to one of the senators. He also said that a gift from a foreign woman would probably be a waste of time. Stephanos said that Valeria Messalina, Claudius's wife, liked gifts and would be the best person to send a gift to, except that getting a gift to her was most difficult because she was inundated with gifts from all parts of the empire. Valeria held a lot of power and influence in Rome as she was the great grandniece of Emperor Augustus and a second cousin of Caligula.

She thought about it for a while and decided to have Alex and Antonio design and fabricate two beautiful vases to give to Valeria. Her first thought was to contact the Roman friends of Stephanos whom she met at the café in Athens. She was hoping that they had some contact with government officials in Rome since they were having Markos Shipbuilding build military cargo ships for them.

Aside from all that, water was flowing quite well in the spring. The spring rains were above normal. Ragamuffin spent a lot of time at the pool and sunbathing on the spa rooftop. She and Mary-Beth would grind wheat together and then swim in the pond or sit in the spa for a while. I was tagged to heat the water for the spa. The old iron pot still worked. One of the iron pieces was rusting off. Father wasn't sure how to fix it. The pot was too big to work with in his small forge.

The lakes didn't freeze over for the third year in a row. There was no ice to put in the fruit drinks. The grapes were doing quite well. It took several years before the new plants would mature. We still haven't mastered the fine art of wine making. Rabbi Zachias kept giving us advice, but we must be doing something wrong. Every visitor who stopped by gave us some sort of advice, but to no avail. Little Gaius didn't seem to care. He ate half the grapes before they were harvested.

Captain Madera was making regular trips back and forth between Beth-Gebar, Athens, and Alexandria. He was transporting amphoras to Athens, then back to Beth-Gebar to pick up amphoras for Ptolemy, and then dropping off Egyptian cotton products in Beth-Gebar to be taken over the coastal range. Everyone was making money. Bribes to the village mayor were on the increase, Father was making good money storing goods on his property with no questions asked, and Rachael was hauling in a whole bunch of gold and silver from amphora sales.

The increase in the local economy stirred the villagers to step up the pace to build and complete the rock jetty. The plan was to make it L-shaped and then build a wooden pier on the inside that will be sheltered from the sea. Father led the efforts to build the pier, and the mayor led the effort to build the jetty.

Chapter 16

RACHAEL MARRIES STEPHANOS

Silvanus, son of Matthias, son of Gaius, to my descendants. Volunteers from the village either hauled or rolled rocks down from the wadi toward the village. It took most of the winter to complete the jetty and pier. As they extended the jetty, it took more and more rocks as the water depth increased. Father had to put logs along the length of it as that was the only way to drag or roll large stones to the end. One day, we felt a minor earthquake. An hour or so later, a huge wave came down the coast. It was large enough to lift the logs off the jetty as well as lift the fishing boats off their moorings. Nothing was really lost, but a lot of work was needed to repair the damage.

Father fabricated a pile driver that worked off of the jetty. Once the framework was finished, he led a team of villagers to cut planks for the top of the pier. A sawmill was built to make planks of the same thickness. Two people would work the saw for about an hour, and then someone would sharpen the blade with a stone. Father lashed the planks to the pier framework in such a way that the ropes weren't exposed to traffic on the pier. When finished, the pier was wide enough to handle donkey carts. Later on, Father had to set the jetty ends of the framework in concrete, as the pier tended to move too much in heavy seas and when ships tied up to it.

Captain Madera was pleasantly surprised when he showed up for his first spring run to the north. His ship was loaded with Egyptian cotton cloth destined for Athens. He made his usual grumbled complaint about having to go out of his way to stop into Beth-Gebar. A hug and a peck on the cheek from Ragamuffin, and he would become his usual jovial self. His rough and gruff character of old seemed to have disappeared. Years of being around Ragamuffin seemed to have changed him. He would probably sail to the Gates of Hercules and back if Ragamuffin asked him.

He had little room for amphoras. His ship was quite loaded down. He did agree to take six amphoras and the two vases that Alex and Antonio made. He really liked the vases and suggested that she have the potter make a couple for Rhodora. Ragamuffin said that one of the vases could go to Rhodora, and that she would only send one to Valeria. When the captain heard that name, he asked her if she meant Valeria as in the wife of Emperor Claudius. She told him her strategy to make connections with Rome, and the captain laughed and almost fell overboard when he stepped backward toward the rail. He told her to be careful of Valeria, as he heard that she had a similar evil mindset as Caligula. He said that she was a very powerful woman who would make Cleopatra a pussy cat in comparison.

The seas were a bit rough, but normal for that time of the year. Rhodora and Stephanos were happy to see them. Rhodora loved the vase. Stephanos wanted a couple for the atrium in the house that he was building for himself. The house was closer to the shipyard and a little higher on the hill. He gave her a walk through and showed her the water pipe coming from the spring, which was quite a distance away. He reminded her of Grandfather Gaius who built an elaborate piping system at home.

He asked her what she thought about the house layout and what she would do to improve on the design. She suggested a few things, such as a centerpiece for the atrium that displayed flowers in season, more storage space in the kitchen, and a lower railing on the veranda so that it didn't block one's view of the Aegean when sitting down. She also suggested that the servant who attended the front door should not have to sleep in a space inset to the atrium wall. A small room off to the side of the atrium would be better and the insets on both sides of the atrium could be filled with art work.

He liked her suggestions and made the usual arrangements to visit her favorite restaurant and his exclusive café. She told him about the vase that she had Antonio and Alex make for Valeria Messalina. His stoic demeanor mellowed a bit as he smiled and said, "You mean the wife of Claudius, the emperor?" She said, "Yes." He inquired as to why she wanted to do that. She explained how false rumors about her were spreading around the ports of the Aegean Sea and as far away as Alexandria, and once those rumors were dispelled, she feared the Romans would not be so kind to her when she stirred up trouble in the cities where she preached the gospel message of Jesus Christ. She said that having a true connection with Rome would be of benefit, especially if she became a Roman citizen.

Stephanos said that buying her a Roman citizenship was not a problem despite the fact that she is a woman. As for connecting to Rome, he said that Valeria was probably just as hostile to Jews and Christians as her powerful family was unless of course it worked to her advantage to gain more power in Rome. She probably would like to become the first woman emperor of Rome. Stephanos said that it's not beyond the realm of possibilities that she would have Claudius murdered just to take his throne. The army loves her, and the senate hates her. Fortunately, Claudius has the army under his thumb.

While at the café, Stephanos introduced Rachael to Mario Estes, a shipping magnate and the owner of a huge wine region in Italy. Mario liked to travel and search for new wines and grapes for his vineyards. He imported a lot of wine from Greece. He was a ship-building expert and served Rome by overseeing Roman ships built in Italy and Greece. He spoke fluent Greek and was quite mellow and friendly, probably from the wine he was drinking. Stephanos told Rachael to avoid him as he was quite the womanizer. He told her that the best way to get her vase to Valeria was through him. He was known for greasing the palms of senators and tribunes alike.

Stephanos suggested giving Mario a couple of vases on her next trip. Mario seemed to set the standard for art displayed in several of his villas. What Mario bought, all his wealthy associates had to have. If Mario liked a certain wine, everyone else had to have that wine in their cellar.

With that, Rachael asked Rhodora if she could have the vase that she gave her. Rachael explained her strategy to give a vase to Mario and have him give one to Valeria. Rhodora was more than happy to be part of the scheme. Rhodora just laughed and told her that she was beginning to think like a real woman but told her that she liked her pirate slaying image better. She said that a house without humor and laughter is dead. Rachael promised to replace the vase with one that was even better. Rhodora told her not to worry about it, and that if any one needed décor, it was Stephanos and his new house.

She said that his house was too stoic, just like Stephanos. Rhodora told Rachael that she should get Stephanos to mellow out his house with art work the way she was mellowing out Stephanos with her good looks and smiles. Rachael blushed at her comment.

A few nights at the café made Rachael decide to learn Latin. She noticed Latin being spoken by several people. There seemed to be a lot of Roman influence in that part of the city. The two ships that were due to be launched in the spring were delayed further into the summer. Markos was having trouble with some of the hull fittings, and that put a lot of pressure on the family as the Romans were anxious to get more ships into service. More ships were being lost at sea than were being built. That put a heavy demand on shipbuilding.

One evening while having dinner at the restaurant, Stephanos had the waiter serve a covered dish surrounded with various fruit. He told her that she had to eat the fruit before lifting the cover to see what delicacy was under it. Rachael slowly ate the fruit while they talked. He seemed a bit nervous as she took her time eating the fruit. When it came time to lift the cover, he asked her to guess what was under it. She said that it was probably her favorite dessert, baklava with strawberries on top.

As she lifted the cover, her eyes grew wide as she saw a set of beautiful earrings and a matching finger ring in the center. Stephanos reached over with his right hand and grabbed her left hand and proposed to her. With teary, sparkling eyes, Rachael said yes.

The news of their engagement brought lots of excitement in the family. They planned on getting married late in the summer after the two ships were delivered. Stephanos didn't want to get married when things were stressful. Mario was excited to hear the news and suggested that they honeymoon at his villa on the island of Crete. Stephanos took him up on his offer. Mario was leaving as soon as the ships were delivered and loaded with cargo for Italy. His interest seemed more focused on shipping amphoras filled with his Greek wine than getting the ships to Rome in one piece.

Captain Madera celebrated the news with wine aboard the ship. Rachael wanted to check on how well Arion was doing in delivering amphoras along the Grecian coast. She talked Captain Madera into sailing to Neapolis to check on Arion and suggested that he could make a killing on transporting grain to Sidon. He began to call her Captain Rachael, as his life seemed to rotate around her whims and fancies. He didn't complain much as between her and Ptolemy, he was making money hand over fist.

Arion, Rosa, Hermes, Emma, and the children were glad to see Rachael show up. They heard rumors of her whereabouts but didn't know what was happening in the amphora business. For some reason, merchants were buying her amphoras all along the coast. Rachael checked the amphoras coming from Akim. She said that the art work had improved due to Antonio's visit but had room for further improvement.

She filled them in on the news of her engagement to Stephanos. Hermes said that he and Emma will most likely attend the wedding. Captain Madera said that he would make a special trip to transport everyone to the wedding, including the family in Beth-Gebar. Arion suggested that his ship may be more suited to transporting personnel, and said that he could outfit it in short order. Rachael and Captain Madera took him up on his offer.

With that, Captain Madera picked up some grain for delivery to Sidon. Arion was planning another trip to Akim to deliver some potter wheels and pick up more amphoras. Rachael decided to oversee the building of a church in Neapolis. She used her share of profits from amphora sales to purchase building material. A church member donated land, and labor was strictly on a volunteer basis.

A Christian apostle visited the church and stayed several weeks. He taught the congregation many things concerning the mind of Christ and how they should live. He stayed in Rachael's room while Rachael slept on the floor in the atrium. He, Rabbi Uzziah, and Rachael discussed many subjects. He prayed over the both of them and blessed them when he left.

Rachael visited Rabbi Uzziah several times. He told her that he had to make a tough decision. One that had to do with giving up his old way of life and taking on a new way of life as a Christian. He was wondering if he could survive pouring new wine into an old wine skin. Rachael suggested that he could pastor the new church. His knowledge of the Hebrew Scriptures along with the good news concerning Jesus the Christ would go hand-in-hand in helping the church grow and prosper.

Meanwhile, on a return trip from Thessalonica, Arion mentioned that he heard that Markos launched one of his ships and that the other one should be launched in a few more weeks. He also found out that the first ship would be loading cargo in Athens and Thessalonica, and that merchants were required to use Rachael's amphoras. It turned out that the amphoras in storage in Thessalonica were selling at three times the original costs. Rachael was a bit puzzled by Arion's comment on the selling price.

Rachael asked Arion if he would deliver some grain to Sidon, as she wanted to talk to her parents about her engagement to Stephanos. Arion agreed as he wanted a break from the usual routine of running back and forth between Akim and Grecian ports.

The trip was uneventful. The family was excited over the news. Mother said that she was afraid to travel to Athens by ship or by land

and declined to attend the wedding. Joseph and Mary-Beth thought it best to stay and take care of their new baby as well as little Gaius and Priscilla, as Stephanie and I were planning to attend. Antonio had married a local Phoenician girl while Rachael was away, and he said that he would attend, but his new wife declined. She had family to stay with while he was gone.

Rachael waited for Captain Madera to return from Alexandria as she wanted to travel to Athens and visit with Stephanos and family. It was several weeks before he showed up. His plan was to deliver amphoras to Athens and was very happy to see Rachael. Rachael had Alex and Antonio make four decorative urns, two for Rhodora and two for Stephanos.

The trip to Athens was slow at first, and strong winds made for a rough remainder of the trip. Several amphoras broke during the transit. Rhodora was pleased with the two urns and placed them at the atrium entrance. Rachael had spent quite some time shopping with Rhodora and visiting restaurants and cafés with Stephanos. He said that the second ship was about to be delivered. She asked why the amphoras were being sold at such a high price. He said that he and members of the consortium had fronted money to purchase her amphoras, and that creating a demand for her standard fitting amphoras meant for huge profits for the investors.

Rachael was a little upset over others making three times what she made on the amphoras and mentioned it to Stephanos. Stephanos said that the consortium members made seven times more per amphora than she did as their overhead cost was far less than hers. Rachael's mouth dropped when she heard that. Stephanos said that she could have his profits if she was really upset over that. Rachael smiled and simply said, "What's fair is fair."

They talked about the wedding and decided on an early fall wedding. She said that Arion would transport her family to the wedding, and that Hermes and Emma would be attending. He was thinking about using the Parthenon for the wedding, but Rachael preferred a place where there weren't any idols. Stephanos thought about it and said that there wasn't any place in Athens that didn't have some idol attached to it. He said that they could have the wedding at his new home as it was twice as big as his parent's home, and that the court-yard had enough space for the wedding and reception. He said that the landscaping should be completed by then, and that his friends could deliver enough flowers to make the atmosphere most elegant. She liked the idea.

Rachael met with Captain Madera and told him about the prof-its that the consortium members were making on her amphoras. The captain laughed and said that Stephanos is a chip off the old block. Rachael told Madera to sell all future amphoras at half the price that the consortium members were selling them. She told him to get the word out to the shipping agents. He had already delivered half his cargo but said that he could easily sell them at the pier, as several merchants had already approached him to purchase them.

Rachael asked Captain Madera to inform Arion and Hermes about the wedding date and also asked him to tell them to sell the amphoras from Akim at half the price the consortium was selling them. Once the second ship was delivered, the demand for amphoras will double. Captain Madera mentioned that Markos was modifying a couple Egyptian ships to handle Rachael's amphoras. Once they are delivered, he said that Ptolemy would probably make a killing on the amphoras that he has been ordering from Rachael. Madera said that it wasn't a good idea to undercut Ptolemy on his purchases.

The second launch was successful. The owners immediately put it into service and its hull was filled with Rachael's amphoras that contained wine, nuts, grain, olive oil, and spices. Mario sailed with the second ship to Italy. Father, Antonio, Stephanie, and I sailed with Arion to Athens for the wedding. Hermes and Emma decided that the trip was too much for Emma, and that the children needed her attention.

The wedding was held at Stephanos's new home. Stephanos told me that the Roman garb that I was wearing was a bit out of place and found me a nice Greek outfit. With a few modifications, Stephanie wore her wedding dress. It fit in perfect with the dress styles of the wealthy class of attendees invited by the Markos family. Rhodora wanted to know where she got such a beautiful dress and commented on her matching jewelry. Stephanie captured the attention of a number of men with her good looks and smiles. One gentleman told me that I had to be someone of importance to have such a lovely wife. In a kidding way, he said that such beautiful women were reserved for the elite.

Stephanos agreed to let Anatolios, the pastor of the Christian church whom she met quite some time ago, administer the wedding vows. Stephanos was not tied to any of the Greek gods and was showing a great deal of interest in Rachael's Christian faith. I couldn't believe my eyes when I saw Rachael in her wedding dress. It was a flowing long white dress. Her bracelets and earrings really sparkled in the sunlight. Her hair was braided in an elegant fashion. It was a stark contrast to the Ragamuffin we knew as a child who tended to walk around in unkempt clothes and raveled hair.

Stephanos and Rachael took up Mario's offer to use his villa on Crete as a honeymoon spot. The beach was beautiful, and Mario had arranged for a couple of locals to take care of them for the two weeks that they were there. Stephanos congratulated her on selling her amphoras at half the consortium prices and making a goodly amount of money. She apologized for competing against the investors in his consortium and offered to cover his losses. He smiled as he declined her offer and used her quote, "What's fair is fair." He told her not to apologize as business is business, and friends were friends, and besides, he had sold his interest in that particular consortium investment knowing that Rachael's competitors would soon be copying her design. He said that the investors will not lose money but will not make the killing that they hoped for. He said that the consortium investors already called foul when they found out that Rachael was now his wife. They accused him of insider trading but took the whole thing with a bit of humor. Few people knew that the consortium basically ran the country. Stephanos told Rachael that her newly acquired wealth could someday get her invited into the consortium brotherhood. She would be the first woman to be a member if it was to come to fruition.

Chapter 17

THE ENTERPRISE

Silvanus, son of Matthias, son of Gaius, to my descendants. We all returned home safe and sound. Captain Madera kept us informed on Rachael's activities. She was spending a lot of time with Anatolios, as his church seemed to be the most active in the city. She learned a lot from copies of new letters from the apostles. Healings took place on a regular basis, and worship services were expanding to the point where they needed a larger facility than Anatolios's home. The walk to Anatolios's home was a fair distance, and Rachael would sometimes spend the night at Anatolios's place and walk home in the morning.

She spent time listening to the philosophers who met near the Acropolis. She loved to hear Erastus speak. His political views were more in line with Judeo-Christian morals and ethical standards than the others. She found it very difficult to reach the philosophers with the gospel. Erastus was tall with white hair and beard. He dressed well and had a soft voice, yet he projected well in the small theater. He would sit with Rachael and take the time to discuss numerous topics with her.

Rachael was planning on starting a home church with the hope of expanding to a larger church building. The walk to Anatolios's home was quite tiring for her. Stephanos offered to front the money for a church building. He owned some land higher on the hill that was about halfway to the local marketplace.

Speaking of Captain Madera, he showed up with a load of Egyptian cotton destined for Damascus. He handed father a bag of gold, probably worth on the order of forty denarius. A denarius was worth about twenty-five denarii. He wanted Father to look after it for safekeeping and told Father to use it himself if necessary. He told us that he and Ptolemy had partnered on buying the amphoras shipped to Alexandria and held them until the Egyptian ships that Markos was overhauling were delivered. They charged three times the purchase price and split the profits. He got the idea from discussions with his brother, Markos, and his son, Stephanos.

Captain had another bag of gold that was worth three hundred or so denarius. He said that he was going to give the gold to Rachael to help her in her ministry. He wined and dined at our place while his ship was in port. He really liked the pier. He said that there was a plague in Egypt, and that a lot of people were dying, and said that he was staying away from Alexandria for a while until things settled down. He and Ptolemy decided to work out of Caesarea unless the plague made its way into the Palestine area. His next plan was to load the ship with amphoras and deliver them to Athens, and maybe get in a last-minute grain shipment from Neapolis.

It wasn't long when, of all people, Cleo showed up in a chariot. He and one of the palace guards, Cato, traveled all the way from Caesarea with a short overnight stop in Tyre to visit with Flavius and Abigail. From what I gathered from Cleo and second hand from Rachael's discussions with Mario Estes, Mario delivered the vase to Valeria Messalima and told her it was from Rachael. She inquired as to who Rachael was, and Mario told her that she was of the House of Gaius located near a small Phoenician fishing village. He also told her that it was said that she defeated pirates off the coast of Troy, and that it was rumored that she fought against a Roman centurion at the age of twelve or so and won the battle. Valeria couldn't fathom a woman being aboard a cargo ship and having the strength to defeat pirates and a centurion to boot.

Apparently, she liked the vase but told Claudius that she was upset that Mario was always one step ahead of her in the latest art world. Pilate, the former procurator of Jerusalem, was visiting from the northern territories and was with Claudius at the time. Pilate told her that Rachael was the sister of Abigail who married Flavius the current procurator of Tyre. He also said that she was a close friend of Patricia, the daughter of Marcus—the current procurator of Troas—who was his personal assistant while in Caesarea.

Pilate said that Marcus's son, Cleo, was an artist and a good friend of Rachael. He said that Cleo was a bit of an oddity but an excellent administrative assistant, and Pilate said he wished that he had brought Cleo to Rome with him. Pilate said that Cleo could be tasked to visit Rachael and obtain some of her latest art work before Mario got his hands on it. Valeria liked the idea and had Pilate write an order for Cleo to do just that and not to spare any money. She said Rachael was to be paid well for her talent. Little did she know that it was Antonio's artwork.

Cleo and Cato remained for several weeks while they worked with Antonio to produce some rather interesting art. Cleo still liked painting pictures of bugs and came up with an idea to form different bugs on the sides of some urns and paint them with their original colors as close as possible. Alex, the potter, helped them select the material, as when heated, some of the minerals in the paint changed color when fired. Cleo would accentuate different parts of the bugs to add humor to it. I told Cleo that he would probably be either boiled in oil or given a high military commission for his work. He said that if Valeria didn't like it, he would say that Antonio did it.

Cleo made small honey jars with bees painted on the side. He painted a bee on the inside bottom so that when the honey was used up, she or someone would see it. It took awhile to get the bee color correct because every time they fired the clay jar, the color would change. I found some white rock that when ground up and fired, turned yellow.

Antonio made some nice urns with colorful flowers and birds painted all around it. He would paint the birds, and Penelope would paint the flowers. He designed tree branches on some of them and avoided geometric figures, which seemed to be the common thing to do when adding dimension to the surface. Cato helped out a lot. He was good at making and mixing paint. He enjoyed the pool and spa and could not get over the variety of food that we served him. He said that the drought had a measurable effect on the types of food being served to the soldiers. Cato said that most of his wages were spent eating at the cafés along the waterfront.

I asked Cleo how he was going to get all the artwork to Caesarea without damaging them. He said that he hadn't thought about that yet. I suggested that he hire Captain Madera to deliver them to Caesarea on his next trip south and to get permission for him to dock without having to pay a fee or any import taxes on items delivered. Cleo said that he could easily arrange for all of that and left us with a sizable amount of money for our efforts. Alex and Antonio couldn't believe the bag of gold and silver coins that Cleo left for them. A gold denarius was worth twenty-five silver denarii.

I noticed the size of the silver denarii coins. They were smaller than what we were used to. Apparently, Rome was making denarii with more copper and less silver. That meant a lower exchange rate with the Greek drachmas. I suspect the Greeks will follow suit and make their coins of the same weight of silver. It makes for an easier exchange. Otherwise, money exchangers would take advantage of people when weighing out the coins. The cost of goods seems to be on the rise.

Alex cut back on amphora production, as the demand for them slowed during the winter months, and competition was on the increase. It was a month or so before Captain Madera returned from Neapolis. He had dropped off grain in Sidon and stopped by to pick up a few amphoras to be delivered to Ptolemy in Caesarea. He was glad to deliver Valeria's artwork for Cleo as it meant no import taxes on the amphoras.

He said that all was well with Stephanos and Rachael. Apparently, Rachael was having a church built near their home. He said that an architect friend of Hermes from Sparta was hired to design the church.

Rachael said that she thought that she was pregnant and needed a few more days to know for sure. Little Gaius heard stories about Kaysi and wanted a pet dog. It took awhile to find the right dog. Gaius and Priscilla had a great time with him. They named him Kaysi. The vineyard produced an abundance of grapes this year. We made excellent wine from them; however the volume of wine was limited by the amount of grapes that Gaius and his friends left behind. There was always a bowl of grapes on the kitchen table. We were all guilty of eating them.

Father was experimenting with making mortar. He mixed limestone, crushed shells, and various crushed rock to see what worked out best. When he got the slurry just right, he would add some of Antonio's paint and see how it looked. He eventually covered the brick walls of our house to see how long it would last. The walls looked great when we finished. The color changed a bit as you walked around the house, but one only noticed it when up close.

Chapter 18

THE ARTIST COMMUNITY

Silvanus, son of Matthias, son of Gaius, to my descendants. Valeria loved the artwork that Cleo sent her. The word got out in Rome, and people were asking Mario where they could get some of the same artwork. Valeria was happy that she was now one up on Mario in having the latest artwork from the east. Mario didn't mind as he was arranging for shipment of more artwork to sell to his merchants. I suggested that Captain Madera could ship them to Athens, and Mario could in turn ship them to Rome.

Flavius mentioned that Cleo was transferring to Rome. Antonio wished Cleo was still around, as he was quite helpful in sculpting bugs and painting them. He trained some of the girls from the village to take over Cleo's work and found that some of them were quite creative.

Alex was getting good at firing the clay pieces. Antonio talked to artists in Tyre and invited them to produce unique artwork to be shipped to Rome and other cities along the Italian coast. He told them that all work has to have Rachael's stamp on the bottom to make it authentic. The stamp was in the form of the Greek letter rho. Father made a small metal stamp with a long rod on it. Antonio would impress it on the bottom of clay artwork, and heat it up when stamping glasswork. Some artists moved into the community, and after years of people moving out, people started to move in. Shops in Sidon and Tyre were selling artwork from Beth-Gebar.

Romans seem to like the words, Rachael, Phoenician, and Beth-Gebar. The interesting fact was that Rachael was nowhere to be seen in Beth-Gebar as she was living full time in Athens. Alex and Antonio took full advantage of her name and were becoming quite wealthy. Father, Joseph, and I were paid quite well. We took turns carting clay down from the hills, cleaning it, and storing it in Alex's new warehouse that Father and I built. Even Roman soldiers were stopping into the village to purchase gifts for their friends and relatives.

Jewish resistance seemed to be on the rise. A number of skirmishes between them and the Romans have been reported. The resistance began to irritate the Romans, so much so, that Claudius ordered all Jews out of Rome. News arrived that Valeria may have been killed. No one was certain, but rumors have it that she tried to have Claudius assassinated.

We haven't seen Rachael for quite some time. Captain Madera would give us updates on the church-building progress. He said that it was coming along real nice and said that they have to hide marble from the Romans as they tend to confiscate it for Roman projects. Stephanos was providing wood that he salvaged from dismantled ships. Stephanos never threw anything away. If there was a possibility that he could use it, he saved it.

A stone mason from Sparta was hired to fabricate the columns in front of the church. Hermes recommended him. Hermes had the stone mason carve the Greek letters alpha and omega on the columns closest to the entrance. Alpha was on the left and omega was on the right as one enters the patio. The columns were connected to the facade with arches and a nice roof. This made for a nice open air walkway and meeting place for social events. The sanctuary was strictly used for prayer, worship, and pastoring the flock.

Mario Estes provided the tiled floor. He said that Italian tile was the best. He even had a circular area designed in the center of the floor of the sanctuary that included the letters alpha and omega.

They had cut into the hillside to get sand and gravel to fill the church as it was being built. This allowed them to easily place each layer of stone blocks. Once the roof was finished, the sand and gravel was removed and taken southwest of the shipyard as Markos wanted to expand his shipyard in that direction.

Life has been fairly routine for the last three years. The artist community was still flourishing. Because of Jewish hostilities, Flavius thought that it might be better for Abigail and him to transfer to a more northern location. The Jewish resistance seemed to be gaining strength. Abigail was safe in the palace but wished that she could move back in with us for a while. Here, she could roam about with a lot more freedom and with no threat from Jewish reprisals. Mixed marriages between Romans and Jews were not tolerated. In turn, Roman officials considered Jews married to Romans, especially officers, as potential spies.

Captain Madera has been considering getting out of the shipping business. His health was deteriorating. The harsh sea conditions along with too much wine seemed to be taking its toll. He was our main source of information on how well Rachael was doing. His last report said that the church was finished and said that it looked beautiful.

He also said that Rachael and Stephanos were considering building an amphitheater on the hill next to the church, as when guest speakers come to the church, the sanctuary was not big enough to handle the crowds.

Rachael was making some headway with the philosophers who met near the Parthenon. One of the regular visitors was deaf in one of his ears. Rachael laid hands on his ear and prayed for a healing. He received his hearing in front of everyone, and Rachael told them that her God healed him, and that it was a demonstration of His power. She spoke about the powerless nature of their gods, and that the only way to heaven was through Jesus Christ. Erastus and a few others eventually turned to Christ and began to visit her church. Some would walk a great distance to attend church services on the Sabbath. She would eventually hold church services in the middle of the week and left the church doors open for anyone who wanted to come in and pray and spend time alone with the Lord.

Rachael would stay late and pray with people who stopped by. Stephanos would often stop by to escort her home when it was dark or when a storm was brewing. They would stop at one of the cafés on the way home and have a late meal together. They had one child. A beautiful baby girl. They named her Elizabeth. Captain Madera thought that she was pregnant again when he last saw her.

Captain Madera had stored a lot of money at our place. There were many bags of gold in the form of rings, bracelets, and small ingots. He had a chest full of silver drachmas and denarii. For some reason, he didn't want Markos or Stephanos to know about it. He seemed to be holding some kind of secret. He was a very cautious individual when it came to money. On one hand, he was generous with his giving. I had never heard of him cheating a crew member out of his wages. On the other hand, he was smart in saving for the future. He attended our church meetings and stayed with us when he arrived in port. Antonio and his family were attending on a regular basis as well. We thought about building a large church building to handle the membership. There was room this side of the cemetery to do so, but Father thought that putting it on top of the hill would be better. It would stand out as a Christian church where people could see it from a distance and also present a nice, peaceful atmosphere to view the Mediterranean and surrounding area.

Joseph and I started the church effort by building a nice pathway from the village side of the hill. Many church members participated in the effort. Most of the pathway was sandstone. It was easy to carve out steps, but in some places, it tended to crumble from too much use. We cemented together all kinds of flat stones to make the crumbled areas look nice. Father was getting good at making and mixing concrete. The Roman road builders would be proud of him as they were masters in building roads and using concrete.

Leveling the top of the hill took a great deal of time. While volunteers worked that area, Father was locating limestone blocks for the building. The church was three years in the making. It was small but adequate for its members. A Christian brother from Antioch would cart tile down to us when he had a chance. He designed a circular arrangement at the entry way and had carved the Greek letters alpha and omega, in two of the center tiles. A stone worker in Ephesus heard about our efforts and made enough pieces to build four narrow columns in front, just above the stairway. The back of the church faced Jerusalem, the holy city, so that when the congregation prayed, they would be facing Jerusalem. The courtyard faced the Mediterranean. It was a pleasant view when gathering to have meals and conduct outside worship services. We eventually paved the courtyard with bricks and put in cabanas to shade people from the sun. Mary-Beth, little Gaius, and Phyllis kept the church grounds swept clean. Joseph planted some nice trees and put in flower pots. Keeping everything watered was a major task.

There was a lot of sickness in the village this winter. It seems like everyone came down with some sort of illness. Our family seemed to have weathered things quite well. Little Gaius, who is not so little anymore, seemed susceptible to something on a regular basis. Regardless of how he felt, he was always up and running around. He insisted on doing his chores. He had his special plants to water and wanted no one else to water them.

Rabbi Zachias was bedridden for quite some time. We prayed for him regularly. One day, I walked to the synagogue and took him some fresh fruit. That morning, I prayed, laid hands on him, and commanded the sickness to leave. I felt the Spirit in a powerful way. He said that my hand was extremely hot when I touched him. Shortly after leaving, he got out of bed and was seen walking the synagogue grounds. Zachias said that he didn't know what happened, but soon after I left, the sickness completely disappeared.

Captain Madera showed up for the last time. Rachael came with him. Rhodora offered to watch her two children. She had a baby boy. They named him Alexander. Stephanos was a fan of Alexander the Great. The Romans didn't like that name, which pleased him to no end.

The news was that Claudius was dead, and that Nero became the new emperor. It was rumored that Nero was persecuting Christians, probably because of their association with Jews. It seems that the conflict between the Jewish resistance and the Romans in Palestine got worse every year. More and more Roman soldiers were being sent to quell riots and track down rebel forces.

Rachael thought that we were in danger by staying in Beth-Gebar and offered a place for us to live near her home. She reminded us about Daniel's prophecy that predicted the destruction of Jerusalem and the sanctuary forty years after the crucifixion of the Messiah, our Lord Jesus Christ. Rachael said that Jews and Christians would be safe in Athens. Markos and Stephanos had strong relations with Rome. It would not be of benefit to Rome to lose one of their prime shipbuilders. Rachael said that Stephanos was a member of the Greek resistance, a well-kept family secret. Some of his money made its way to support the resistance. Mario had warned them to watch out for Nero, as many considered him a tyrant of the worst kind.

Rachael and Captain Madera stayed for several weeks. The return trip to Athens was Madera's last voyage. His plan was to sell the ship. The ship had little life left in it. Years of being battered by storms had taken its toll. Captain Madera decided to sail south with a cargo of amphoras. He wanted to discuss the sale of the ship with Ptolemy. He hoped Ptolemy would let him sell the ship in Athens and forward the proceeds of sale to him. That way, Captain Madera had a way for him and Rachael to return to Athens with a load of amphoras and make a few drachmas before retiring from his life at sea.

Ptolemy was actually nice to Captain Madera in that he told him to keep the proceeds of sale as a bonus for their long-term relationship. Rachael wanted to head north to Troas and visit with Patricia as she thought that it may be the last time the two of them would meet. Rachael figured that her at sea traveling days were coming to an end. That was another reason for wanting our family to move to Athens. She missed her family a lot.

We decided to let Arion take over Madera's task of shipping amphoras to Athens. The demand for amphoras was dropping. Rachael cut back on shipments from Akim and slowed down Alex's production to meet actual demand. Rachael asked Madera to travel to Neapolis via Troas to ask Arion to take over Madera's shipping route. Madera didn't mind at all. He figured Athens could use some last-minute grain shipments from Neapolis to help pay his crew and give them a decent bonus. He hoped that the new buyer would hire his crew.

Captain Madera mentioned that Cleo was transferred to Rome. Apparently, Pilate was not well and needed support as hostilities in the northern territories were on the increase. Madera had dined at Peter's restaurant before departing Caesarea, and Peter told him that Cleo had become a Christian and wondered how he would fare under Nero's rule.

After the amphoras were loaded, Captain Madera and Rachael prepared to get underway. Before leaving, I suggested that Rachael talk with Marcos and Stephanos about building a nice passenger ship. There seemed to be a greater need for people to travel across the Aegean Sea these days. The family walked with the Captain and Ragamuffin to the ship. After hugs and tears, they departed Beth-Gebar, perhaps for the last time.

Chapter 19

THE TRIP NORTH

Silvanus, son of Matthias, son of Gaius, to my descendants. It was months before we got the word. It turned out that Madera's ship hit a large storm before making it to Troas. The storm was so violent and long-lasting that the ship was blown into rocks somewhere south of Ephesus. As the ship broke up, Rachael had fallen into the water and seriously injured her right shoulder. Although she didn't know it at the time, she had dislocated it. She thought she heard the captain yelling for her, but the noise and wave action from the storm drowned out her response. She had landed on a floating piece of the ship.

It was dark, and Rachael could barely see the silhouette of the distant shore. She tried to use her left arm, but it caused extreme pain in her right shoulder and forced her to lie still. Her feet were in the water, and she went in and out of consciousness several times. She awoke in the morning to find her head bumping against a loose piece of wood. The bumping caused some bleeding. She tried using her left arm to paddle to shore, but every movement caused pain in her right shoulder. The waves were still high. Every bit of motion caused a lot of pain. She also felt pain in her lower right leg.

Eventually, she maneuvered herself into a position where she could use her left arm to slowly propel herself to shore. Fortunately, the wind and currents were helping her. The sun was fairly bright as the clouds disappeared. The water was cold. An occasional shiver added pain to her shoulder.

It was late afternoon when Rachael reached shore. The waves on the shore were throwing her every which way. She eventually was able to roll into the surf and get into a kneeling position. As she did so, the pain in her arm got worse. She had to hold her injured arm with her left hand, and slowly stand up. That was when she felt more pain in her lower right leg. Regardless, Rachael limped ashore and lay down on the sand. She was totally exhausted. Every breath was a moan. Every once in a while, she would cry from the pain while praying for help.

As the sun was going down, she got up and limped toward some rocks and leaned against one that was least painful to her shoulder. As darkness set in, Rachael made it to the edge of the woods and curled up next to a tree. Her undergarment was still wet when she awoke in the morning. The cold night caused her to shiver, and the resulting pain made it difficult to sleep. She wished she hadn't stripped down to her under garment, especially during a storm where she could have used the extra warmth. She was upset that she had on her good sandals and wished that she had left them on the ship. It was a while before she realized that if she left them on the ship, they would have been lost.

Her face and arms were slightly sunburned. She held her right arm as she limped down to the beach. Rachael looked up and down the beach to see if anyone else survived. All she saw were pieces of wood from the ship. She decided to walk north along the shoreline in hopes of finding someone or perhaps some water as she was quite thirsty. Her left arm was weak from using it to paddle toward the shore.

Rachael spotted a small stream coming down the shallow cliff. The water was quite refreshing. She sat next to the stream with her feet in the water to cool off and collect her thoughts. She grimaced as she noticed a slight swelling in her lower right leg. Rachael decided that hiking up the stream was her best chance to find people or a road. People seemed to congregate along sources of water. The hike up the cliff was quite difficult. Once on top, she was able to follow the stream for a great distance. She had a difficult time dealing with the spider webs. About the third spider web that crossed her face, she decided to find a stick and wave it in front of her as she walked. The only problem was that when she waved the stick, she had to let go of her right arm. It became a war between spider webs and pain. Eventually, she held her arm and the stick at the same time, with the stick pointing forward guarding her face.

A nice pool and a small waterfall came into view. She decided to stand in the waterfall for a while to wash the salt out of her garment. Her hair was filled with sand from the sea shore, and her garment was a total mess. After awhile, with much difficulty, she was able to remove her garment. Any movement of her shoulder meant extreme pain. She sat on a stone and used her feet to scrub her garment. Hunger set in, and she decided to walk further before finding a place to spend the night. She kept a sharp eye out for snakes and listened carefully for creatures that could be lurking about.

Rachael found a tree that had strings of bark and pulled off a number of strands. She took three strands and braided them together and added more and more strands to make a long braid. She had to rest her right arm on her leg while she leaned over and made the braid. Then she wrapped it around her right forearm and up and around her neck to form a tourniquet. It was approaching darkness when she finished.

Rachael walked for another half hour before settling down next to a tree. As she began to doze off, she heard voices. She got up and decided to walk in the dark toward them. After stubbing her toes a few times, she saw a campfire and several men sitting around it. She approached the men and greeted them. They all immediately jumped up and wrestled for their swords and what weapons they could reach for.

There was total shock on their faces when they realized that a lone woman was in their presence. Only one of them could speak Greek. The others spoke a Syrian dialect. The one who spoke Greek appeared to be the leader of the group. He asked a lot of questions. At first, he didn't believe her as he said that women don't ride cargo ships unless they are slaves or prisoners destined for Rome. She asked him if he knew where the nearest city was as she needed a physician to look at her injured arm. He said that Ephesus was a four days' walk.

The leader's name was Hani Habib. He told her that he was a one-time pirate and spends his time as a highwayman, that is, robbing travelers of all sorts. He offered her some meat that was hanging over the fire. It tasted real good. Hunger caused her to eat it rather quickly. She thanked him and asked him if she could sleep by the fire. He wrapped his cloak around her as she sat next to the fire and talked. She asked him why they were there, and he said that they had attacked a group of Roman soldiers, and the soldiers were too much for them to handle. He said that most Roman soldiers fight like girls; however, this group was of a different breed. They killed several of his men and had been relentlessly chasing them.

She asked why they gave up being pirates. Hani said that a Roman galley chased them ashore and burned their ship. They killed half of his crew. She asked where this took place, and he said that it was off the coast of Troy. Rachael wondered if he was the same pirate who attacked Captain Madera's ship.

Hani said that he had lost some of his crew on a botched attack involving a cargo ship. Rachael inquisitively asked him to describe the botched attack. What he described was the incident involving Captain Madera's ship. Hani said that he thought there was a girl on board, and that she shot fire arrows at his sails, and that she also shot a short arrow that struck his knee. He showed her the scar. She said that she felt sorry for the pain that he encountered. He said that he was still searching for the sea captain and the girl that caused him so much grief.

She told him that she was surprised that a girl was on board the ship as cargo ships don't allow women on board. With that, she fell asleep. Exhaustion overcame pain, and after a good night's sleep, she awoke to find a cloak under her head for a pillow and another cloak covering her feet.

Hani noticed the necklace that she was wearing. The beads and the gold pendant told him that it was quite an expensive piece. Rachael offered it to him for his trouble and told him to thank the others for lending her their cloaks. He said that he had too much good stuff to get rid of already and didn't need any more.

Hani gave Rachael the rest of the meat that was left from the night before. He told her that he had to leave, and that he must stay one step ahead of the Roman soldiers who were pursuing him. She asked him where and how far the nearest road was. He pointed in an easterly direction and said that it would take her at least a full day to reach it and another two or three days to make it to Ephesus to the north. He said that if the Romans didn't get her, the bears will, and that it would be better if she tagged along with them. She said that she needed to get to a physician to get help for her shoulder.

He told her to follow the stream and it would take her to the road, and that she was on her own. As she began to walk away, Hani gave her his cloak to keep her warm and protect her from rain. She hugged him with her left arm and thanked him for his help and offered to repay him if the chance ever arrived. He turned and waved good-bye. A very short time later, she heard a noise behind her. It frightened her. She breathed a sigh of relief when she discovered that it was Hani. He said that he couldn't walk away and leave a nice lady to fend for herself, especially, a severely injured lady. It wasn't long, and the others joined him. Her pretty smiles and sweet voice made them fall in love with her. She was the best thing to come into their lives in recent times.

They had no more food, but drinking lots of water from the stream seemed to help. One of the men made her a nice walking stick. It helped reduce the pain in her right leg. They reached the road just before dark. Hani said that there might be some travelers nearby who would have some food that they could steal. Rachael told them that if they wanted the privilege to travel with her, they must promise not to rob anyone. Hani had to think about that for a few seconds. He pondered the words *privilege* and *not robbing anyone*.

Hani then asked her if she perhaps was the captain of the ship that she was on. With that, they camped near the road as a couple of the men searched for game. The impending darkness meant that they had to work fast. They found a deer near the stream, and with a couple of arrows, they dropped it quickly. They didn't want to have to chase after it during the dark.

Rachael watched Hani use flint and a knife to start a fire. She commented on his skills. The more she commented on how well he did this or did that, the more of a liking he took of her. The next day, they followed the road toward Ephesus. They lived off of venison as they traveled. It rained that night, and a couple of the men sat close to her with their cloaks over their heads and trying to keep the rain off of her at the same time. The men took turns while others slept.

Hani figured that they could reach Ephesus by evening the next day. It rained during most of the morning. Hani walked without his cloak. Rachael felt bad about that but knew that Hani would not have it any other way. Around noon, they were surprised by a large contingent of Roman soldiers. Hani and his men didn't draw their swords as they knew that it would be a waste of time. A centurion asked him to identify himself, and before Hani could speak, Rachael said that he was a ship's captain, and that the storm destroyed her cargo ship. She chose her words carefully so as not to be caught in a lie. Rachael didn't say that Hani was the captain of her ship.

The centurion was a little suspicious and said that women don't ride or own cargo ships and asked what her name was. She responded with Rachael. One of the soldiers approached the centurion and told him that he thought she looked familiar and said that she was seen at the palace in Troas. With that, Rachael said that she was good friends with Marcus and his daughter Patricia. The soldier also said she was known to have defeated some pirates off of Troy a few years back.

Hearing that, Hani's eyes opened wide and stared at Rachael. He said, "Defeated pirates off of Troy?" Rachael hit him with a backhand to his midsection and told him to be quiet. He asked why, and she told him that it hurts her shoulder when she hits him with her left hand.

Rachael told the centurion that her sister is married to Flavius the governor of Tyre. The centurion said that he knew Flavius and had a lot of respect for him. Rachael asked if there was a physician in

Ephesus who could help her with her injured shoulder. The centurion said that there was a physician at the garrison and one in the city. He recommended the physician at the garrison and told her to drop a few names such as Flavius, Marcus, and his name, Titus.

He said that he had more urgent matters to deal with; otherwise, he would have them escorted to Ephesus. He said that finding Hani Habib was of higher priority. With that, they parted company.

Once the Romans were out of sight, Hani looked at Rachael and asked her if she was the girl on the ship that shot him with an arrow. Rachael put her hand on his shoulder and smiled as she told him that she would have hit him in his chest, but she wasn't used to shooting arrows from a moving ship. Hani turned to his men and explained that Rachael was the one that shot him in the knee. Rather than show him any sympathy, they all started to laugh. Hani began to laugh himself as he tried to threaten her about getting even. Rachael then told him that she just saved him and his men's lives from the Roman soldiers, and that they now owed her their lives. He mentioned that they would not have been in that predicament if they had not offered to escort her in the first place. She then told him that she did not ask for their help, and that they were free to go at any time. Hani realized that arguing with her was a losing battle.

After dropping the right names, the guard at the garrison arranged to have her escorted to the physician. Hani stayed with her as the physician examined her shoulder. He said that the arm was out of the socket and knew how to fix it. He said that it will hurt, and that her arm would need a lot of therapy to regain its full range of motion. Apparently, the physician had experience with such conditions, as many torture victims were brought to him with joints out of place.

Rachael fainted when the physician adjusted her shoulder. After the physician fashioned a nice tourniquet, Rachael thanked him and leaned on Hani as she left the garrison. She asked a few people if they knew where there was a Christian church and told Hani that the Christian brethren would take care of her until she recovered enough to return to Athens. When the brethren found out who she was and that she was my sister, she had more help than you could shake a stick at. She thanked Hani and his men for their help and forced Hani to take her necklace as a gift. Hani said that he would keep the necklace as a remembrance. Rachael also told him that he should give up the life of a highwayman, settle down, get married, and live a good life. He said that he would think about it.

The Christian women took excellent care of her. The local physician provided therapy for her shoulder. The range of motion increased as the weeks went by. Rachael had a letter sent to Stephanos explaining what had happened. It would be a couple of weeks before he would receive it. She told him that she didn't want to take another voyage until her shoulder completely healed.

The physician told her that he thought her leg probably had a stress fracture and that she should stay off of it for a few weeks to let it heal. Rachael couldn't use crutches because of her shoulder. That meant sitting around a lot, and when walking, she used a cane and the help of the lady in the home where she was staying. A man named John regularly spoke at the church. She met with him often and learned a great deal concerning the ways of Christ. He wrote down his account of what he knew and experienced while with Jesus. He said that Mary, the mother of Jesus, lived on a hill near a spring above the Roman palace. The brethren offered to copy some of John's writings for her. Rachael gladly took up their offer.

John mentioned that the Asian churches were growing in huge numbers as a result of apostles traveling through the region. However, he said that the mystical and demonic power of the Babylonian priesthood was quite pervasive in most cities in the region. According to John, when the Babylonian empire fell to Cyrus, king of the Medes and Persians, Babylon decayed into ruins. As a result, the Babylonian priesthood fled to Pergamos and became the seat of Satan. Many years later, Attalus III bequeathed his kingdom, Pergamum, to Rome. As a result of this marriage, he suspected that the power of the priesthood would shift to Rome. The priesthood formed an alliance with Mark Antony, after which, Mark ordered that all the scrolls in the Pergamum library be sent to the library in Alexandria. With Mark Antony's defeat at Actium, the power of the priesthood seemed to be shifting back to Rome. He told Rachael to warn the Christian brethren to stay strong in the word and not allow the priesthood to compromise the true word of God and to beware the Antichrists.

A sea captain stopped by and visited with her. He was asked by Stephanos to check in on her, and that if she was ready to travel, he would take her to Athens. Rachael wanted a couple more weeks to recover and told him to tell Stephanos that all was well, and that the Christian brethren were taking most excellent care of her.

The women taking care of her got to hear Rachael's life stories. They were in awe of what she and her family had accomplished and experienced. The stories concerning her encounter with pirates, challenging a centurion, and dealing with highway robbers left them awe struck. Gossip concerning Rachael spread like wildfire. Even the governor's wife heard about her.

Rachael heard that Hani Habib and his men were later arrested and put in prison, along with several others found along the highway. Commander Titus was committed to ridding the highway of robbers and any other kind of vermin that seemed out of place. The news of Hani's arrest pleased the local populace as Hani was known to terrorize the community. Other than Roman soldiers, Hani never really harmed anyone. He just took any valuables that travelers were carrying with them.

When Arion got the word that Rachael was in Ephesus, he sailed there directly from Athens. Hermes was with him when they met up with Rachael. The women outfitted her with nice clothes and a pair of new sandals before undertaking the voyage to Athens with Arion. She treasured the copies of John's writings. She collected as much money as she could from Arion and the crew and left it under her pillow in the house where she was staying.

Stephanos and Rhodora were relieved to see her arrive. They had been worried sick the whole time. It was a couple of months before she got rid of the cane. She turned the amphora and artwork business over to me to handle. Hermes worked as a shipping agent for Arion and eventually stopped shipping amphoras from Akim as it was no longer cost effective. Rachael settled down and focused on raising her children. She taught them to read and write in Hebrew and Greek. She now had the time to learn Latin and helped Stephanos as an interpreter when he met with Romans who didn't speak Greek.

Chapter 20

THE INHERITANCE

Silvanus, son of Matthias, son of Gaius, to my descendants. A couple of years passed since Rachael's adventure in Ephesus. Arion kept us informed on what everyone was doing. He would bring letters from Rachael when in port. The pottery business began to slow. The demand for artwork came to a practical halt. Rome was in turmoil under Nero. People seemed to be more focused on entertainment than in collecting artwork. Money was spent going to theaters and especially attending the arena where gladiators fought with each other and Christians were being slain.

Influence from the consortium in Athens kept the amphora business alive. Everyone accepted the fact that Captain Madera did not survive the shipwreck. Father and I decided to keep his money for safekeeping in the event we were forced to move because of increasing hostilities between the Jewish resistance and Romans. We felt that captain Madera wanted the money to be used by us anyway.

A lawyer from the consortium stopped by and met with Markos, Stephanos, and Rachael. He said that Captain Madera left a will with him, and that given the word of his possible demise at sea, the lawyer waited the usual two years before releasing any money held at the consortium under Madera's name. Apparently, to Stephanos's and Rachael's surprise, he owned half of the shipyard. Neither Rachael nor Stephanos knew this. It was a well-kept family secret. Madera left his half of the shipyard to Stephanos and Rachael to be split evenly. Markos was surprised, as he thought Stephanos would inherit all of it. The lawyer also said that there was a sizable amount of money invested in the consortium that Madera gave to Rachael. It was on the order of 140,000 drachmas. Stephanos didn't realize that Madera had that much money invested in the consortium.

The lawyer told Rachael that unless she became a member of the consortium, she would have to withdraw her shares. Stephanos said that women weren't allowed to be members of the consortium. The lawyer said that he could meet with the directors and have the rule changed so that Rachael could be a member. He said that technically, a lady from Rhodes inherited her husband's wealth and used him to keep the money in the consortium. She was in a sense an indirect member. He said that the time has come to let women become members especially if they become widows.

Markos and Stephanos told the lawyer to make it happen, and if the directors did not cooperate, he told them to tell them that Markos would be most unhappy. Apparently, Markos and his shipbuilding empire had majority control in the marketplace and Greek economy as a whole. The wealthy establishment respected his position.

There were no ill feelings between Stephanos and Rachael over the inheritance. His love for Rachael and the children was more than his love of money. Markos, on the other hand, was not happy with splitting the shipyard between Stephanos and Rachael and Madera giving his wealth to Rachael. If something happened to Stephanos, Rachael would get it all. But then again, he figured his grandson, Alexander, to be in line downstream.

Rachael had acquired a sizeable fortune from amphora sales, and combined with her inheritance, she had become the wealthiest woman in Greece. It wasn't long before Rachael was granted membership in the consortium. There was an elite group of which she was not a member that met secretly from time to time. It was sort of a circle within a circle. Government officials would occasionally attend these meetings. Stephanos cautioned Rachael not to ask any questions or mention any knowledge of this group. Aside from that, it wasn't long before Rachael was selected to lead most of the consortium committees.

Now that she was part owner, Rachael would occasionally visit the shipyard. Stephanos always made sure that she was escorted when walking aboard the ships that were being overhauled or under construction. On one ship visit, she noticed workmen standing around a seam that the owner claimed was intermittently leaking. Rachael walked over and got a closer look at the seam and the adjoining rib. She noticed that a knot on the other side of the rib had split off and was jammed into the seam. It could not be seen from the side that was leaking. She showed this to the foreman and suggested that he have a shipwright chip the defective part of the knot away, as when the ship flexes in a storm, the knot would put pressure on the seam and cause it to leak. The foreman motioned to a shipwright standing nearby, and he did what she suggested. As she began to walk away, she turned to the foreman and told him that he should reseal the seam after the shipwright was finished. He gave her a respectful nod as she left.

When they tested the ship at sea during a decent wind, Rachael went with them. She wanted to see if the fix actually worked. There were no leaks. On the return trip to the shipyard, she noticed that the ship was making slow headway in a broadside wind. She checked the angle of the sails and noticed they were not properly set to take maximum efficiency of the wind direction. She mentioned this to the navigator, and he said that the sails looked okay to him. She made a right angle with her two index fingers and then formed a triangle with her thumbs and showed him the angle they should be at when the wind was directly broadside. He asked her where she learned that, and she gave Captain Madera the credit. The navigator humored her and had the sail angle adjusted to Rachael's recommendation. To his surprise, the ship's speed increased significantly.

It wasn't long before she gained the respect of the whole shipyard. On another occasion, she stopped by when Mario Estes and Stephanos were negotiating to build another ship for Rome. After listening for a while, Stephanos asked Rachael for her opinion. Mario was a bit perturbed that he was asking a woman to intervene on their negotiations but knew that she owned a sizeable portion of the shipyard.

Rachael said that the estimated cost for the ship was too low. She cited the fact that the contract cost was in denarii and not in the weight of silver. She said that Rome had reduced the size of the denarii, and that drachmas were being adjusted to the same weight to make for a balanced exchange rate. She told him that the suppliers sold their material based on a certain weight of silver, which meant that the actual cost of the ship had to be adjusted upward to compensate for that.

She also said that the upfront advance should be at least a third of the final estimated cost, as most of the initial cost was material for the ribs and planking for the hull. A smaller upfront advance would force the shipyard to have to borrow money from the consortium, putting the shipyard at risk, not to mention a cut in the profits.

Mario tried to explain Rome's reason for adjusting the size of the coin and not having enough money to cover the upfront cost. He said that the cost of running the empire was forcing these changes as well as having to increase taxes. Rachael told him that coining more money and raising taxes will eventually cause the empire to self-destruct and suggested that Rome slow down on their construction efforts. She said that Marcus, the governor of Troas, mentioned time and time again that Rome's budget should be balanced, the treasury should be refilled, public debt should be reduced, the arrogance of officialdom should be tempered and controlled, and the assistance to foreign lands should be curtailed lest Rome become bankrupt.

Mario was speechless. Stephanos weighed in and told Mario that Rachael was correct in her assessment, and that if Rome wanted a high quality ship, they would have to pay a little more up-front and cover the cost of inflation. Mario shook his head and said that Nero will have him crucified when he hears about the cost of his ship. Rachael put her hand on his shoulder and told him not to worry, and if Nero complains, just blame it on a pirate slaying Amazon woman from Phoenicia who drives a hard bargain. Mario added, "And a beautiful woman at that!"

They all agreed to meet at the café for a bit of social life. That evening, Rachael asked Stephanos if Mario agreed to her terms, and he said that Mario agreed to a 12 percent increase in estimated cost, and mentioned that Mario is a member of the consortium and has a vested interest in whatever transactions take place in Rome. Rachael asked him if that was really ethical, and Stephanos said that power and corruption goes hand-in-hand, especially when dealing in government matters. He said that if you want to survive in this world, one must go with the flow.

It has been awhile before any significant news arrived. Two apostles were killed at the direction of Nero. Peter was crucified, and Paul was supposedly beheaded. It was sad times for Christians. However, despite Rome continuing to execute Christians, the body of Christ continued to grow in huge numbers. I figured that eventually Rome would have to give into the Christians, or a time will come when the empire will no longer be able to prevail against them.

The most shocking news came when Arion told us that Captain Madera showed up in Athens. Apparently, he was arrested near Ephesus and imprisoned. He and two crew members survived the shipwreck only to be captured by a Roman centurion named Titus. Captain Madera tried to explain to Titus and the prison guards that he was not a highwayman robbing travelers as he was accused of, and that he was the survivor of a shipwreck.

While in prison, Madera would share sea stories with Hani Habib and other prisoners. One day he noticed a necklace that Hani was showing a fellow prisoner. Madera recognized it as a necklace that Rachael wore before his ship went down in a storm. When asked where he got it, Hani told him the story of his encounter with Rachael and how he took care of her while escorting her to Ephesus. The excitement of knowing that Rachael was alive and safe filled Madera with a newness of life.

Whenever a new guard appeared, Madera would plead his case with him. Eventually, one of the guards recognized Madera as being a ship captain and told the captain of the guard. A short investigation was made, and he and one of his crew members were freed. The other crew member died while in prison. Hani Habib was due to be transported to a local mine to work as a slave laborer. Madera, wanting to return a favor for taking care of Rachael, told the captain of the guard that the person they thought was Hani Habib was really his ship navigator. The captain of the guard said that he would look into the matter. Madera figured that if they questioned him on his navigation skills, being a former captain of a pirate ship would be to his advantage.

When Captain Madera arrived in Athens, he was very thin and gaunt-looking. The time in prison had taken its toll. Rachael and Rhodora did their best to nurse him back to health. When he found out that his wealth was in Rachael's hands, he just smiled, nodded his head, and stroked his beard. Madera knew that after two years, if a person didn't show up, his wealth was given to his next of kin, and there was no recourse if that person showed up in the future. Rachael offered to return his wealth to him, but Madera turned it down.

There was a time when Markos would have tried to get Madera to have his wealth returned to him as he wanted Stephanos to get it all. However, it seemed that Rachael's short visits to the shipyard have been quite profitable for both himself and Stephanos. Markos was taking a more and more liking to Rachael. Rachael insisted that captain Madera move into the guest room at her home.

A letter arrived from Rachael. Apparently, she was selected as head of the consortium. That would make her the most powerful woman in Greece. Her decisions at the shipyard had a long-term impact on the Italian shipping industry. She was definitely making waves in Italy, not to mention her business relationship with the Ptolemy family in Egypt.

Madera spent a lot of time at the church. He fell in love with the building. Eventually, he dedicated his life to follow Jesus and was baptized. Rachael was very excited over this and sent us a letter within days afterward. The church membership was growing. Christians were on edge because of Nero. An edict could come down any day to slay all Christians.

Our church membership in Beth-Gebar reached about a hundred. The pool was used to baptize new believers. Stephanie gave birth to twins, a boy and a girl. We named them Isaac and Rebecca. Joseph and Mary-Beth now have three children. Our houses were fixed up rather nicely. Stephanie did an excellent job designing the interior of the atrium. She even had Antonio paint the columns in front with spiraling florals and birds. We purchased wheat and spelt from Arion when he arrived to pick up pottery. We used Hiram to grind the grain for us as Mary-Beth and Stephanie were too busy with the children. Father and Mother were slowing down. Age was catching up with them.

Hermes and Emma were thinking about moving back to Beth-Gebar. Emma missed the village and her friends. Hermes's knees were giving out on him, which limited his ability to ride ships. He told us on his last visit that all his bones seemed to creak, and that his joints were very stiff. Joseph and Mary-Beth said that he could have his house back if they decided to make the move. Father and Mother invited Joseph and Mary to move in with them. The children could take over the girls' room and the guest house.

The Romans were moving in more and more troops to quell the ever increasing Jewish uprisings. The Jewish resistance was more determined to rid Judea and Palestine of Roman rule. Flavius said that Jewish terrorists slaughtered Roman troops at Masada and now were in control of the fortress. This did not bode well for all Jews in the Region. Word has it that following this incident, the leader of the temple in Jerusalem stopped the daily sacrifices, something to with appeasing the Romans. This did not bode well, as the prophecy in

Daniel stated that the destruction of Jerusalem would occur about three and half years following the cessation of the temple sacrifices.

Flavius suggested that because we are Jews, we should consider relocating for a while until hostilities settle. Father spoke to Arion on his next port visit, and Arion said that he would help us relocate to Athens or any other place he chose. Father talked to Antonio and asked if he would like to move on to our property in the event our family had to move, and he agreed. Antonio would essentially become the caretaker until we returned. Joseph and Mary-Beth said that they preferred to stay. Joseph said that, although a Jew, he could easily claim Phoenician decent having a similar language dialect that was common in the village. The only drawback was the Christian church that we built at the top of the hill. Nero was still persecuting Christians in Rome, and if Rome defeats the Jews, he may turn his full attention to the Christians whom he saw as a sect of the Jews.

It's been two years since the Masada incident, and Jerusalem was near defeat. Nero's reign as emperor came to an end. No one knew who was really in charge. Cleo sent us a message and suggested that we depart as soon as possible. He said that the Jewish attempt to fight against Roman world order would come to an end. Lots of soldiers were entering the port at Caesarea.

Father kept the sign that said "House of Gaius, Friends of the Romans" on the main gate. Many soldiers were seen marching south. Father didn't invite the officers to our home when they camped in the nearby field. He did talk with them and directed some spring water their way. The fresh cool water alone was enough to gain their trust and friendship.

Arion and Father talked, and he asked Arion to tell Rachael that we would like to move to Athens within the year. Arion said that he would do that. He also said that Captain Madera passed away, and that Rachael was quite saddened over it.

Arion met Patricia in Troas awhile back. Patricia told him that half of the garrison was ordered south to Jerusalem. She also said that Marcus may be headed to Rome if Vespasian is selected as the new emperor. Vespasian envisions a greater Rome and had many construction projects planned. He needed a good administrator and knew of Marcus's talents.

Interestingly enough, Patricia mentioned that Cleo was in Rome serving in an administrative capacity. He was in charge of making sure that the farming regions of the empire were properly taxed, and that enough food was being delivered to support the Roman military as well as the populace in Rome. He used Christian prisoners at the Coliseum to deliver grain and other produce from one distribution point to another. No one seemed to question him when some of the prisoners never returned. He tried to save as many Christians as possible without raising suspicion.

Many Christians lived in caves or underground passages along the Appian Way. They built catacombs for their dead. Cleo used Christian prisoners to deliver and bury Christian martyrs outside the city. Again, not all the Christian prisoners returned. Not all the grain carried to Rome made it to the city. Cleo was looking after the Christians. We all figured he would someday be fed to the lions. However, Cleo always had a good song and dance when confronted by his peers or those higher in authority. Marcus will probably lose what gray hair he has left when he gets to Rome and finds out what his son, Cleo, has been up to. Cleo will not have Patricia at his side to protect him.

The time to move has come. Vespasian has ordered the final assault on Jerusalem. His son, Titus, was put in charge to make the assault. Arion arrived, and we were loading up what belongings that made sense. We gathered fruit for the voyage. Mary-Beth made several loaves of bread for us. We told Mary-Beth and Joseph that we would return as soon as possible. The future of Israel was uncertain. Mother was quite ill and decided to stay. Father decided that it was best for him to stay and take care of Mother. Stephanie was sad to have to leave, but thought it best for the family as a whole. Little

Gaius and the rest of the children were excited about traveling on a ship.

I am going to seal this scroll in one of Antonio's beautiful urns. Once sealed, all the urns will be placed at the end of the secret room in the cave. I made an insert in the room to house all the scrolls. I will cover it with rocks and sand in hopes that they will not be disturbed by anyone until I return. I showed little Gaius where I hid them and told him that he must pass the location of the urns on to his son in the event he or I never make it back to Beth-Gebar. My plan is to continue writing after settling in Athens.

EPILOGUE

W hile the book was being edited, I glanced through some of the pictures of my trip to Greece. My jaw dropped as I glanced at the picture of Nicholas and me standing at the front of the ship that transported the urns to Turkey. The name of the Greek ship was clearly visible in the background. Although a slight spelling difference, the name was *Rachel*.

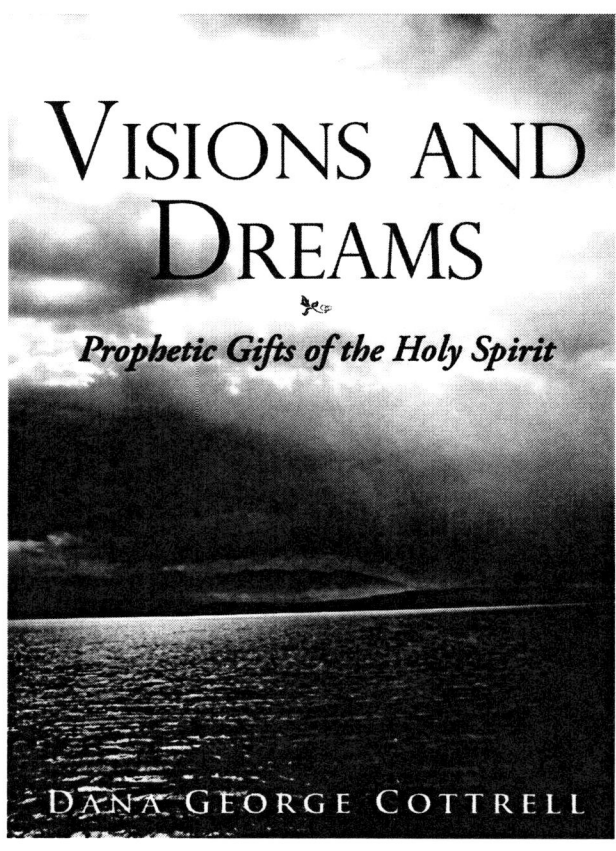

VISIONS AND DREAMS

Prophetic Gifts of the Holy Spirit

DANA GEORGE COTTRELL

This book is based on prophetic visions and dreams that author Dana George Cottrell has experienced over a twenty-three-year period. The intent of the book is to aid those who receive the gift of visions and dreams on how to handle and interpret them, as well as to provide information on the subject to those interested in the topic. Numerous visions and dreams are shared along with their respective interpretations and comments.

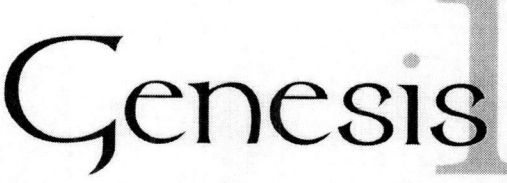

A STUDY GUIDE TO GENESIS 1

Genesis 1

The Design and Plan for the Kingdom of Heaven

THE BEGINNING

DANA GEORGE COTTRELL

This book, based on exegetical theology, intends to present a unique, theological sound interpretation of each of the seven days of Creation, which will in turn lead to a much greater in-depth understanding of the Holy Scriptures—an understanding that will provide a refreshing wind to the churches. The book will engage readers in a spiritual archaeological digging, showing how the first five days of Creation relate to the design and plan for the kingdom of heaven, how the sixth day refers to the implementation of the kingdom, and how the seventh day reveals the handing of the kingdom to the Father. This concept is the unveiling of a mystery that has been either hidden or lost since the Scriptures were written. Knowing this vital information, the reader can embrace a depth to the Creation story that will impact his or her understanding of God and the future He has planned for His creation.

ABOUT THE AUTHOR

Dana George Cottrell was born in St. Stephen, New Brunswick, Canada, and raised in northern Maine. He graduated from the University of Maine with a bachelor of science degree in electrical engineering, and he holds a master of arts degree in biblical studies from the Mission Bay Christian Fellowship School of Ministries in San Diego, California. He has recently authored two books titled *Genesis 1: The Design and Plan for the Kingdom of Heaven and Visions and Dreams*.

www.danacottrell.net

CPSIA information can be obtained
at www.ICGtesting.com
Printed in the USA
FSOW01n1952281216
28914FS

9 781681 978482